AGENT PRIME

JAKE BIBLE

SEVERED PRESS
HOBART TASMANIA

AGENT PRIME

OTHER BOOKS IN THE GALACTIC FLEET UNIVERSE

Salvage Merc One
Salvage Merc One: The Daedalus System

Drop Team Zero

Outpost Hell

Roak: Galactic Bounty Hunter
Nebula Risen- A Roak: Galactic Bounty Hunter Novel
Razer Edge- A Roak: Galactic Bounty Hunter novel

Galactic Vice

1.

"Rylia Five?"

The words hung there, unanswered for several seconds before the man being addressed looked up from his holo vid and turned to regard the questioner.

"Excuse me?" the man asked.

Bright red eyes, beady and small. Bald head, wrinkled brow, teal-blue skin that sparkled in the dim light of the public transport car. Possibly human, but from a lineage that veered off from Earth-pure millennia earlier. Not that Earth was very pure anymore; a slagging orb of toxic waste and a billion poisons was all that planet held.

"Are you speaking to me?" the man asked when the stranger only smiled at the first question.

"Those boots," the stranger continued. "That's Hoocahna snake skin. Those snakes only live on Rylia Five. Just wondering if you were from Rylia Five. Not many people are."

The man with the boots looked the stranger up and down. Average height, average size, above average looks. Sandy blond hair with deep brown eyes and light tan skin. A smile playing at the corners of his mouth. Just another basic human being in a galaxy many thought had been overrun by the species.

"I'm sorry, but I was in the middle of watching a holo. Do you mind?" the man with the boots responded. He looked up and down the transport car. They were the only ones riding that specific car. Every other seat was open and empty. "Perhaps you wouldn't mind sitting somewhere else? Lots of room."

"Of course. Lots of room." The stranger mimicked the man with the boots, looking up and down the transport car. "Except I like to have a chat with folks when I'm riding the transport. Makes the time fly by."

"So do holo vids," the man with the boots said, waving his wrist at the stranger. "See? You can watch whatever you want. Quietly. Over there."

"Over there?" the stranger asked, pointing to one of the many empty seats. "Or how about over there?"

"Wherever you want," the man with the boots said. "As long as you stop bothering me."

"Bothering you? Apologies. Didn't know I was bothering you."

"You do now. Maybe leave me alone, please?"

"Since you said please."

The stranger stood up from his seat, studied the transport car for a minute then moved off to one of the empty seats. He wiped it off with his hand and sat down, his eyes locked onto the man with the boots.

After a couple of minutes, the man with the boots glanced up from his holo vid and glared at the stranger.

"Are you going to stare at me the entire ride?" the man with the boots spat. "Do I need to call security?"

"Sorry."

The stranger grinned then turned to look out the window by his seat at the dark and roiling skies of Egthak, a planet made up of mostly beaches and scrublands, all boxed in by tumultuous oceans. A massive storm system was on the horizon, moving quickly toward the small slice of continent where the truly brave decided to set up civilization.

"Primed," the stranger said under his breath.

"What was that?" the man with the boots snapped. "I told you to leave me alone. I'm calling security now."

"If that's how you feel," the stranger replied.

"What? You have done nothing but harass me since you stepped into this car," the man with the boots almost snarled. "All I have done is try to watch my holo until we arrive at the station. Just a little bit of relaxation before a very important meeting."

The man with the boots waved a hand over his clothes which were of a stylish cut, obviously business formal, but not expensive. If they'd been expensive, the man with the boots would have hired a private roller or hover car, not taken the public transport.

"So stop talking to me," the man with the boots demanded.

"Interview?" the stranger asked.

The man with the boots gawped. He blinked those bright red eyes over and over then shook his head.

"You're mental, you know that?" the man with the boots said. "Mental enough that I am calling security."

He waved his hand across his wrist, banishing the holo, and brought up a glaring red display interface. The holo interface flashed twice then went green.

"There. Security is called," the man with the boots said.

"Good. That means we have three minutes to talk before they arrive," the stranger said and leaned forward, resting his forearms on his knees. The stranger was dressed in casual attire—sturdy pants, a basic long-sleeved shirt, nice, comfortable shoes. He plucked at a bit of fuzz on his pants then focused his entire being onto the man with the boots. "Listen carefully."

2

"What? What are you on about?" the man with the boots exclaimed. "You had best get up and get—"

"Shut up and listen, Mr. Gor'bun," the stranger said.

"How do you know—?"

"Roshall Gor'bun," the stranger said with a sigh. "Recently laid off by Tremmle Corp due to some irregularities in your filing of shift records. Why was that, Mr. Gor'bun?"

"Why was what?" Mr. Gor'bun asked. "How do you know that?"

"Hows are pointless topics," the stranger said. "The topic at hand is whether you want to stay alive or not. When security gets here, you will tell them that I was behaving strangely—"

"You have been!"

"—and you will leave with one of them while the other questions me. Go willingly with the security officer, answer questions truthfully then wait with the person until the transport stops. Once we reach the station, wait until I exit this car then you exit. If I look directly at you, get back on the car. If I don't look directly at you then wait for the transport to leave and walk over to me. I'll get you away from the station and to safety."

"You're mad," Mr. Gor'bun said. "I'm not doing any of that."

"Less than a minute," the stranger said. "I was told to say that Herra Mor'ta says hello, if you don't want to listen to what I have to say."

Mr. Gor'bun's teal skin managed to almost turn white at the mention of the name Herra Mor'ta.

"That's a name you know," the stranger said. "A name you shouldn't know unless you were doing much more than misfiling shift records. You accessed data in the Tremmle Corp mainframe that you were not supposed to access. We know all about that. What we don't know is whether that little breach was an accident or deliberate."

Mr. Gor'bun began to open his mouth, but shut it with a snap when the stranger pointed a finger at him.

"Not my place to ask or to hear," the stranger said. "My place is to get you away from the station safely and into the hands of those that will make sure your knowledge doesn't get you killed."

Mr. Gor'bun was silent for a couple seconds then said, "Killed...?"

The stranger didn't have time to answer as two security officers burst through the connecting airlock of the transport car. They glanced at Mr. Gor'bun, but dismissed him right away before stomping down the aisle towards the stranger.

One of the security officers was a short, squat fellow with sheer white bristles sticking out of every millimeter of skin not covered by his uniform; a conglomeration of many different, and somehow compatible, galactic races. The stranger furrowed his brow as the officer locked onto him and approached, hand on a small pistol still holstered to his hip.

The stranger barely gave the oncoming officer a glance. The second security officer was the one to pay attention to. A full-blooded Gwreq—stone-skinned, four-armed, humanoid, and over seven feet tall—the officer stopped in front of Mr. Gor'bun, blocking the stranger's view of the teal-skinned man. If the Gwreq officer was bought then all it would take was one hard, quick backhand and Mr. Gor'bun's neck would be turned to jelly.

"You," the bristle-haired officer said as he stopped just out of the stranger's reach. "Up. Let's go. No more bugging hard-working passengers."

"Does something about me say I'm not hard-working too?" the stranger asked. He looked around the officer at Mr. Gor'bun, but the man was completely blocked by the Gwreq standing guard.

"Eyes on me, slagger," the bristle-haired officer ordered. "That gentleman is not your concern. How about you get up now and come with me before I have to get drastic?"

"Wouldn't want you to get drastic," the stranger said and slowly stood up. "Where are we going?"

"Gonna take you up front so I can do a full scan," the bristle-haired officer replied. "Match you against the database."

The stranger nodded. "Good idea. You'll see I'm clean."

"That so? We'll see," the bristle-haired officer replied. "Get walking, slagger. And eyes forward. No need to try to intimidate the gentleman as you go by."

The stranger did as he was told, barely able to squeeze past the bulk of the Gwreq officer as he walked down the aisle towards the airlock. The Gwreq reached out and grabbed his arm, stared him down, then sneered and let go, turning back to address Mr. Gor'bun. The stranger was pleased to hear a normal, boring round of stock questions come from the Gwreq's mouth as he and the bristle-haired officer reached the airlock.

2.

"That's odd..." the bristle-haired officer said as he stared at the holo display and the data readout that scrolled by, fading out as it reached the surface of the small desk in the transport's security kiosk. "What did you say your name was again?"

"Sno. Denman Sno," the stranger replied. "You have it right there. Next to my picture and my stats."

"Yes, well..." The bristle-haired guard stopped the data scroll and grabbed at the pic that was displayed prominently in the file. He stared at the pic then stared at the stranger then back at the pic. He humphed and continued the scroll before he became frustrated and banished the holo altogether. "Not even a smudge on your record."

"I play by the rules and keep my nose clean," Sno said.

"A little too clean," the bristle-haired officer said. "Maybe get out more. Find a mate, go to a club, stop harassing transport passengers."

"Like I said, I was only having a chat with the man. Don't know why he took offense," Sno said.

"My colleague will find out," the bristle-haired officer said dismissively. "But other than being annoying, you've done nothing that I can hold you for."

"Good thing," Sno said. "We've reached the station and I have a cab waiting."

"A what?" the bristle-haired officer asked.

"Taxi," Sno said, but the officer's puzzled features didn't change. "A roller for hire?"

"Kip driver. Got it," the bristle-haired officer said and nodded with understanding. "Taxi? That one of those city-planet names?"

"I guess so," Sno said. "Am I free to go, officer?"

"Yeah. Go. Get along with you." The bristle-haired officer opened the kiosk and pointed. "Out of my sight. And stop being weird!"

Sno smiled, nodded, left.

"Only plan on seeing the beaches," Sno said as he hurried off towards the closest exit.

"Not gonna see much in this storm!" the bristle-haired officer called after Sno.

Sno gave an over-the-shoulder wave and stepped off the transport car and onto the station platform. The air was thick and warm and charged with electricity. Sno felt the hairs on the back of his neck stand up, and he moved quickly to one of many columns staggered along the platform that held up the long, wide roof.

It was at that moment that Sno wished he'd come armed. But no way to sneak a pistol worth a damn onto a public transport. Scanners would have found the weapon instantly even with the shielding tech that all his pistols contained. Egthak had a very strict no-weapons policy and had developed tech to back-up that policy. It should have made the planet safer, but as the hairs on the back of Sno's neck continued to stand up, he knew the safety was an illusion.

Weapons were plentiful if one knew where to look or who to comm.

Sno studied the platform. Not a single person around. That should have been a good thing, but it wasn't. There was no reason for the platform to be deserted. Not at that time of day and that time of week. There should have been at least a dozen other passengers milling about, either headed towards or coming from the expanse of beaches that were only a short roller ride away.

The oncoming storm could have been a reason for the lack of others, but Sno knew better. He fixed his eyes onto Mr. Gor'bun as the man finally exited the transport. Mr. Gor'bun completely ignored Sno and walked briskly towards the station's small building. Sno cursed under his breath, glanced around, still saw no one then moved to follow.

Sno made it a meter before Mr. Gor'bun reached the station building's doors. The doors slid open with an automatic hiss and Mr. Gor'bun was inside. Then the world turned bright white and Sno was lifted off his feet and sent flying against the side of the transport that had just started moving again.

Pain radiated out from Sno's back as his shirt, then his skin, was nearly scraped free of his body by the moving transport. Twisting hard and fast as the vehicle's momentum sent him spinning and ricocheting back at the station platform, Sno managed to tuck a shoulder and roll a few meters, to avoid getting his skull bashed in by the platform's brutally hard surface.

What he didn't avoid was the burning debris that represented the remains of the station building. Piles of scorched refuse sat there and Sno found himself smack in the middle of a circle of flames and thick, acrid smoke. His shirt in tatters, he ripped it off his body and tore a long strip to wrap around his nose and mouth as the smoke assaulted his lungs.

Sno squinted through the pungent clouds and tried to find some semblance of life, but all he saw were the battered and burnt bodies of the few travelers, or workers, that had been waiting inside the station. Mr. Gor'bun's corpse was nowhere to be seen. Sno was not surprised.

There were more than a couple of piles of burning matter that could or could not have been living beings before the explosion.

Tapping at his wrist, Sno activated his comm and waited for the chime in his ear to tell him the connection was active and secure.

"Agent Prime requesting extraction," he stated when the chime finally came.

There had been a significant delay. Sno wondered if the incoming storm was messing with the connection. It shouldn't, considering his comm was next-gen quantum tech, but then every planet was different and had its issues.

"Repeat, Agent Prime requesting extraction," Sno stated once more. The sound of emergency alert sirens grew in the distance and Sno swore. "Shit. Hey! Anyone on the damn comm?"

Still no response.

The wind had picked up considerably, chilling the sweat on his torso, giving him a shiver despite the heat radiating off the wreckage that surrounded him. Sno studied the piles, found a route out, and made his move, leaping across two smoldering piles of debris before getting clear of most of the mess.

The emergency alert sirens grew louder.

Without a thought, Sno stripped a corpse of its jacket and shirt, put them both on, and limp-sprinted to the end of the station platform, heading for a copse of scraggly trees that stood swaying in the wind. Other than a pile of boulders a few meters away, the trees were about all the cover there was for as far as Sno could see. It struck him that the station was a strange place for Mr. Gor'bun to disembark, but the desolation of the area did provide excellent range of views for whoever was coming for Mr. Gor'bun. Visibility was completely unobstructed in all directions other than the copse of trees.

Sno wondered if the station's destruction was meant for him as much as for Mr. Gor'bun. A solid pair of binocs would pick Sno out easily. His face wasn't exactly supposed to be known wide, but Sno had made plenty of enemies across the galaxy over the years as an agent for the Fleet Intelligence Service's Special Service Division or FIS-SSD.

"Where is my damn backup?" he muttered as he made his way to the trees and found some cover from both the increasing winds of the storm and any possible eyes tracking him. They'd know where he was, but he wouldn't be an easy target any longer. The smoke back on the platform had probably been all that stood between him and a plasma blast between the eyes if someone had obtained a rifle and was gunning for him.

Sno swiped across his wrist and brought up a holo of his comm system. Aural implant was in the green. Transmitter and receiver in the green with all planet-wide spectrums fully open. Main channels and sub-channels were accessible. No trace of jamming. The comm itself wasn't the issue.

The far-off sirens went silent. Sno frowned as he looked towards the destruction. No vehicles. No rollers or hover cars; no emergency swift ships. No sign of emergency personnel anywhere. The vehicles never made it to the explosion site.

That got Sno moving. Either the emergency vehicles had been called back, which meant someone in power on Egthak had made a request. Or the vehicles had been stopped and possibly destroyed just like the station. Sno hadn't heard any explosions, but a molecular disruptor would do the trick with barely a sound. Emergency vehicles weren't shielded against violent tech like that.

Sno stood at the edge of the trees for a moment then sprinted as fast as he could to the stand of boulders a few meters off. He'd made it halfway before the trees behind him were engulfed in flames. No sound of a weapon discharge or incoming projectile. They simply caught fire, sending flames arching far, far into the sky.

Sno dove for the boulders. He rolled and came up with his back against the stone. His ears were on overdrive, listening for the approach of enemies. Nothing. No crunch of wheels or hum of a grav engine. No footfalls of boots running his way. Nothing except the crack and pop of the trees burning.

There were times in Sno's career where he sometimes, and only sometimes, wished the SSD didn't have a 'no AI agents in the field' policy. He had old friends that swore by their AI counterparts. Whether simply assistants or ship pilots, everyone said having one made all the difference. But the SSD couldn't take the risk of an AI going rogue. Didn't matter if the AI was mainframe-based or a physical android, the SSD didn't trust them and refused to allow agents to use them in the field.

Sno knew of a couple exceptions, but those were extreme cases where the director in charge had put in a special request. That knowledge didn't help him much at that moment. What would have helped was an AI to call who could bring his ship to his current location and get him all the Hells out of the situation he found himself in.

Which was what?

A destroyed transport station, a dead asset, and a copse of trees spontaneously combusting? What kind of situation was that?

Waiting, listening, calculating, Sno stayed put, his back firmly against the boulders. Without new intel, he wasn't going anywhere.

Thirty minutes. An hour. Two hours. Sno waited. There was a protocol in place. No contact after four hours and the local FIS liaison would be forced to take action. Unfortunately for Sno, that meant another few hours of bureaucratic back and forth before a decision was made to send out local friendlies to find him.

Unlike the SSD, the FIS never deviated from protocol. That made Sno's job extremely difficult at times, and damn near impossible at others, but in the end, asses were covered and the Fleet Intelligence Service could survive another round of Galactic Fleet Council reviews which meant the SSD survived another round of reviews. To Sno's superiors, surviving those reviews was more important than Sno's actual survival out in the field. Or that was how it felt most times.

So, Sno waited. It was all he could do.

3.

The swift ship was a two-seater. It came in low and fast, a blip on the horizon then a blob then a fully formed vehicle shooting straight at where Sno still sat, back secure against a couple tons of stone. Shaped like a large needle with four stubby wings spaced evenly around the aft end, the swift ship lived up to its name in all ways.

Sno watched the ship come in fast then do two low, quick circles of the area before landing a quarter click from the boulders. Sno didn't move. The swift ship had no markings, nothing to indicate it was from any specific agency. It could have been his rescue or it could have been part of the same entity that had blown up the station and killed Mr. Gor'bun.

So, Sno waited. Some more.

The cockpit of the ship opened up top and two lines of liquid metal alloy deployed from just under the seal, quickly forming into a multi-runged ladder for the pilot to climb down. Sno did not recognize the pilot, but that didn't mean anything. The Egthak liaison never gave Sno a list of trusted local contacts and Sno never asked for one. Safer that way.

"Hail there, friend!" the pilot shouted as she stepped onto the ground and swiveled her head in Sno's direction.

No binocs, so she must have had ocular implants in place or there would have been no way she could have seen Sno up against those boulders.

Sno did not respond. He waited quietly and watched as the woman approached his position.

Humanoid and bipedal, the woman could have been human, but it was hard for Sno to tell. She was dressed in a pilot's uniform complete with headgear that obstructed any decent study of her specific anatomy and race. He could see that her skin was a bright orange, but that meant nothing. Most humans had bright-colored skin, along with a dozen other bipedal races.

And those were the races Sno knew of; the galaxy was a vast place and new civilizations were discovered yearly, added to the list of Galactic Fleet allies, or Skrang Alliance allies, or coalition of independent planets that swore allegiance to neither the GF nor the Skrang, blaming both for the War that nearly destroyed half the galaxy so many years earlier.

Despite his inability to accurately identify the woman's race, Sno had no regrets regarding his lack of ocular implants. Too many planets, systems, stations, and cities flagged anyone with more than a simple aural implant for comms and holo display implant for connecting to the grid. Once flagged, that person was tracked relentlessly, depending on the security measures in place for said planet, system, station, or city. In Sno's line of work, he couldn't afford to be constantly monitored. That kind of non-stop surveillance ruined an agent's career quickly.

And Sno liked his job.

The pilot slowed when Sno still didn't respond to her cheery hails. She didn't stop completely, but her eager gait became hesitant, wary.

"Denman Sno, yes?" she said when she was only a few meters away. "I sure hope so because I raced against that storm to get here, and we only have about twenty minutes before it turns the atmosphere into an unnavigable mess."

"Pass phrase," Sno said, still seated on the ground.

"Excuse me?" the woman asked. At that, she did stop. "Pass phrase?"

Sno cocked his head, but said nothing else.

"Uh... No one gave me a pass phrase," the woman said. Steely gray eyes blazed with danger. The woman's hand went to her hip, but there was no holster or weapon there. The hand fell away empty and her fingers began tapping the side of her thigh. "If I'm supposed to have a pass phrase, then you are shit out of luck, friend. All I have is a swift ship idling back there with an empty seat inside that has your name on it. If your name is Denman Sno."

"Sorry. Wrong guy," Sno said. "Maybe check at the station ahead."

"Station ahead...? Are you daft? This is the only station that is no longer a station on the entire line," the woman snapped. "I was sent to pick up Denman Sno at the station that is no longer there. That pile of smoking rubble fits the description." She pointed a finger at Sno. "And you fit the description of Denman Sno. Either you want a ride back to Egthak City or you don't. Better tell me now because I need to get back to my ship and take off ASAP before that shit storm comes down on us."

"Who sent you?" Sno asked.

"Don't know the gentleman's name," the woman replied immediately. "Only name I got was Denman Sno. But he was a Dornopheous. You know, those putty people? All one big blob constantly moving unless you scare them then they turn into a puddle of fear at your feet. You ever been around a Dornopheous before?"

"I have," Sno said and stood up slowly, wiping grit and sand off his ass as he stretched his legs and watched the woman carefully. "Dornopheous give you a name?"

Alarm bells were going off in Sno's head. His local FIS liaison was not Dornopheous. The man had been a halfer, part human and part Spilfleck, a lizard race with neck frills that extended whenever they became excited or frightened. The only Dornopheous Sno knew was...

"Don't answer that," Sno said before the woman could reply to his question. "You already said you only have one name. I think I know who sent you."

"Great on you, friend," the woman said, bowing and twisting at the waist so she could sweep an arm back towards her ship. "Would you care to grace me with your presence in my ship so we can leave before we're torn apart by fifty kilometer-wide cyclones?"

Sno glanced past the woman, past her ship, and saw what was coming straight for them. She was right, the storm had worsened and they were dangerously close to being overtaken by it.

"Yes. Thank you," Sno said and started jogging towards the ship.

The woman joined him, matching his pace as they both hurried to the swift ship and climbed inside. The cockpit closed and sealed and the ship lifted off before either Sno or the woman had finished strapping in.

"AI?" Sno asked as the ship turned, banked, and shot across the sky towards Egthak City.

"What?" the woman asked. "Oh, no, not AI. Simple identification protocol I created. I activated it when I left the ship so it would be ready to take off as soon as I was back aboard. Like I said, friend, we're cutting it close."

Sno nodded. He was seated behind the pilot in a simple jump seat. No safety frills or extra padding. A place for his ass and a place for his back; cross-strap harness to keep him in place if the flying got dicey. As he studied the swift ship, he realized he was safe. Contractors and illicit operators liked bells and whistles. They liked spending money on equipment that made their jobs easier and lives more comfortable. Sno hadn't met a single contractor or operator that wasn't that way.

But the swift ship he was in was so stripped down that Sno wondered if it even had basic tech interfaces. He leaned slightly forward and was amused at the sight of the woman piloting the ship with a very retro-looking flight stick. Nothing indicated that she was jacked into the controls with implants or physical enhancements. Throttle and flight stick, that was about all Sno could see other than some simple holo navigation displays.

"Got a question, friend?" the woman asked.

"Name?" Sno replied.

"I have one," the woman responded.

She didn't give him her name and Sno didn't press. He never confirmed with her that he was actually Denman Sno, so fair play with her being coy too.

"I'm going to drop you off on the outskirts of the city," the woman said. "I was told to bring you in to a specific landing zone, but the way you're acting, I think you might prefer an indirect delivery. You'll be about a two-kilometer walk from the landing zone, so it's not much of a hike, but it gives you a chance to observe the location before heading in."

"That's nice of you," Sno said. "Where'd you learn that bit of trade craft? Not here on Egthak. Nothing happens on Egthak."

"That's not true or I wouldn't have been sent to fetch you, friend," the woman replied with a snicker. "Plenty happens on Egthak, just like any other planet. And what makes you think I'm using some type of trade craft? Common sense says that you're in some sort of trouble and I'd rather not get too close to whatever climax or conclusion your trouble leads to."

Sno liked the woman. She wasn't from Egthak, the automatic motion of going for a holstered pistol told him she was used to having a weapon on her at all times. So not from Egthak. But she was a professional. Sno just couldn't figure out at what.

"Deliveries," the woman said without Sno asking a question. "I'm a courier. Plain and simple. I get goods delivered fast, friend. That's my job. Wasn't expecting to pick up a quick gig like this while here on Egthak, but you never turn down a job when one is placed before you. Especially when it pays in chits, not credits. Cash in hand always gets my attention."

"Good to know," Sno said. "I don't have any chits on me, so I hope you've already been paid."

"Handsomely and upfront," the woman said. She cleared her throat. "I'm going to ask a question that I want you to answer."

"That a threat?"

"Not specifically, no. But I would like to know if you destroyed that station back there. And if you did, will you riding in my ship end up with me catching blow-back from that destruction?"

"I didn't and it won't," Sno replied. He felt comfortable answering those questions. "Care to tell me your name now that I've been a huge help?"

Sno could only see the back of the woman's head, but he caught a tightening along the skin of her jaw and assumed she'd grinned.

"Maybe sometime," the woman responded. "Not today. You're too much of a wild card for me to be giving you my name. We meet again and we'll see then. Okay, friend?"

"Okay, friend," Sno replied.

Ahead on the horizon were signs they were approaching Egthak city. Small dwellings that were scattered about quickly became densely packed until they were wall to wall and gave way to taller and taller buildings. The storm had kicked up so much dust that Sno could only make out the outlines of the modest skyscrapers that constituted the center of Egthak City.

"Gonna put down in about two minutes," the woman said. "Right over there by that strip of shops. Once on the ground, you'll want to head northwest until you reach a primary school. Landing zone was supposed to be the sports field. Another reason I'm not going there. I'm not about to tear up some kids' sports field because a Dornopheous paid me a bunch of chits."

She laughed.

"Oh, and reach behind you. Should be a shirt back there that fits. I always keep extras lying around. That one you have on, well…stinks like death and smoke. Change it."

Sno was really liking the woman. He reached behind him and pulled out a shirt that looked like it would fit. It neither looked nor smelled completely clean, but it was better than being dropped off in Egthak City with the nasty shirt he had on.

4.

The swift ship took off and was gone before Sno made it past the first shop in the strip of buildings. A part of Sno was hoping he'd see the pilot again. She had guts and didn't seem like the type that got caught up in intergalactic intrigue on a regular basis. Sno could use someone like that in his life.

The shops to Sno's left were closing up as the storm bore down on Egthak City. Sno glanced over his shoulder to see a wall of dust fueled by massive storm clouds heading straight for him. It would still take a good hour or so before the storm hit, but that didn't put Sno at ease.

Once the storm slammed into Egthak City, Sno's chances of finding answers to the day's insanity would be close to impossible. An attack like that was carefully orchestrated which meant there would be an escape plan in place for the perpetrators. That escape plan would already be rolling along, and Sno needed to hurry if he was going to catch even a hint at who was behind it all.

He broke into a jog and hurried past the strip of shops, turning at the corner of the next street and heading northwest as the pilot had said to do. Sno knew he was taking a risk trusting the swift ship pilot, but every instinct in him said she was on the level.

Sno continued jogging, passing another row of shops then a couple of apartment buildings, until he came to a street sign that pointed to the primary school. He took that turn and slowed then stopped as he scanned the area for threats.

"Hello?" Sno called into his comm. "Someone confirm you hear me."

Still no answer. Sno doubted it was a tech issue. The instincts that told him to trust the swift ship pilot told him that his backup was dead. Or captured. But dead was more likely. Even captured, they would have found a way to get some type of message to him even if it was only a series of panicked clicks.

Sno spotted the sports field and walked slowly towards it, all senses on high alert for the next attack. It would be coming, he knew that for sure, but the when and where were impossible to predict. If he was a betting man, which he was, he would say an open sports field made one convenient spot for an ambush. All it would take was a nicely placed sniper to cap off Sno's day.

As Sno passed the posted entrance to the sports field, he caught sight of a Dornopheous standing close to a row of practice equipment on the opposite side of the field. Sno had no idea what kind of sport the equipment was used for, since he hadn't studied Egthak's sporting culture before setting foot on the planet, but it looked like the sport certainly was full contact by the way the equipment mimicked the size and shape of many of the galaxy's races.

The Dornopheous turned and gave Sno a cautious wave.

"Trel'ali," Sno muttered. He took a deep breath and moved across the open sports field, his neck hair standing straight up once again.

"Sno," Trel'ali said when Sno reached him. "Been a while. Nice shirt."

"Thanks," Sno said.

Trel'ali, like all Dornopheous, was a semi-solid pile of putty that stood erect, his eyes level with Sno's. He waved a half-formed hand at Sno and motioned for them to get out of the open and over to a covered stand of seats.

"Not happy to see you, Trel'ali," Sno said, following the Dornopheous to cover. Sno fought back a sigh of relief when they stepped into the shadows and moved behind a short plasticrete wall. "What happened today?"

"That's a question a lot of beings are asking themselves right now, Sno," Trel'ali said once they were semi-secure behind the wall.

An ambitious sniper could use concentrated plasma, or a highly volatile laser stream, to hit them behind the wall, but those would be even harder weapons to import. A basic plasma rifle blast would be stopped by the plasticrete long enough for them to seek better cover. The looks on both men's faces said they were keenly aware of that.

"My backup?" Sno asked.

"Dead," Trel'ali confirmed.

"I guessed as much," Sno said and sighed. "How'd you get involved?"

"I was in the area," Trel'ali said in a tone that said he wasn't going to answer any detailed questions on the subject.

"Lucky me," Sno said.

"Extremely. What happened to the swift ship? Pilot was supposed to land here in the field."

"The pilot thought that was a stupid idea. And she didn't want to ruin the field."

"Huh. Not my instructions, but you made it here all the same."

"And why am I here and not at the docking ports? I shouldn't be on this planet anymore."

"You'll be leaving as soon as the storm passes."

They both turned to face the direction of the incoming storm. The wind had picked up and it pulled and pushed at flaps of Trel'ali's putty body.

"I don't know Egthak all that well," Sno said. "This a bad storm?"

"Bad enough," Trel'ali replied. He formed an arm and held it out. A holo appeared showing the corpses of Sno's backup team. They'd been brutally hacked to death. "I'm calling this a local issue. I think they got word of your operation somehow and decided to blow that transport station as a message to the Egthak authorities. The state of the bodies is consistent with other local murders claimed by an upstart terrorist cell."

"Upstart terrorist cell?" Sno scoffed. "These aren't preschoolers here. There's no upstart to it when they end up killing three FIS operatives."

"Of course. My apologies for the flippant term," Trel'ali replied, his putty head bowing to physically emphasize his verbal apology. "But, I do believe these killings and the attack on the station are local, not galactic. Bad coincidence."

"How'd you get involved? Gerber contact you directly? I'd think it'd have to be Gerber and not Crush. Considering."

"Yes. Considering…"

Sno waited, but Trel'ali didn't elaborate. He left their troubled history untouched between them for a minute before he said, "You going to tell me what's next or do I have to guess?"

"Here," Trel'ali said, all business. He stretched his arm towards Sno and a new holo appeared. "Safe house. One hundred percent clean. Go there and hunker down. When the storm is almost past then make your way to the docking ports. Port Eleven will have your ship waiting and ready."

"I didn't land my ship at Port Eleven," Sno said.

"I had it moved and scanned," Trel'ali said. "It's being watched closely, so no need to scan it again when you get there. Take off and do not look back at Egthak. I will handle the terrorist cell and make sure your colleagues are avenged."

"Avenged? This personal for you, Trel'ali?"

"It always is, Sno," Trel'ali replied as he waved his arm at Sno. "Take the holo and coordinates. Get to the safe house. Hunker down then—"

"Get to the docking ports," Sno interrupted. He waved his wrist through the holo and the image was transferred with a soft bleep. "Anything else I need to know?"

"If there was, I would tell you," Trel'ali said with a quick nod. He turned and walked off without another word.

Sno watched him go, the Dornopheous disappearing into one of the sports field's entrance tunnels. Sno counted to sixty, scanned the area with his eyes then left the sports field through a different entrance tunnel.

Once away from the primary school, Sno brought up the holo, memorized the coordinates of the safe house and the map to get there then deleted the holo permanently. If he was killed and his wrist implant was hacked, no one would know about the safe house. That was for Trel'ali's benefit. No need to burn a good hiding place.

It took Sno a good hour to walk the streets of Egthak City before he reached the safe house. He'd taken a convoluted, circuitous route to ensure that he wasn't being tailed. By the time he slid in through the house's back door, the storm had hit the city full on and the sky had become nearly pitch black with dark clouds.

Sno didn't bother turning on any lights in the house. He did a quick scan of the place then found a chair in the front room and sat down. He sat there stock still and listened to the storm grow and growl around the house. Soon it was louder than a battalion of heavy rollers.

Sno stood, picked up his chair, and moved it to a corner of the room that gave him a view of every entrance. Hearing was gone, even with enhanced listening through his implant. The storm was too loud. So he sat back down and watched and waited. If anyone came for him, he may not hear them, but he'd see them.

The storm raged on.

5.

The storm didn't let up for most of the evening and far into the night. By the time it began to slack enough that Sno thought he could handle walking through it towards the docking ports, it was the early hours of the next morning.

Sno had been awake for thirty-four hours straight. He was exhausted, but that exhaustion was only background noise. His real mission was dead and his new mission was to make sure he didn't end up the same way. Mortal survival tended to trump exhaustion. Sno's field training and years of experience kicked in. Time to go.

Finding a towel in a dusty closet, Sno made another covering for his mouth and nose, wrapped and tied the towel around his head, and left the safe house, eyes checking every direction at once to find the attack. No attack came. Sno moved quickly away from the safe house, his shoulders up to his ears and head down to minimize the discomfort of the blowing dust that swirled hard around him.

Street lights glowed dimly as their halogens fought against the end of the storm. The light gave the street, and the next, and the next, an eerie feel. The world was a dim orange-pink haze of half-obscured solid objects and shadows that stretched on for eternity.

Sno kept walking, once again taking as indirect a route as he could without getting completely lost himself. Even with the cover of the storm haze, Sno would have spotted a tail if someone had been following him. He brought up a scan holo from his wrist and checked for snooping tech that may have been tracking him, but the display was clear. No drones or follow bots anywhere around.

The wind slowly began to ease up as Sno grew closer to the docking ports. Lights were coming on in the buildings around him and a few faces appeared at windows as storm shutters irised open. Sno picked up his pace so he could reach Port Eleven without being hassled by any curious locals. Egthak wasn't exactly a bustling tourist destination, but it did a good business amongst galactic travelers. Even still, a man out walking the dark streets while an active storm was still blowing about would eventually raise a few eyebrows.

The docking ports were only a couple blocks away, but Sno stopped dead in his tracks as he watched a very large shadow appear under the street light at the corner ahead of him. The shadow had to be over ten feet tall and almost as wide. There were very few races in the galaxy that had those proportions while still looking as solid as that shadow did.

Chassfornian.

"Damn," Sno muttered as he quickly looked for an escape route.

Dealing with a Chassfornian would not be a good thing. They were massive creatures. Built like giant mastiffs, but bipedal. Once used as shock troops in the War, none of the other races would deal with them anymore due to their intense need to kill anything they came in contact with, even supposed allies. They were usually with a handler to keep them in check since their default personality was pure, homicidal rage. Sno did not see a handler around.

A lone Chassfornian, off leash and waiting for him. Certainly not a good thing.

The space between the two buildings on his right was just wide enough for Sno to fit through. He ducked into the narrow corridor and sprinted as fast as the width between the buildings would allow. By the time he reached the end, his shoulders, hands, and elbows were scraped and shredded. So much for the shirt the swift ship pilot had given him.

Sno paused at the end of the space, ducked his head around, saw no sign of trouble, especially not a waiting Chassfornian, then burst from cover, his legs moving as fast as they could. The exhaustion was creeping from background to foreground, and Sno had to will his legs to move one in front of the other in order to keep from stumbling. Every rapid step was a deeply intentional action.

He was down the street and only a block from a side entrance to the docking ports when Sno felt more than saw a hunk of the closest building come part and rush him side on. Before Sno could react, he was hit so hard that he nearly bent completely over sideways, his cheek close to touching his ankle. Pain radiated up his leg, his side, and through his ribs.

But Sno didn't have time to worry about the pain. He was flying through the air and about to collide with an ancient-looking roller. Sno tried to twist his body into as small a projectile as possible, but there was no time. From collision with the huge form to flight to collision with the roller was a second at the most.

Sno's other side exploded with pain as he slid down the surface of the roller and crumpled onto the street.

He forced himself to get his hands and feet underneath him. Then he forced himself to breathe and haul his ass up onto his feet. Just in time to be sandwiched up against the roller.

The Chassfornian laughed, actually laughed at Sno as the man cried out in pain.

"You mine," the Chassfornian said, his voice a timbre that was almost inaudible due to the low register. There had to be some races that couldn't hear the being at all. "Mine for the bounty."

Bounty? Sno couldn't figure out what the being was talking about. What bounty? On who? Him? A bounty? Hits had been called out and paid for on SSD agents before, but no one had ever offered a bounty. A bounty was too public, too out in the open, too known. A bounty meant someone was sending someone else a message.

Sno was lifted several feet into the air, his body clutched in the Chassfornian's claws like a child's rag doll.

"You Sno?" the Chassfornian asked.

Sno wasn't going to reply and make the being's life easier. Not that he could reply since he could barely take in enough air for breath let alone for words.

The Chassfornian's eyes blinked several times and a holo erupted from the being's right wrist. It was a holo of Sno. The image spun three hundred and sixty degrees then blinked away.

"You Sno," the Chassfornian confirmed for himself. "I get more you live."

The only thought Sno could muster that didn't have to do with the intense pain he was in was that he'd never heard a Chassfornian talk before. He knew they had speech skills, but not once in his career with the FIS and SSD, or his time with the Galactic Fleet military, had he ever heard a Chassfornian utter any sound that wasn't a murderous war cry.

"Wrong...guy," Sno finally managed to utter.

"No," the Chassfornian said and hoisted Sno up over his shoulder like a sack of vegetables.

Sno grunted with pain, his ribs protesting the rough treatment loud enough that he saw specks and stars in his blurred vision.

Sno was carried towards the docking ports. There was a slit in the metal alloy fence just large enough for the Chassfornian to fit through. The storm hadn't quite passed fully, so there was plenty of gloom for the being to take advantage of to get across the several meters of open ground from the fence to the first docking port.

"Who...?" Sno asked, unable to get out more than the one word. His ribs felt like splinters and each splinter was jabbing deep into his body, causing him to shudder and shiver with agony.

"No talk," the Chassfornian said as they passed the first then a second then a third docking port before coming to a fourth.

Docking Port Eight read the sign to the side of the port's entrance. There was no building, no hangar, just a wide-open landing circle ringed by a barely perceptible energy shield. The Chassfornian walked right through the energy shield to the ship waiting in the landing circle. There was a hiss and spark of static electricity that tickled at Sno's skin, but no debilitating shock like there would have been if the Chassfornian's biometrics hadn't been keyed in properly.

Sno was able to get a look at the ship and that's when the real panic set in. Skrang tech. The ship was not GF and was not part of any GF allied contractor or manufacturer line. It was Skrang Alliance all the way and the day's events began to click into place.

"No," Sno grunted and started to squirm in the Chassfornian's unbreakable grip.

"Shut it," the Chassfornian barked, ignoring Sno's feeble attempts to get free.

Sno went still. Not because of the Chassfornian, but because he'd found what he'd been squirming around to see. There was a raw spot on the back of the Chassfornian's neck where the kill charge had been removed. That told Sno that the Chassfornian had been one of the elite shock troops back in the War, part of a squad that had been sent out with full autonomy to murder everything in sight. The kill charge was simply a failsafe in case the Chassfornian decided he didn't want to go back to base and get caged up again. Press of a button and the being lost its head. Literally.

Even though the kill charge was gone, that spot still held value to Sno. There was a nerve cluster under the skin that was as sensitive as the being's gonads. All Sno needed to do was hit that spot with enough force and the Chassfornian would drop. Hopefully.

Sno threw an elbow into the spot and the Chassfornian slowed then stopped walking. It dropped Sno onto the ground and took a couple of steps back. The being's huge eyes studied Sno as it rubbed at the back of its neck.

"Ow," the Chassfornian said. It took a few more steps back, rubbed even harder. Then a few more steps as it rolled its head on its neck. "Ow."

Sno watched from where he'd been dropped. He had no choice. The fall from shoulder to ground had been nearly ten feet. All of Sno's concentration was on keeping his lungs pumping as his ribs insisted that they try to tear through and out of his body. Sno would have welcomed a ribless bit of relief, but that was wishful thinking.

The Chassfornian shook its head back and forth then let its hand drop away from its neck.

"Stupid," the Chassfornian said.

The being took one step towards Sno. That was the last step it took.

Chassfornian pulp exploded everywhere as the docking port's energy shield evaporated and a swift ship dropped from the sky directly on the being. Hair and blood and bits of bone coated Sno like a gory wave.

"Come on!" the swift ship pilot shouted as the cockpit shot open. "Get your ass up and in!"

Sno opened his mouth to let the pilot know that getting up of his own accord was not in the cards. Instead of words coming out of his mouth, a hunk of Chassfornian cheek rolled inside and Sno struggled not to vomit as he spat the grisly morsel out onto the ground.

The swift ship pilot cursed and swore as she jumped out of her ship and hurried over to Sno. She grabbed him under the armpits and hauled him to his feet. Sno was not too proud to scream. He let loose with a cry so loud that the pilot nearly let him go to jump away.

"Hells," the pilot said as she half-walked, half-dragged Sno to her ship.

She shoved him against the side of the swift ship and short, powerful clamps took hold of Sno, keeping him from falling onto his face. The pilot climbed up into the cockpit then waved her wrist over her control console and the clamps began to move, pulling Sno up into the ship. Sno screamed for the first couple of seconds then his voice gave out and he only grunted the last couple of feet before he was tossed into the jump seat.

Before Sno could do more than pull his legs inside the cockpit, the swift ship was already lifting off. Sno somehow managed to get upright and the emergency seat restraints automatically strapped themselves around his body. Sno would have screamed again, but his breath was taken away as he saw three Chassfornians racing towards the swift ship.

"Hold on!" the pilot yelled as she angled the nose of the ship upward and shoved the throttle to full.

The swift ship shot up into the sky then began to shake violently.

"You have got to be kidding," the pilot snapped.

Sno didn't have to ask what the issue was. He could see it plainly.

A Chassfornian was snarling and slamming its forehead against the top of the cockpit over and over and over again. The plastiglass began to crack under the cranial assault.

6.

Barrel rolls.

Simple fix when faced with a raging Chassfornian slamming its forehead against the cockpit hatch. Simple, but not easy.

The Chassfornian gripped that swift ship with all of its strength. Sno thought he could actually hear the hull crumpling from the power behind the being's massive claws. The forehead kept ramming over and over, even as the pilot spun the ship with enough force that it should have thrown the being far and wide.

"Hells," the pilot said again as she tried every maneuver in her arsenal to shake the Chassfornian loose. Nothing worked.

"Hold tight!" the pilot yelled as she sent the swift ship into a nose dive.

Sno couldn't hold tight to anything. His body had pretty much given up obeying, so he sat there, slumped in the jump seat, and prayed the restraints would hold.

The pilot yanked hard on the flight stick and brought the swift ship rocketing back up into the sky. The Chassfornian scrabbled to hang on, but even that large of a being couldn't maintain its grip against the G forces that were shoving at it. With a final roar of rage and bitterness, the Chassfornian was shaken loose and sent falling to the landing dock far, far below.

Sno let out a breath he'd been holding and winced as his ribs protested yet again at even that slight movement of his chest.

"My ship," Sno gasped.

"Gone," the swift ship pilot said.

"What?" Sno asked.

"During the storm," the pilot said and a holo appeared in front of Sno.

The holo was of Docking Port Eleven and Sno's ship. It was a custom-made TL-33 Raven scoop-wing speeder. Four seat bridge with two sleeping cabins, a small mess, a single med pod bay, and a small cargo hold. Four plasma cannons were its only armaments, but the defensive shielding was next-gen tech that almost no one in the galaxy had. The ship wasn't meant for battle, but for fast travel. If it did get into a fight, it could take a hell of beating while it used its natural speed and agility to get as far away from the attacker as possible.

There was a flash and the ship was no longer there. The holo of the docking port was still running, but the ship was barely more than scrap.

Smoking, smoldering pieces and parts littered the docking port's landing circle.

"I was leaving, getting ahead of the rush out of the docking ports when the storm finally passed," the pilot said. "I saw it go up. Obviously, since I caught the holo of it happening."

"How'd you know…?" Sno asked and grimaced at the thousands of stabs of pain in his chest.

"Know it was yours?" the pilot finished for him. "I guessed. Nice ship. Way nicer than the lot that occupy the other ports. I figured it was the perfect ship for an FIS agent. SSD, right?"

Sno didn't respond.

"Don't bother denying," the pilot said as she leveled out the swift ship's trajectory once they'd cleared the planet's stratosphere. "I'm never wrong about ships and their owners."

"The Chassfornians," Sno said quietly.

"What about them?" the pilot asked.

"They…were there…with someone," Sno said and shivered with pain.

"Obviously," the pilot replied. "You ever see a Chassfornian fly a ship? No, because no one has. They'd ram the damn thing into the first ship that pissed them off. Yeah. Someone flew all four of them to Egthak and for a reason."

"Me," Sno said. "Bounty."

"A bounty on an SSD agent?" The pilot whistled low and slow. "What did you do to get that kind of heat?"

Sno shook his head as he closed his eyes. "Don't…know."

"Better think hard," the pilot said as the swift ship fully left Egthak's orbit and shot across the system towards the closest wormhole portal. "I took a risk helping you, and only because I'm hoping to earn some brownie points with the FIS. Maybe land some courier contracts here and there. But if you've got bounty heat on you, then I better drop you at the closest Galactic Fleet station and wash my hands of you."

"Get me to…"

Sno tried to finish his sentence, but he couldn't manage through the pain. He took slow, shallow breaths and tried again, but his ribs would not cooperate.

"Get you to what, spy boy?" the pilot asked.

Sno managed to activate his implant and swipe a set of coordinates up to the pilot. She huffed when she received the coordinates and glanced over her shoulder at Sno.

"You're sure?" she asked.

Sno nodded, but even that hurt. There wasn't a part of him that didn't hurt.

"It'll take about fourteen hours," the Pilot said. "Maybe longer. Probably longer. We'll have a couple of checkpoints to get through."

"No...checkpoints," Sno said and gasped. He struggled to swipe a data file towards the pilot. After three feeble attempts, he gave up.

"Use the interface by your arm," the pilot said as she banked the swift ship down and around a pair of freight cruisers that were approaching the queue of interstellar vehicles waiting for their turn to go through the system's wormhole portal. "It takes a bit longer, but I'll get whatever you're trying to swipe my way."

Sno nodded again, winced at the pain, and slowly, carefully moved his right arm into a long groove next to the jump seat. Instantly, his implant activated and he was able to transfer the data file into the ship's system.

"Huh," the pilot said. "These travel docs legit?"

Sno didn't answer.

"I just need to know if I'll catch flack at a checkpoint for these," the pilot pressed.

Sno didn't answer.

"Fine. I'll use them if needed."

The swift ship was up next and the pilot aimed directly for the center of the wormhole portal. The view of stars and twinkling far-off planets became a swirling mix of a thousand different lights, all strobing together into one brilliant burst of illumination before settling into countless streams and bands of color.

"Rest while you can," the pilot said. "The more sleep you get, the shorter your stay in a med pod will be."

Sno grunted and closed his eyes again. A wave of nausea hit him and his eyes popped back open. He concentrated on the bands of color that swirled around the swift ship's cockpit instead. After a few minutes, his eyes closed on their own and he was finally asleep.

A proximity warning brought Sno awake instantly and he slapped at his side for a pistol, crying out in pain at the sudden movement.

"Relax, friend," the pilot said. "We're coming out the other end to the first checkpoint. The GF sure does like hassling travelers around these systems. Almost wish I could live out with the Edgers and not see another GF blockade ever again."

Sno snorted and shook his head.

"You think...it'd be better out there?" he asked, surprised he didn't convulse with agony over such a long sentence. The couple hours sleep did help. Some. "It's not."

"You've been out to the Edge?" the pilot asked. "How far?"

"All the…way," Sno said.

"Is it as dark and empty as they say?" the pilot asked.

"Darker," Sno replied. "Emptier."

"Hells," the pilot responded and whistled. "Why those Edgers fight for independence out there, I can't figure out."

"Me…neither," Sno said. "But…they do."

The pilot slowed the swift ship as a good-sized Galactic Fleet cruiser moved into position to block the way. A holo popped up in front of the pilot, a frowning Tcherian GF officer staring blankly out of the vid. Tcherians were a chameleon race able to camouflage themselves to fit their surroundings. This one simply looked bored.

"Travel documents," the bored GF officer said. "Please transmit now."

"Here we go," the pilot said and swiped at the holo.

The GF officer nodded, glanced down then looked back up quickly. He cleared his throat, swiveled one of his eyes to look off screen then forced a smile on his lizard face.

"Yes. Sorry about the delay," the GF officer said. "I have put in a clear right of way request for the next checkpoint. Simply swipe your credentials to the Fleet ships you encounter and they will let you pass without stopping. Have a nice night."

"You too, officer," the pilot said as the holo disappeared. She waited until the GF cruiser moved then engaged the engines and steered towards the next wormhole portal. "Care to tell me what that was about?"

"I carry…good papers…with me," Sno said.

"Uh huh…"

Sno felt his eyelids grow heavy again, but before he passed out once more he said, "What's your name?"

"Not sure I want that on record anymore," the pilot replied.

"I'll make it…worth your…while," Sno replied.

The pilot thought for a few seconds and Sno had to struggle to keep his eyes open.

"Velly Tarcorf," the pilot said.

"Denman Sno…" he said before drifting off.

7.

"Eight Million Gods damn, Sno," a voice bellowed, shaking the lid of the med pod as it slowly began to rise. "You care to tell me how that mission went so very, Eight Million Gods damn wrong?"

Sno opened his eyes, but didn't need the visual confirmation to know who was speaking to him.

"B'urn," Sno said as a massive paw reached into the med pod and grabbed Sno by the shoulder, lifting him into an upright position like Sno was made of tissue paper. "You trying to break me all over again?"

B'urn Sc'oll was a crazy mix of races. Part Gwreq (a four-armed, stone-skinned race that were over seven feet tall and tough as titanium), part Leforian (another four-armed, seven-foot-tall race that looked like a mix between a Dung beetle and a Great Dane), Urvein (a bear-like race that usually topped eight feet, covered in bristly fur, and built like a space freighter), and human. Despite having the genetics from two four-armed races in him, B'urn only had two arms. But they were very impressive arms and no one ever chided him for not being part of the quad-appendage club.

B'urn's eight and a half foot frame towered over the med pod, his stone-skinned, fur-covered face glaring down at Sno. He shook that massive head and rolled his eyes up.

"Eight Million Gods," he said to the ceiling.

"Yes. You mentioned them already, B'urn," Sno said. "Care to step away so I can get out of this pod and get dressed?"

"Sure, your highness," B'urn replied, stepping aside as he swept his arm down and gave an exaggerated bow. "My apologies, your lordship."

"Clever," Sno said as he set his bare feet on the ice-cold metal alloy floor of the med pod bay. He looked about, noting the rows of other med pods, only a few in use, and looked about for a cart that should have his personal effects on it. There was no cart. "B'urn? My clothes?"

"Here," B'urn said, straightening up and tossing Sno a thin robe. "Your clothes, what was left of them, are in the lab. Gerber ordered the tests himself. He wanted any trace evidence studied and logged."

"Gerber's here?" Sno asked. "Gerber rarely comes here."

"No shit, buddy," B'urn replied. "Your Egthak mission has caused a shit ripple in the SSD. I guess, and I know this will sound nutso, but I guess when Agent Prime is involved with a terrorist bombing then a fight with some mercenary Chassfornians, all in the same day, that shit gets noticed. Crazy, right?"

"Wasn't in the same day," Sno said as he took the robe and threw it over his naked body, tying the belt tight at his waist. "Took two days to accomplish all of that."

The two walked to the end of the med pod bay and waited for the security protocol to scan and log their credentials before opening the double doors. The doors slid apart and B'urn gave another bow for Sno to go first.

"How's Crush handling this?" Sno asked as they walked down the corridor towards a set of lift doors.

"Crush is raging pissed, buddy," B'urn replied, shrugging his huge shoulders like it was an everyday thing to have the division head raging pissed. "You know Crush."

"So he's quiet and barely blinking all those eyes," Sno stated. He'd been around Special Service Division Commander Crush long enough to know what raging pissed looked like.

"Not blinking any of those eyes," B'urn said.

Sno gave B'urn a side-eyed look of alarm then took a deep breath and stepped onto the lift as the doors slid open.

"Agent Prime."

"Agent Prime."

Two human techs nodded at Sno. He nodded back.

"Nothing for me?" B'urn growled.

"Agent Reign."

"Agent Reign."

"Eight Million Gods damn right," B'urn replied, making sure to smile wide so the two techs got a good look at his razor-sharp canines. "Don't forget it, kids."

"Leave the techs alone," Sno said and waved his wrist over the lift interface.

"Level Eighty-Six access granted," an electronic voice chimed.

"You two can't come," B'urn said to the techs. "Off limits."

"Leave the techs alone," Sno said again then turned to the techs. "Sorry about my colleague's behavior."

The techs nodded and smiled at Sno, their eyes never straying to B'urn.

The lift chimed and the doors opened. The two techs exited quickly. The doors slid closed and the lift continued on its journey to Level Eighty-Six.

"You wanna tell me what happened?" B'urn asked.

"Can't," Sno said. "Have to debrief with Crush first. Once he gives the all clear then I'll fill you in on what I'm allowed to."

"Not even a nibble? A morsel?" B'urn whined. "Come on, Sno. Give me something."

"Trel'ali was there," Sno said after a couple seconds consideration. "He saved my skin by hiring that swift ship pilot. She saved my skin by getting me out of the docking ports before I was torn apart by Chassfornians."

"Chassfornians," B'urn said with a shiver. "I can crush rock with my bare hands, but those beings scare the living shit out of me. I hope the med pod left a couple scars for you to show off. Surviving a Chassfornian attack is an Eight Million Gods damn miracle."

"Yes. I am fully aware of that," Sno said and took a slow, deep breath, beyond thankful his ribs were no longer splintered and trying to tear through his lungs.

The lift chimed and the doors opened onto a good-sized foyer. It was tastefully decorated, nothing too fancy, but there were a few classic prints hanging on the walls, framing a set of double doors directly across from the lift. Sno stepped out and gave B'urn a wry smile.

"You coming in, chum?" Sno asked.

"No, since you aren't going to tell me shit," B'urn said. "Catch up later?"

"Yeah, we'll catch up later," Sno said as he placed a hand against one of the double doors. There was a beep, but it didn't open right away. "Drinks in the observatory?"

"Fair enough," B'urn said. "2100. I'll have the first round waiting."

"Sounds good," Sno said and waited for the lift doors to close before he pushed on the door. It slid wide for him and he walked into his apartment.

Large, yet understated with sparse furnishings and nearly bare walls, the apartment was Sno's home away from home. Being Agent Prime, he could have the pick of the residences set aside for the elite agents of the SSD. There were plenty that were far more extravagant than the one he chose. But Sno liked the simplicity of the apartment.

He first made his way to his bedroom, ignoring the cleaning bots that were busy removing the dust that had accumulated in the apartment during Sno's absence. An electronic voice called from the kitchen, then repeated in Sno's comm, "Would you care for breakfast, Agent Prime?"

"No, thank you, Ledora," Sno said. "I'm not hungry at the moment. Going to have a steam then get dressed before my debriefing with Commander Crush."

"I shall have the bots lay out your clothes while you bathe, Agent Prime," Ledora said.

Ledora was Sno's house AI. With a female voice, Sno referred to it as a she, but in reality, Ledora could pick any of a million different voices, languages, or dialects and her core personality would remain unchanged. She was not an advanced AI, never close to achieving sentience, but she performed her duties of maintaining Sno's Division apartment as well as his personal home on the planet Nab, an Earth-like planet in the Tchor System.

"Ledora?" Sno asked as he tossed the med pod bay robe aside and walked naked into the lavatory. "How is Commander Crush's stock of Klavian whiskey at the moment?"

"I will ask his AI attendant," Ledora replied. Barely a second passed and she said, "He is quite low. Apparently, his ex-wife's family is no longer sharing their stock with him despite it being part of the divorce agreement."

"That's the information I needed. Thank you, Ledora," Sno said as he turned on the steam jets and waited for the shower to fill with moist heat. "Will you have a bottle of my personal stock ready to take to him? I don't want to go into this debriefing empty-handed."

"Your personal stock is low as well, Agent Prime," Ledora said.

"I can get more," Sno said as he stepped into the steam shower and sighed.

"Klavian whiskey is not easy to acquire these days, Agent Prime," Ledora said.

"Ledora? What's the rule?"

"No comm chatter while you are in the shower."

"Exactly. We'll talk once I'm dressed."

"Of course, Agent Prime."

Sno waited for that tell-tale silent void in his ear that said the comm connection had truly been severed. He sighed again and turned his face up to the closest steam jet, letting the heat seep into his skin. No matter what miracles the med pods performed, the med pod bay was always ice cold and Sno hated the cold. He'd been trained and conditioned to handle all extremes of weather and climate, but he never got used to being cold.

Over a decade in the SSD, Sno had been through more extremes than he cared to. He'd been in nearly every habitable system in the galaxy and more than half the uninhabitable systems. He had contacts on close to every planet and station within the Galactic Fleet's reach and more than a few contacts within Skrang Alliance territory.

As soon as he got done with his debriefing by Crush, Sno planned on calling a few of those Skrang contacts to find out what in all the Hells was up with a Skrang ship being used by a team of Chassfornians.

A team of Chassfornians...

Sno had a hard time wrapping his mind around that. Even with a decade of SSD status under his belt, he'd never seen a team of Chassfornians before. Yes, back in the War, he'd witnessed a squad of them take out village after village, station after station, but that had been a military setting and each squad had a set of non-Chassfornian handlers at the ready to rein in the beings if they got out of control. Or to terminate them if they went completely berserk.

Skrang ship and a team of Chassfornians trying to collect a bounty on him. On an SSD agent. A bounty.

Intel on that situation was well worth spending some contact capital on. Even if the mission was dead and Sno wasn't supposed to pursue it, which he was more than certain would be Crush's orders, Sno had no intention of dropping it. He'd get a serious chewing out by Crush if the commander found out, but Sno wasn't one to let a situation like that go.

Skrang ship and a team of Chassfornians trying to collect a bounty on him. Sno shook his head as he turned around and let the steam dig deep into his shoulders.

Close to an hour later, after several alerts from Ledora that Commander Crush was growing impatient, Sno finally stepped out of the steam and dried himself off. He dressed, checked his suit over several times to make sure the cut was right, then grabbed up the waiting whiskey bottle and headed out of the apartment.

"Will you be returning this evening, Agent Prime?" Ledora asked over the comm. "Shall I have dinner waiting?"

"I'll let you know, Ledora," Sno said, activating the lift. "If you don't hear from me, then don't bother with dinner. I plan on having drinks with Agent Reign in the observatory later, so I may grab something to eat then."

"Very well, Agent Prime," Ledora responded. "Please enjoy the remainder of your day."

Sno doubted enjoyment of any kind was on the agenda.

8.

Special Service Division Commander Crush was a Klav. In essence, he was a ball of eyes with several long tentacles sticking out from the flesh that wasn't occupied by eyes. Klavs were known for their brilliant minds, making them some of the best scientists in the galaxy. They also made exceptional whiskey which was prized almost religiously within the Klavian culture.

Sno made sure to hold the bottle of Klavian whiskey out ahead of him so that Crush could easily see what it was. The commander's eyes widened slightly in surprise then narrowed with obvious suspicion.

"You know how much trouble that blown mission caused, Agent Prime?" Crush asked once the two were alone in Crush's office, doors securely shut and jamming tech activated so there was no snooping on the debriefing. "Care to make a guess how many GF agencies I have had to speak with over the past two days?"

"All of them, I would suppose," Sno said. "A team of Chassfornians tends to garner attention."

Crush indicated for Sno to sit. Sno took a seat in a chair directly in front of Crush's desk, but the commander didn't sit. He hovered on three tentacles, shaking with irritation behind his desk. Sno waited for the commander to continue. He'd been in the same situation many times.

"Team of Chassfornians," Crush scoffed. "If I hadn't seen the holo vid from the docking port, I wouldn't have believed it. What in Eight Million Gods' names did you do to warrant a team of Chassfornians being formed to try to abduct you, Agent Prime?"

"A question I hope to get an answer to at some point soon," Sno said.

"No," Crush ordered, five tentacles straightening and pointing directly at Sno. "No and no and no. Do not stir this up more than it already is. Eight Million Gods know that I do not need more comm calls coming into my office because of you. What a complete cock-up, Agent Prime. An A-number-one cock up. Gerber is here. Did Agent Reign mention that Gerber was here?"

Sno didn't respond. He knew Crush well enough not to interject between every bemoaning outburst.

"Any other agent and I'd pull you out of service for a complete and total evaluation," Crush continued. "Any other agent…"

Sno continued to wait.

"Fine. Brief me. Spare no details," Crush said and finally took his seat behind his desk. All of his eyes were fixed on Sno. "Don't keep me in suspense, Agent Prime. Begin."

Sno detailed every step, action, breath from the moment he landed on Egthak to the moment he woke up in the med pod. No supposition or interpretation of events, just a simple recitation of how everything went down as Sno saw it.

"Gor'bun was going to be a solid asset, Agent Prime," Crush said after a few seconds of silence passed once Sno was done speaking.

"Yes, sir, he was," Sno agreed.

"We'll have to start from scratch there," Crush said, but Sno could tell that was a rhetorical statement and not directed at him. "Lot of work to start from scratch, but worth it in the end. I will put Agent Stand on the case."

"Agent Stand is an excellent agent," Sno said. "No one is better at gathering intel in the field than her."

"Yes, I am quite aware of that, Agent Prime," Crush grumbled. "This is my division to run, thank you."

"Of course," Sno said.

Half of Crush's eyes rolled.

"Where does this leave me, sir?" Sno asked. "Is there a new mission?"

"Should there be?" Crush asked. "You had all but two ribs nearly pulverized within you. Your left kidney was shattered and close to unrepairable by the med pod. Fractured bones in both legs and both arms."

"Really? I didn't notice that," Sno said. "The ribs took up most of my attention."

"Yes. You humans and your ribs," Crush said and sighed. "It is too bad we cannot lace your bones with titanium alloy. But you'd never make it through a single scanner in the galaxy without tripping alarms and ending up in a security interrogation room."

Sno was also used to Crush's constant litany of remarks regarding the fragile nature of the human body. Klavs didn't break or bruise, they bounced, and despite being mostly made of eyes, each orb was surprisingly resilient to violence. It was known throughout the SSD, and the FIS, that Crush looked down on the beings that didn't bounce or couldn't take a sharp stick in the eye without crying.

"You could wrap me in plasticrete," Sno suggested. "Leave a couple holes for my eyes and one for me to breath."

"Must we leave a hole for you to breathe?" Crush muttered. "Yes, well, I believe we are done here, Agent Prime."

"Are we, sir? You haven't told me my next mission," Sno said.

"Because you have no next mission, Agent Prime," Crush said, each eye daring Sno to argue. "Not yet, at least. What I would like you to do is go home and take some time to think back on Egthak and what went wrong and how you could have prevented it from going wrong."

Sno started to speak, but Crush held up a tentacle and Sno's mouth closed.

"But do not give Egthak too much thought. Do not dwell on what cannot be repaired. Simply reflect on your actions and how those actions resulted in the failure of the mission."

"If my reflections turn up no actions that contributed to the failure?" Sno asked.

"Do you truly believe that?"

"I'll let you know when I'm done reflecting," Sno said. He raised his eyebrows and Crush nodded his body. Sno stood and dipped his chin. "Then that is that?"

"That is that," Crush replied.

"No new mission? Are you sure, sir?" Sno asked. "As much as I enjoy a holiday—"

"This will not be a holiday, Agent Prime," Crush interjected.

"—I believe I am better utilized out in the field. Sir, that Skrang ship is weighing heavy on me."

"Which is why I am sure you will ignore my orders and call your contacts as soon as you are out of range of Division headquarters," Crush said, looking none too pleased with the idea. "But who am I to stop you? Only your Division Commander, is all."

"A mission would keep me from getting bored…"

Sno let the statement hang there. Crush did not grab for it. All of the commander's eyes glared at Sno.

"Dismissed, Agent Prime," Crush said when it was clear Sno had no intention of leaving before his statement was addressed.

"Yes, sir," Sno said and turned on his heel.

"Agent Prime?" Crush called out as Sno reached the office doors.

"Yes, sir?" Sno replied, turning back to face the commander.

"That swift ship pilot," Crush said. "Worth anything?"

"How do you mean, sir?"

"Is she a good enough pilot to consider recruiting?" Crush said. "We could use another good pilot for extractions. She handled yours without official training."

"She was an excellent pilot, sir," Sno said. "And a pleasant person, as well."

"Pleasant person? Eight Million Gods, Agent Prime," Crush said, exasperated. "I don't care if she's pleasant. You humans and your need to be around beings that please you. It always boils down to your slavery to your sexual organs. Klavs do not have that problem."

"That's because all you need is a good, hard wink and you're satisfied for weeks," Sno said.

Sno left the office quickly, knowing that comment would leave Crush irritated for hours.

9.

The hangar was filled with ships. More ships than most space ports saw in a month. From wall to wall, the hangar was crammed with vehicles of every size and model. The only types of ships missing were the massive ones, heavy cruiser and destroyer classes. Other than that, there were enough ships to launch a small war at any second.

"Sno," Master Sergeant Ho Mix said as Sno stood at the edge of the hangar, eyes scanning the inventory. "What can I do for you today?"

Mix was a human, a bald albino with thick, wraparound, tinted glasses permanently affixed across his eyes. Sno had never seen the man without his glasses on.

"Mix. How are we today?" Sno asked.

"I'd be better if you'd brought your ship back," Mix said as he stood shoulder to shoulder with Sno. "I hear there's a holo of it being destroyed. Never show me that holo, Sno."

"Cruelty like that is not my style, Mix," Sno said. "It was heartbreaking to see, I will admit."

"I'm sure," Mix said and waved a hand towards the inventory of ships. "Crush commed down and said to let you have your pick. He wants you out of headquarters and heading home tomorrow. Tell me which one you like and I'll have it ready to go by the morning."

"Wouldn't happen to have one just like my previous ship, would you, Mix?"

"I might. I just might," Mix said and motioned for Sno to follow him as he walked out onto the hangar floor. "Won't be an exact match. That next-gen shielding takes some time to install. Bring this ship back when you're off holiday and I can add it on then."

"Not going on holiday," Sno said.

"Right," Mix said and continued to thread his way through the many ships.

Some of the ships towered over the men while some barely came above their heads. Sno never could figure out Mix's system of storing ships. It wasn't by class or by size; not by armament or use. As far as Sno could see, the order was completely random. Except Mix always knew where every ship was placed and could walk directly to a ship without hesitation.

And getting them in and out of the hangar was never a problem. The hangar floor was one huge moltrans unit capable of molecularly transporting each vehicle to and from the hangar in the blink of an eye.

Sno had to admit there was probably no one else in the galaxy that could handle placement with the same accuracy as Mix. The man was a genius with a moltrans.

"Here we go," Mix said, pointing to a TL-33 Raven scoop-wing speeder. "Like I said, doesn't have next-gen shielding, but the defenses it does have are more than enough to get you to home. Where is that again?"

"Nab."

"Nab. Right. Nice place, Nab."

"I enjoy it."

"Good thing. Wouldn't be very pleasant living there if you hated it."

"Weapons?"

"Four plasma cannons like your previous Raven," Mix said. "I might be able to boost their power by forty or fifty percent. Give you a little extra punch, if you need it. Make up for the defensive shortcomings. Will that do for you?"

"That'll do nicely, Mix. I appreciate it," Sno said. "What time will the ship be ready?"

"0800 work?"

"0800 works," Sno said. "I'll have Ledora coordinate moving my personal effects aboard as soon as you give the okay."

"I'll comm her in a few hours," Mix said. "Where you off to now?"

"Have some personal business to attend to then drinks with Agent Reign," Sno said. "We'll be in the observatory later if you want to join us."

"Kind offer, but you know how Crush gets when support personnel fraternize with the agents at headquarters," Mix said.

Sno nodded. No more explanation needed.

"See you at 0800," Sno said.

Mix gave him a nod and was already barking orders over his comm for techs and mechanics to meet him at the Raven. Sno walked off, bringing up a holo from his wrist as he wove back through the ships.

"At headquarters," Sno said as he studied the holo of personnel currently stationed at headquarters. "Good."

Once outside the hangar, and walking towards the closest lift, Sno activated a comm signature and waited for an answer.

"No," a curt voice answered. "I just got a comm from Crush saying that I have been assigned as your clean-up agent. So, Denman, the answer is no. A hard no."

"And hello to you too, Agent Stand," Sno said, a smile on his face and a smile in his voice.

"Screw you, Denman."

"Tana. Come on, now. Don't blame me for the shitty assignment," Sno said as he stepped onto the lift and swiped his wrist across the interface. "At least you get to be out in the field. Did you hear? I'm being sent home to think about my actions like a four year old."

"Good."

"Tana…"

"You're going on holiday while I have to sort through your mess and rebuild an operation that took months to build up in the first place. Big, hard, fat, juicy no."

"You talk like that and expect me to stay away?"

The lift stopped and Sno barely waited for the doors to open before he exited. He walked down the corridor with a definite purpose to his stride. When he reached the door of an apartment, he waved his wrist over the interface outside. Sno thought to himself that maybe he should have brought flowers.

"Eight Million Gods dammit, Denman, I said no!"

The door opened and Tana Ashool, Agent Stand, stood there in a tank top and fatigue cutoff shorts. She was a Jesperian, nearly as tall as Sno. Jesperians were a rough-and-tumble race that looked almost exactly like humans. Eye shape and body proportions tended to set them apart, but most races didn't see much of a difference between Jesperians and humans.

One thing that did set Tana apart from most humans, and even most Jesperians, were the ropey muscles that made up her arms and legs. She was a fanatic about staying at her physical peak at all times. Sno usually had the bruises to prove it.

"No," Tana said, feet planted and hands on her hips. "Go play with B'urn."

"We're meeting for drinks later," Sno said.

Sno waited. Tana had said no and he wasn't going to barge into her apartment without being invited. He valued keeping his limbs attached, and despite their relationship, no still meant no.

"Wanted to see you before I leave in the morning," Sno said. "Forced leave."

"Holiday," Tana countered.

"Not a holiday," Sno growled. "Everyone needs to stop saying that. Forced leave."

Tana looked Sno up and down then let her arms fall to her sides. She moved a couple inches out of the way.

"Since I have you here, you might as well brief me on Egthak," she said.

Sno nodded and squeezed past her into the apartment.

Where Sno's apartment was stark, Tana's was flat-out bare. Not a single personal item, piece of art, nothing was there to show that anyone even lived there other than the faint smell of food and the hum of the atmospheric conditioner running through the walls and ceiling.

"Cold in here," Sno said.

"I knew you were coming," Tana said as the door closed.

"But you weren't going to let me in?"

"You want a beer or do you want to waste my time by complaining?"

"Whiskey."

"I have beer."

"Beer it is."

"I'll get you one."

"You having one?"

"Already had four," Tana called from the kitchen. "Switching to water."

"No tacos?" Sno asked as he sat down on the couch.

Tana came out of the kitchen with a glass of water in one hand, a glass of beer in the other hand, and a glare in her eyes.

"Not all Jesperians constantly consume tacos," Tana said. She crossed to Sno, gave him his beer, then stood in front of him, sipping her water, the glare intensifying.

"I thought Jesperians needed tacos to stay healthy," Sno said. He sipped his beer and raised his eyebrows. "Delicious. Yours?"

"My brother's batch," Tana said.

"How is your brother?"

"He's fine. And no, not all Jesperians need to consume tacos to stay healthy. Despite what the galaxy thinks, we are not addicted to the substance. It helps with our metabolism when we are stressed, but my metabolism is just fine, thank you."

"No doubt about that," Sno said as he sipped his beer again and gave Tana a wink.

She sighed and rolled her eyes then plopped down next to him on the couch, tucking her legs up under her as she lifted and pointed her chin.

"Egthak. Talk," she demanded.

"Right," Sno said, setting his beer down on the end table.

He started from the beginning, detailed his encounter with Gor'bun, then moved through each and every event as it had happened until he passed out in the swift ship and woke up in the med pod.

"Who is this pilot?" Tana asked.

"Velly Tarcorf," Sno replied. "Crush is vetting her right now."

"Vetting her? Why? We have plenty of pilots," Tana said.

"She did save an SSD agent," Sno said.

"Convenient, don't you think?"

Sno dipped his chin in acknowledgment. "A little, yes. We'll know more when Crush is done scouring her background."

"I'll need to check her out too," Tana said. "Too much coincidence there. Doesn't feel right that she showed up just when you needed her."

"More than once."

"Exactly. More than once." Tana's eyes narrowed. "Different GF agency? Freelancer? Hired by a syndicate? Opportunist?"

"Or a swift ship pilot that was hired by Trel'ali like she said," Sno said. He reached for his beer, downed it, and stood up. "You said no, but I pushed anyway. That wasn't fair. I only wanted to see you before I take off in the morning. I'll leave you to your evening. I'm going to eat and meet B'urn in the observatory for drinks. Whiskey drinks."

"You're leaving?" Tana asked. "You pull your charming shit, drink my beer, dump a bad mission on me, and you're leaving to go eat then drinks with B'urn?"

"You want to come for drinks? B'urn won't mind," Sno said.

Tana stood up and stripped off her tank top. She started on her shorts then frowned at Sno.

"Get naked, asshole," she said. "Then get that naked ass into my bedroom. You'll be skipping dinner."

"Will I?" Sno said, smiling wide as Tana's shorts slid down her muscular legs. "I'm pretty hungry."

"Cute," Tana said as she grabbed Sno and pulled him to her. She kissed him hard, let her hand slide down to his crotch, and cupped him. She gave a small, hard squeeze and Sno gasped. "Get. Naked. And. Into. My. Bed. Now."

"Yes, ma'am," Sno said.

Tana bit his lip then slid past him, making sure she put plenty of sway into her hips as she walked to her bedroom. Sno left a trail of clothes as he quickly followed behind her.

10.

The whiskey tasted like liquid smoke and unfulfilled dreams. Sno closed his eyes and smiled at the lingering burn that slowly faded from his tongue.

"You gonna screw that glass or drink from it?" B'urn asked as Sno opened his eyes.

"Cute," Sno said, turning his attention to the observation deck's massive plastiglass window that looked out onto the Scortuer Neu Nebula, a massive cloud of swirling blue and emerald green gasses.

"Love this view," B'urn said as he downed his glass of whiskey then refilled it, offering the bottle to Sno when he was done.

Sno took the whiskey and filled his glass as well then set the bottle down on the floor. He eased his body into the back of the padded bench, sipped more whiskey, and watched the tendrils of nebula gasses chase each other out in space.

"A bounty on an SSD agent," B'urn said, shaking his huge head. "What is the galaxy coming to?"

"That is not the question I care about," Sno said. "My question is why a team of Chassfornians, which I'm still mentally grappling with, why that team had a Skrang ship on Egthak. Did the Skrang put the bounty out on me or was that ship simply a vehicle the Chassfornians purchased on the black market?"

"Not a very low profile choice," B'urn replied.

"Unless they needed to get through Skrang Alliance territory without being stopped at every Eight Million Gods damn checkpoint," B'urn said. "The Skrang love their checkpoints more than the GF does."

"Hard to fathom."

A puff of aquamarine gas exploded out from the nebula then was sucked back in, creating a swirling vortex. Sno smiled at the display of nature's magnificence.

The two agents sat there in silence for a long while before B'urn cleared his throat and set his empty whiskey glass aside.

"How much trouble are you going to get yourself into while on holiday?" B'urn asked.

"Forced leave."

"S'mantha."

"I'm sorry?"

"If you're going to give your holiday a fake name, why not a pleasant one like S'mantha. Forced leave is a little clunky."

"Cute."

"You know, you're the only person that uses that word to describe me."

"Irony."

"I assumed as much. You going to answer my question?"

"What was the question again?"

"How much trouble are you going to get while on S'mantha?"

"On S'mantha? How provocative, Agent Reign."

"Answer the Eight Million Gods damn question, Sno."

"I don't expect to get into any trouble while I'm on forced leave."

B'urn chuckled as he refilled both glasses. "What you expect and what happens are two very different things, Sno."

"My plan is to do as I was told and rest and recuperate while I am home on forced leave."

"You can stop saying forced leave now. I get the point. Everyone in headquarters gets the point."

"While I rest and recuperate, I may reach out to some contacts so I have a better understanding about what happened on Egthak."

"Agent Stand has the Egthak assignment now. You planning on stepping on her toes?"

"Not at all. I'll be discrete. Her rebuilding of the Egthak mission and my conducting a personal inquiry into my experiences on the planet will never cross paths. No reason they should."

"You believe Egthak was a coincidence," B'urn stated. "If you'd been on any other planet, carrying out any other mission, the results would have been the same."

"I suspect as much."

B'urn shook his head. "That's worse. Means this Chassfornian business really is all about you, not about the Division."

"Could be."

"You need company on holiday? I can wrangle some leave time and join you. I do love that beach of yours."

"The neighbors complained of your nude swimming each morning last time you visited," Sno said and laughed. "I like my privacy too much to invite you this time and deal with neighbor complaints for weeks after."

"They can't handle the B'urn," B'urn said. Sno groaned.

"I am going to need alone time for this, B'urn," Sno said. "No offense."

"I figured, but thought I'd ask," B'urn replied.

Sno nodded and stood up.

"Where the Hells do you think you're going?" B'urn asked, picking up the whiskey bottle. It was empty. "Oh. Shit."

"And that is my cue to call it an evening," Sno said. "Agent Reign."

"Agent Prime."

Sno gave B'urn a warm smile then made his way out of the observation deck and to the closest lift. Even with time spent in the med pod earlier, Sno was exhausted and he barely paid attention to the lift ride until he was in his foyer and staring at someone he never expected to see.

"Major General," Sno said and gave the man a crisp salute.

"General now, Sno," General Ved Gerber said. "Pay attention."

The man was in his late fifties, heavy wrinkles from dealing with extreme weather, not because of advanced age, coupled with more than a few battle scars, crisscrossed his deep brown face. Gerber stood with his back ramrod straight, his muscular body fit tight inside his Galactic Fleet uniform. His black hair was shorn close to his scalp, a hint of grey at the temples and above the ears.

"At ease, Sno," Gerber said and pointed at the apartment door. "Going to invite me in?"

"Of course, sir," Sno said and hurried to open the doors, gesturing for Gerber to enter first.

Once Gerber was over the threshold, Sno made a cursory search of the foyer, hunting for the tell-tale signs of shielding tech. After some dustup with the GF Council a few years back, Gerber always traveled with a contingent of personally selected bodyguards, each known to use shielding tech to cloak their presence. But Sno saw nothing in the foyer except a floor that was in need of a shine. He made a mental note to tell Ledora to take care of that.

"Drink, sir?" Sno asked as he moved past the general and motioned for the man to take a seat in the living room. "Are you hungry? I can have Ledora prepare an appetizer or even a meal if you haven't eaten."

"Kind of you, Sno, but I won't be long," Gerber replied as he sat down in the middle of a rather Spartan and severe couch. The general grimaced. "Do you actually sit on this, Sno? What a horrid piece of furniture."

"I don't spend much extended time here, sir," Sno said as he took a seat opposite the general in a chair just as severe as the couch. "How can I be of service this evening, sir?"

"By doing as told and going home for a much-needed holiday," Gerber replied.

Sno didn't bother to correct the man.

"Of course, sir," Sno said instead. "Commander Crush suggested as much and I believe he is correct when it—"

"Stop spewing crap, Sno," Gerber said tersely. "I don't need to hear it. What I need to hear is that you will go home to Nab and not reach out to every contact you have in this Eight Million Gods forsaken galaxy. Because if you do that then you will be stirring up shit I do not want you to stir up."

"Sir...?"

Gerber leaned forward, sneered at the lack of give in the couch cushion, then rested his forearms on his knees and locked eyes with Sno.

"We became aware of the bounty on you shortly after you landed on Egthak," Gerber said. "I sent Trel'ali to back you up in case exactly what happened were to happen. Good thing, don't you think?"

"I appreciate the help, sir," Sno said. "But why choose a non-GF operative? Wouldn't another SSD agent have been a more secure choice?"

Gerber waited, blank-faced.

"Unless you suspect the Division has been compromised," Sno said after a second's thought. "Do you, sir? Could the Division be compromised?"

"Any agency within the Galactic Fleet system of bureaucracy can easily be compromised, Sno. That is the very nature of bureaucracies. They are easily corruptible because they lack incentive to stay true other than personal pride and patriotism. Neither of those elements are very lucrative and most employees of the Galactic Fleet machine do not come from a place of vast family wealth such as you do, Sno."

"I wouldn't say vast, sir," Sno responded.

"Don't be modest. You are rich. More so than the majority of beings in this galaxy, Sno. Never forget that," Gerber chided. "Privilege should not be ignored or taken lightly."

"Of course, sir."

"So, are we in agreement?" Gerber asked.

Sno raised an eyebrow. "Sir?"

"That you will do as you are told and let what has happened on Egthak rest until you are told to do otherwise," Gerber said. "Use your holiday as an actual holiday. Relax. If you are needed, then I will contact you personally. Until then, find something to occupy your time. Invent some new cocktail you can impress females with. Eight Million Gods knows you enjoy doing that."

"I'm not sure how to take that statement," Sno replied.

"Take it how you will," Gerber said as he stood up. "As long as you take it home, stay home, and do not stir shit up. Don't make me regret letting you out of my sight, Sno. Commander Crush is not standing between us on this. If you disregard my request, it will be me you will deal with, not Crush. Understood?"

"Loud and clear, sir," Sno said, standing up as well. "I'll show you out."

"I'll show myself out, Sno," Gerber said. "Oh, and Sno?"

"Yes, sir?"

"We never had this conversation. There will be no data logged that I was in your apartment or even on this level."

"Yes, sir. Understood."

Sno watched the general leave then let out a long sigh once the man was gone.

"Ledora?"

"Yes, Agent Prime?"

"See if Mix can have my new ship ready a couple hours earlier, will you? I'd like to leave headquarters before the docking ports get busy."

"I will contact Master Sergeant Mix right away, Agent Prime."

"Thank you, Ledora. Wake me an hour before departure time, please."

"Yes, Agent Prime."

Sno made his way to his bedroom, stripped down to nothing, yanked back the sheets, and collapsed into bed. He was asleep within the minute.

·

11.

The lines of landing pads were a busy blur of ships appearing, taking off, and ships landing then disappearing. Sno stood by the safety rail of one of the many landing pads, waiting for his new ship to materialize before him.

"You had your house AI call me to get an earlier launch time," Mix stated. "Seriously, Sno?"

"I tried, Mix," Sno said, pointing his chin at the hustle and bustle of ship activity on the landing pads. "Wanted to avoid this and get to the wormhole portal before a queue started."

"You're going on holiday, Sno," Mix said and shook his head. "You can afford to wait in the queue like everyone else that isn't Agent Prime."

"But I am Agent Prime," Sno said with a smirk.

A ship materialized two landing pads from Sno and Mix pointed. "Go get on your ship and out of my hair, will ya? I got real work to do."

Sno waited for the low chime in his comm to tell him it was safe to walk around the rail and out onto the landing deck. He skirted the empty landing pad and made his way to his ship on the next landing pad. A hatch slid open and a set of stairs descended once Sno was close enough.

"Engines are warmed and ready, Agent Prime," Ledora said in Sno's comm. "We will lift off as soon as you are secured in the pilot's seat."

"I'll handle liftoff, Ledora," Sno said as he walked up the steps, through the hatch, and down a short, narrow corridor to a ladder.

He climbed the ladder, walked down another corridor, past the hatches to the two cabins and the mess, climbed a second ladder, and was on the bridge. Sno made his way past the two rear seats and sat down in the pilot's seat. Straps automatically secured around his torso as an electronic voice ticked off items on the launch checklist that every ship was required to perform.

"Are you certain, Agent Prime?" Ledora asked. "I am more than capable of handling liftoff."

"I know you are, Ledora," Sno replied. "I feel like flying, is all."

"As you wish, Agent Prime," Ledora said. "Checklist is complete and flight control has given the all-clear for the ship to launch, Agent Prime."

"Thank you, Ledora," Sno said as he swiped his wrist across the control console and brought up the flight interface. A couple of adjustments to the configuration and Sno was ready. He dialed in flight control's comm signature. "Special Service Division Agent Denman Sno lifting off."

"Good flying," a voice replied as Sno took off from the landing pad, turned the ship 180 degrees, angled the nose slightly, and aimed for the space above headquarters that had been specifically cleared for his ship. "Eight Million Gods speed to you."

"Appreciated," Sno said as the ship shot away from headquarters and out into the tangled mass of shipping routes that surrounded the massive complex.

It took only a few minutes to reach the wormhole portal queue and Sno eased back in his seat as he waited for his turn. His mind was filled with conflicted thoughts. Even after a good night's sleep, General Gerber's request to go home and sit tight weighed heavily on Sno's mind. He'd met personally with the general on more than a few occasions, but he'd never been told to specifically do nothing before. He was Agent Prime, the FIS's top SSD agent. Having him go on holiday and sit on his hands was like setting a pistol aside in gunfight and picking up a laser blade.

To Sno, the request didn't make sense.

"Ledora?" Sno asked.

"Yes, Agent Prime?"

"Make sure the bots have the house spotless when I arrive."

"Of course, Agent Prime. They are already working hard to eliminate all traces of dust from your extended absence. I have also taken the liberty of alerting your neighbors that you are not to be disturbed while on holiday. It is the high season on Nab and many of the estates are currently occupied."

"Thank you for that," Sno said as his turn came up in the queue. "I am not in the mood for reminiscences."

"I assumed you would not be, Agent Prime," Ledora said. "I have received favorable responses from all but one of your closest neighbors."

"All but one," Sno said with a smile. "I can guess who the holdout is."

"That would be a Ms. Veben Doab," Ledora said.

"I know," Sno said.

The wormhole portal flashed a brilliant white and Sno accelerated into trans-space.

Most of the process was automated, despite Sno insisting on doing the piloting. There were few races in the galaxy that could handle the disorienting effects that entering trans-space had on the body. Humans were not one of those races. The ship's portal protocols filtered out the majority of the visual mess that would have sent Sno into a semi-coma while also adjusting the grav drive so that Sno didn't feel like his insides were being torn apart.

Once the ship had stabilized, Sno was able to blink a few times and smile at the swirling mass of chaos that filled his ship's view shield. Virtual instruments on the control console beeped and blinked, all part of elaborate holo simulations so beings knew the ship was working. Sno hated those simulations and knew Mix had engaged them on purpose to mess with him because of his request to have the ship ready early.

Sno smiled and banished the virtual instruments. He set up a protocol to alert him when the ship was about to exit trans-space. Then he eased back farther in his seat and activated his comm. He waited for the all-clear sound to tell him that his comm was encrypted and secure then dialed in a specific signature.

"You have been graced with reaching Ms. Veben Doab, but unfortunately, I am unavailable at the moment," a woman's cultured voice said. "Please leave your comm signature and any message you would like. I might return the favor. I might not. The whims of a woman such as myself cannot be predicted."

Sno's smile widened. "V, it's Denman. I'm on the way home and need to make sure you aren't there waiting for me. I've had a bad week and need some time alone with my thoughts before I decide whether or not to be social. I can already feel your eyes rolling, but it is true. Give me a couple of days to settle in before you bypass my security protocols and grace me with your presence."

Sno almost disconnected.

"Oh, and I know you have been raiding my liquor stock, so please replenish the pantry before I arrive, will you? Love you, V. See you in a few days."

Sno disconnected and checked his travel status. Two hours before exiting trans-space. Three more legs of similar length and three more wormhole portals to go through before he reached the Tchor System, home of the planet Nab. That gave him some time to begin his own self-debriefing.

"Ledora, please integrate memory data into the ship's console, specifically of my mission on Egthak," Sno said.

"I will need authorization to override the ship's security protocols, Agent Prime," Ledora responded. "I am a house AI and not cleared for mission recall."

"Right. New ship," Sno said. He waved his wrist across the control console and toggled through the security protocol menu. He found personal memory data to ship integration and authorized Ledora's access to that as well as several other of the ship's functions that would make his journey much easier.

"You are now cleared, Ledora," Sno said. "Please begin integration."

"Thank you, Agent Prime," Ledora replied.

Like all SSD agents, Sno had a memory recall chip embedded deep within his brain. It wasn't like playback from an ocular implant, but it worked well enough in case an agent was incapacitated or couldn't quite recall a specific memory.

The view shield changed views and became a holo vid of Sno's perception of events on Egthak. He scrolled through the timeline quickly, from the moment he set foot on the planet, to the moment he was whisked away by Velly Tarcorf. Then Sno toggled back to the first minutes of the mission and let the vid play at normal speed.

Before the holo could progress too far, an alarm alerted him that he was about to exit trans-space. Sno paused the holo vid and returned the view shield to the swirling mass of trans-space that enveloped his ship.

In a blink, Sno was out of the wormhole portal and navigating quickly towards the next portal he'd need to use to continue his journey. He piloted around larger ships easily and raced to get into the next queue.

The wormhole portal was within sight when alarms began to blare. Sno scrambled to bring up his security interface, seeing almost immediately the threat his ship's defenses had detected.

Skrang.

Three Skrang light fighters were on his tail. Sno banked right and put the ship into a steep, twisting dive to evade the fighters. The maneuver didn't work. The Skrang stayed on his tail and matched him move for move.

"Ledora! Send a message to Division now!" Sno ordered.

"I cannot, Agent Prime," Ledora replied. "All comms have been jammed."

"How?" Sno exclaimed. "Light fighters don't have that strong of tech."

"I am uncertain, Agent Prime," Ledora replied. "As you know, I am a simple house AI protocol. I can assist with minor tasks needed to maintain a household properly and to make your life more comfortable. Tracking the origin of comms jamming technology does not fall into the category of household maintenance."

"It'd make my life a lot more comfortable," Sno grumbled as he brought the ship up into a steep climb and activated the plasma cannons.

He set the cannons to auto and painted each fighter as an enemy. That left Sno to pilot the ship while the cannons waited for the perfect moment to fire. Unfortunately, auto for plasma cannons on an official Galactic Fleet ship meant that they would not fire unless it was absolutely certain that no civilian ships in the vicinity would be put at risk. There were plenty of civilian ships in the vicinity, all headed towards the wormhole portal that had been Sno's original destination.

"Dammit, Ledora! Find a loophole in your programming and help me out here!" Sno shouted as the aft shields began taking fire from the Skrang fighters. "There has to be something in your protocols that can allow you to override your limitations if my life is in danger!"

"I am afraid not, Agent Prime," Ledora responded. "An SSD agent is trained to evade capture and defend his/her/their self. Reliance on an artificial intelligence is against regulations and can be considered a breach of confidence."

"Idiotic bureaucratic regulations," Sno snarled.

The ship shook from several more plasma impacts. Sno checked his shields and was happy to see them holding at over eighty percent efficiency. That number dropped to seventy percent then sixty percent in less than two seconds as Sno was unable to avoid a massive barrage of plasma fire from all three Skrang fighters.

"To Hells with this," Sno said and braked hard.

The ship slowed then came to an almost dead stop as fore thrusters engaged and halted all momentum. The Skrang fighters shot past the suddenly stationary ship as Sno took over manual control of his plasma cannons. The targeting system was still locked onto the ships. Sno didn't hesitate. He fired all four cannons, sending blast after blast of plasma fire at the Skrang.

Two of the fighters took enough damage that they broke off from the third and retreated deeper into the system. The last Skrang fighter avoided most of the blasts sent at it and dove fast. Sno went to follow, but quickly realized his ship simply didn't have the agility needed to keep up with the Skrang fighter. The enemy ship was suddenly back behind him and working at dropping Sno's shields.

"Could have used that next-gen tech," Sno snapped as he employed every skill he knew as a pilot to try to shake the fighter. But the Skrang pilot was too good and Sno didn't come close to shaking the fighter loose.

"Alright, Ledora, the main task I need you to focus on is getting the comms back up," Sno ordered. "Jamming tech or not, the comms have to be considered—"

"Comms are no longer jammed," Ledora stated. "Once two of the three fighters disengaged, communications was restored."

"Then get me some help!" Sno shouted.

"I have already put out a distress call to Division headquarters. It has been received and emergency assistance is on its way."

"ETA?"

"Five hours. That is the fastest a Galactic Fleet ship can reach you."

"There aren't any GF ships in this system?" Sno shouted. "How is that possible?"

"This system is uninhabited, Agent Prime. There is no need for a Galactic Fleet presence," Ledora responded in no different a tone than if she'd been reporting that the ship's mess was out of lemons. "Five hours is as soon as a ship will arrive."

"I may be of service," a voice broke in.

There was a flash and Sno's ship rocked slightly. All alarms and alerts went silent three seconds later.

"The Skrang light fighter has been destroyed," Ledora reported. "You are free to approach the wormhole portal now, Agent Prime. I have called off the Galactic Fleet ship that was en route. I did report the incident to Division and was told that you are expected to file a full report once you reach Nab."

"Who destroyed the fighter?" Sno asked. "Whose voice was that?"

"I am sorry, Agent Prime, but I do not understand the question," Ledora replied.

"The voice that said they could be of service? The voice that broke into my comm right before blowing up the Skrang fighter? That voice!"

"I am sorry, Agent Prime, but there is no record of a comms interruption nor of another ship in your vicinity."

"Check again, Ledora," Sno snapped. "I heard a voice and someone blew that fighter out of space for me."

"I have checked all systems and there was no voice interruption," Ledora reported. "There is also no record of another ship firing on the Skrang light fighter."

"Then how was it destroyed?" Sno shouted.

"It blew up, Agent Prime, for lack of a better term."

"It did not simply blow up. Someone fired on it and blew that fighter up. I want to know who it was."

"Understood," Ledora responded.

Sno waited as he aimed the ship for the wormhole portal. There was no longer a queue as all ships in the system had quickly moved to as safe a distance as they could get from Sno's unfortunate dogfight.

"Ledora?" Sno asked. "Have you found anything?"

"There is nothing to find, Agent Prime. The ship was not fired upon. It exploded on its own. My previous statements still stand."

"Then what have you been doing this whole time?" Sno asked as he waited for the go-ahead to enter the portal and trans-space.

"I was remaining quiet so I did not upset you by repeating my statement," Ledora said.

"Coward," Sno muttered as the ship was granted access and shot through the portal, once again launched into the swirling chaos of trans-space. "We're going to have to do something about your protocols when you accompany me in the field."

"You know I am strictly forbidden to assist you in the field, Agent Prime," Ledora said. "You are journeying home and that is why I am here to assist you."

"Some assistance," Sno growled.

He tried to relax, but his adrenaline was too high.

"I want all data from the Skrang encounter delivered to my household system for analysis later, Ledora," Sno said. "I'll look it over myself once I'm home."

"Of course, Agent Prime," Ledora said. "It is my pleasure to help."

12.

Nab was the seventh planet from the Tchor System's star. It was one of four planets in Tchor that were habitable by the majority of galactic races. While considered "Earth-like," when comparing it to the clean, livable Earth of many millennia ago, the topography and climate wasn't anywhere near as diverse as ancient Earth.

In reality, Nab could be more closely compared to the long-gone Earth country called Switzerland. It was a planet of mountains and alpine lakes. There were no oceans for the fifteen moons to influence. The planet's orbit around its star was equal to two and a half Galactic Standard years, meaning that seasons went on for months and months.

Sno was more than glad he was arriving in what was considered early summer for the area of Nab where his home was located. The time of year was paradise, despite the fact that the majority of homes around the lake would be occupied. But Sno had taken care of that. Almost.

Set on the edge of a two-hundred-foot cliff overlooking one of the grandest alpine lakes on the planet, Lake Go'Ilve, Sno's home had been in his family for generations. Nab wasn't where he was born, and wasn't considered his ancestral planet, but it was where he had spent a good deal of his childhood. So when his parents passed and all familial holdings were left to him, he liquidated most assets, but ended up keeping the Nab estate as his primary residence.

More than a few visitors had asked why he didn't quit working and live on Nab full time. The majority of those visitors had no idea what Sno's actual employment was, they simply believed the story he told them that he was a former soldier turned GF bureaucrat that now worked as a business consultant. If that was his real job, Sno probably would have quit and retired to Nab. But the lure of being Agent Prime meant he would most likely die in service to the GF before he had a chance to retire.

Sno was fine with that outcome.

The landing pad next to Sno's estate house had just finished rising from the subterranean hangar and was barely locked into place when he set his ship down. Several servant bots approached the landing pad, waiting for their master's orders.

"Ledora, I'm going to need a soak," Sno said as he opened the ship's side hatch and walked down the steps to the landing pad.

"Of course, Agent Prime," Ledora responded in his comm. "I will prepare the tub immediately. Would you care for food and drink as well?"

"Yes. That would be perfect," Sno said as he walked to the landing entrance of his estate house.

The sky was a brilliant blue, almost as clear as a flawless sapphire, and the sun's rays glinted and sparkled off the vast lake far below the estate. Sno took a brief moment to take in the view then proceeded inside.

He'd only managed about three steps into his house before he knew he wasn't alone. Even if the smell of cooking and the sound of soft music hadn't given away the occupancy, Sno would have known. His house had a feel to it when it was empty, a feel he'd known most of his life. That feel was absent.

"Denman? Is that you, love?" a voice called from the kitchen. "I've cooked! Come try!"

Sno was not surprised to hear the voice of Ms. Veben Doab.

He made his way through the side corridor that connected the landing pad entrance with what his father had called a "mud room." The mud room was almost as big as Sno's residence back at Division headquarters. Sno stripped off his flight jacket and removed his boots, setting both in their appropriate places on the wall, before taking a deep breath and continuing his journey to the kitchen.

Sno walked through a massive pantry, fully stocked with almost every delicacy available on Nab, and came out into a steam-filled kitchen. The steam was pungent, causing Sno to sneeze instantly.

"Oh, this spice will do that to you," Veben said, tipping a wine glass in Sno's direction as she busied herself at the twenty-burner range set against the kitchen's opposite wall. "Careful not to open the cooker. If the spice doesn't cook fully down, then it can be caustic to humans."

"Lovely," Sno said as he gave the cooker on the counter to his left a perfunctory glance before navigating his way around the huge center island and over to the beverage counter set up close to the massive farm sink that took up half of one of the kitchen's walls. Sno found the opened bottle of wine and poured himself a glass. "You got my message, I see."

"Of course I did, love," Veben replied, stirring something thick and brown in a large cook pot. She turned, took a sip of her wine, and gave Sno a wide smile. "Load of shit that message was, love. Never tell me what to do. You know that."

Stunningly beautiful, the woman was in her late seventies. She had eyes that could pierce the most inhospitable planet's crust. Those eyes twinkled with mischief as she sipped at her wine then turned back to her cooking.

Ms. Veben Doab was human…maybe. Sno suspected she was a Jirk, a race of beings that killed and skinned other races, taking their victims' forms by sliding inside the corpses' removed skins. Jirks were a race despised by almost the entire galaxy, including the Skrang.

But Sno had never shared his suspicions with anyone, not even Veben. If she was a skintaker, then she had taken her skin decades earlier and settled, never bothering to acquire a new one. While the original acquisition was murder, Sno never brought it up since Veben had been nothing but kind and wonderful to him his whole life. There wasn't a memory of the house that didn't include the woman.

And Veben knew it, obviously, since she helped herself to the estate house as if it were her own.

Veben's own house was modest in comparison. A small villa about two kilometers down the road. Veben's estate bordered on Sno's, but just like the villa, was a fraction the size. But Veben lived alone, had for as long as Sno knew her, and always said that if she needed more space, she'd simply come visit the Sno estate.

"How has work been, love?" Veben asked.

Sno's hand paused as the wine glass was almost to his lips. He eyed Veben carefully, noting the tone in her voice.

"Why do you ask, V?" Sno responded.

He had a small pistol, a Defta Stinger which shot poisoned flechettes instead of plasma, on his right hip. He always carried it when traveling. His hand instinctively wanted to go for the Stinger, but that would have been ridiculous. He was in his own house, enjoying a glass of wine, while one of his most trusted friends cooked in his kitchen.

"Relax," Veben said, turning to give him a grin. She looked him up and down. "Love, would I allow any threat or harm come to you?"

"I should hope not," Sno said. "What aren't you telling me?"

"You mean, what haven't I had time to tell you," Veben stated. "We've barely exchanged pleasantries."

"V…"

"You have a guest in the sitting room," Veben said and waved a hand at Sno. "I'd go introduce you, but the little man keeps undressing me with his eyes and it's most…distracting."

"Not offensive?" Sno chuckled.

"At my age, love, a man, any man, undresses you with his eyes and you do not get offended," Veben said. She held up her glass of wine. "You drink and hope for an evening of intense pleasure. Been a while since I've had one of those that wasn't assisted by a bot."

"A delight as always, V," Sno said, setting his glass down. "Sitting room, you say?"

"Sitting room, I say," Veben said and gave Sno a dismissive wave. "Go socialize while I get dinner finished. It'll only be a few more minutes."

"I thought the spice in the cooker had to cook down a while more?" Sno replied.

"That's for tomorrow's lunch," Veben said.

"Will you be joining me for lunch?"

"You're home, silly boy," Veben said with a laugh. "You know you can't get rid of me."

"I may have work," Sno said.

"You're supposed to be on holiday," Veben said then gave one more dismissive wave. "I have my sources, love. Go chat with the old man then wash up for dinner."

"Yes, ma'am," Sno said as he left the kitchen and moved at a brisk pace to the sitting room.

The Sno estate's sitting room was a good deal larger than most of the conference rooms back at Division headquarters. But the headquarters conference rooms did not have bookshelves filled with ancient, rare books, nor a view out onto a gorgeous lake.

Sno found a short, hunched over old man with a heavy backpack standing at the main picture window, staring out at the lake.

"Hello?" Sno said.

"Oh, Mr. Denman Sno. Agent Prime. You have arrived," the old man said, turning to face Sno.

"It is my house," Sno said.

The man had to be in his late seventies, or maybe early eighties, with a heavily scarred, weathered face. But, despite his hunched nature and wizened features, the old man's eyes sparkled with life and danger. Sno knew that look. It was not a look to take for granted.

"You are?" Sno asked, walking to a drink cart across the room. "Cocktail? Wine? Beer?"

"If you have wubloov, that would be great," the old man said. "I know it is strong, and can cause hallucinations if consumed in too large of quantities, but it sure would hit the spot."

"I don't keep wubloov on hand," Sno stated. "Tarmelian brandy?"

"Oh, decadent," the old man said and clapped his shriveled hands together.

Sno smiled, poured two glasses of brandy, and crossed to the old man. He held out one of the glasses and waited for the man to take it.

"I mean you no harm, Agent Prime," the old man said, eyeing the offered glass.

"I do not think that you do," Sno said.

"Yet your body language tells me that as soon as I take hold of that glass, you will take hold of me," the old man said. "I believe you would win in a physical contest, Agent Prime. No need to get grabby."

Sno set the glass down on a small end table next to a large, cushiony chair that was angled perfectly to catch the picture window's natural light. An excellent reading spot, Sno had always thought.

"There," Sno said, taking several steps back. "Enjoy the brandy without fear."

"Oh, I'm afraid I cannot do that, Agent Prime," the old man said. "Fear is my constant companion."

"Isn't it for all of us," Sno said.

The old man tilted his head then smiled broadly at Sno. He nodded and fetched the drink from the end table. Sno did not move a muscle.

"Delicious," the old man said after sipping the brandy.

"No point in having it on hand if it isn't," Sno responded. "So… Who in all the Hells are you?"

"Down to business…," the old man sighed.

"Your name," Sno demanded in a quiet, firm voice.

"Ah, yes, my name is Pol Hammon," the old man said. "Perhaps you've heard of me?"

Sno tried not to choke on the sip of brandy he'd just taken.

"I see you have," Pol said, the smile leaving his face. "Good. Then we can skip the backstory. I need your help."

"Is that so?" Sno said. "A legendary dark tech like you needs my help? I've always assumed that the great Pol Hammon could manifest any help he needs. Why come to me for assistance?"

"Because it is the Galactic Fleet that is after me," Pol said. "Along with most of the galaxy. And the Skrang. Lest we forget the Skrang. I decided I'd go straight to the Special Services Division and cut myself a deal. Which I have. Care to listen?"

Several pieces of the past few days clicked into place inside Sno's head.

"Sit," Sno ordered. "Let's start at the beginning."

"Yes, let's," Pol said and took a seat in the cushiony chair.

13.

Sno took his own seat in a short couch opposite Pol's chair.

By opposite, it was several meters away since the room was quite large. But it was still close enough for Sno to watch every single detail of the old man's face. Sno needed to see the lies and the truth clearly and even as scarred a face as Pol Hammon had, it would give up both under Sno's trained gaze.

Sno sat rigid, rage coursing through him as Pol revealed what had been done. But Sno kept himself in check despite the nearly overpowering need to strip off all his clothes and hunt for the foreign object that had been forced on his person.

"You thought you could use me as a mule?" Sno said, his voice even and cold.

"A mule? Well, that is one way of putting it," Pol replied. "And it was only for a short period. Your return trip to your headquarters. Luckily, despite the Skrang interference, you made it there alive and the transfer was complete."

A mission gone horribly wrong, the target asset dead, a Chassfornian hit squad, Trel'ali's involvement, the swift ship pilot. Sense was being made of the chaos.

But the main piece that suddenly found a home was the fact that General Gerber had come to see Sno personally and insist he take a holiday. After a botched job like Egthak, Sno should have been put on official administrative leave and been waiting for a hearing before the GF Sub-committee on Covert Affairs.

All of that told Sno that the mission, the real mission, had actually been accomplished. Roshall Gor'bun had been a smokescreen. A fatal one for the man.

"Who was it?" Sno asked.

"I'm sorry?" Pol replied then held up his empty glass. "May I?"

Sno nodded and watched the old man haul himself out of the chair and go to the drink cart. Pol poured a hefty amount of brandy into the glass then returned to the chair. He groaned as he sat back down.

Sno didn't believe any of it. The old man was more than physically capable. The groans, the innocent looks, the victim tone—all an act.

"Who was it?" Sno asked. "The person that transferred the data to me? Who was it?"

"I do not know his name," Pol said. "But he was one of the security guards on the transport you were on with Mr. Gor'bun. A

Gwreq maybe? A simple sub-dermal data patch on the underside of your wrist. Then everything went wrong and you know the rest."

"Went wrong? I almost died," Sno said. "Those Chassfornians were not kidding around."

"Yes, that," Pol said and grimaced. "We knew there could be issues with the Egthak terrorists, hence the transport station blowing up, but no one saw the Chassfornians coming. I didn't even know they were still allowed to move about the galaxy in squads like that."

"They aren't," Sno snapped. "By GF law, they can never gather in groups larger than two."

"GF law..." Pol snickered. "Quaint."

"This data that you transferred onto me," Sno said. "It was retrieved at headquarters while I was in the med pod." A statement. Pol nodded. "And what is this data? What was I transporting for General Gerber?"

"He didn't tell you?" Pol asked.

"No."

"Then it is not my place to either."

Sno laughed. "You are in my house, drinking my brandy, and telling me a story that is a little hard to believe. If there was ever a place to tell me what that data was, this is that place. Unless you want me to call the local authorities and have you arrested for trespassing."

"I'd prefer that did not happen, Agent Prime," Pol said. "We both know that as soon as I am in the hands of your local authorities, everyone in the galaxy will know of my whereabouts. Your local authorities are, shall we say, bought and paid for?"

"I do not doubt it," Sno said. "So tell me what I want to know and you can avoid all of that."

"Perhaps you should contact General Gerber."

"Perhaps I should. I need to report my run-in with three Skrang light fighters, anyway."

"Oh, yes, the Skrang fighters."

"Yes. Oh. Skrang fighters. You didn't happen to have anything to do with one of them blowing up for no reason? Hack the fighter's engines remotely? That's something you can do, if your reputation is even close to reality."

Pol shrugged. Sno glared.

The two men watched each other for a few moments then Sno activated his comm.

"General Gerber," Sno said. "Secure signature. Agent Prime authorized."

Sno waited as the comm signature went through a thousand protocols in order to ensure a secure connection. Pol only watched with indifference. That told Sno plenty. The old man wasn't even twitching in his seat. If he'd been full of crap, he would have been nervous for Sno to call Gerber.

"Agent Prime," General Gerber answered. "Have you met your guest?"

"He's here in my sitting room with me," Sno replied. "Enjoying my brandy."

"Has he told you what your mission is yet?" Gerber asked.

"My mission? No, he told me I was a mule for a secret mission on Egthak."

"Your word, mule, not mine," Pol said and sipped his brandy.

"What's this about another mission?" Sno asked, ignoring the old man.

"I need you to transport your guest safely to Galactic Fleet main headquarters," Gerber said.

"So much for a holiday," Sno said.

"Did you truly believe I would send you home on holiday, Agent Prime?" Gerber laughed. "Perhaps those Chassfornians knocked a few brain cells loose."

"Time frame?" Sno asked, ignoring the dig.

"ASAP," Gerber replied. "Take a day or two to rest up from your journey home. Fighting Skrang is never relaxing."

"You know?"

"I know."

"And?"

"And not surprising. Once you have delivered your guest to GF main headquarters then you will be filled in on the whys and whats that you are authorized to know."

"I appreciate that."

"I don't have to fill you in on anything, Agent Prime, so drop the sarcasm."

"I like to consider it more wit than sarcasm."

"You've considered wrong."

"My apologies, sir."

"Deliver your guest ASAP, Agent Prime. That is your priority from this moment on. Are we understood?"

"Yes, sir. I'll have him to main headquarters by the end of the week."

"Sooner."

"I'll assess the situation and try, sir, but no promises. Delivered alive and in one piece is the goal, yes?"

"Of course."

"Then I'll make sure that happens. If I can get the guest to main headquarters before the end of the week, then I will. Otherwise, I'll do what's needed to keep him alive and in one piece. Is that fair enough, sir?"

"This mission has zero room for error, Agent Prime. Get the guest to the destination. If you fail, there will be consequences well beyond the end of your career."

"I will complete the mission, sir. Is there anything else I need to know?"

"You have all you need, Agent Prime."

"Then thank you for the mission, sir. I will alert you when it is completed."

"Goodbye, Agent Prime."

The connection ended and Sno sighed.

"How much can you tell me?" he asked Pol.

"I can tell you everything," Pol said offhandedly. "But it is best you know nothing beyond what you already do."

"Which is zero," Sno said. He glanced down at his empty glass, but set it aside on an end table instead of getting up to fill it. "Sounds like you and I are taking a trip together."

"Excellent," Pol said and finished off his brandy.

"You've had enough," Sno said as Pol moved to stand up. He thought for a moment then continued. "My ship has already been clocked by the Skrang, so it is too hot to take. Do you have a ship?"

"I do not," Pol said. "Transportation is up to you, Agent Prime."

The smirk on Pol's face infuriated Sno. But he tamped down the anger and took a few deep breaths. Pol's smirk widened until Sno locked eyes with the old man. He must have seen something in Sno that he did not like because the smirk died away fast.

"It could take me a day or two to figure out how to get you from here to GF headquarters."

"Main headquarters," Pol said.

"Yes. That's what I was told."

"Good, because only the GF main headquarters will do. If you take me to any of the regional headquarters, then I will most certainly end up dead within twelve hours of landing. You, Agent Prime, have a bit of a traitor problem, evidenced by the Skrang attack on your ship en route to Nab."

"A valid theory," Sno said and rubbed at his eyes. "But until proven, it's only a theory. I refuse to consider someone in the Special Service Division is working for the Skrang until I see detailed evidence to the fact."

"I do not blame you," Pol said. He closed his eyes and smiled. "Mmmm. What a delicious aroma."

"Boys? Food is ready," Veben called from the sitting room doorway. "It is a lovely evening. Shall we eat out on the veranda? I do love to watch the boats on the lake when I eat."

"A great idea, V," Sno said and stood up. "I can always throw Mr. Hammon here over the edge if he annoys me."

"Please, call me Pol if you're going to threaten me with violence, Agent Prime," Pol said, the smirk back.

"Then you can call me Sno," Sno said.

"No Denman?" Pol asked.

"Sno will be just fine," Sno replied and waved an arm, indicating for Pol to take the lead.

"Oh, you two are going to be highly entertaining at dinner," Veben said with a full, throaty laugh.

14.

Dinner was eaten and finished with minimum hostility. Veben looked disappointed.

"Dessert?" Veben asked as bots rolled around the table, clearing empty plates and partially finished platters and dishes of food. "I made the most exquisite TLonga Squid cheesecake."

"Oh, I had a slice of that when I visited Jafla Base once," Pol said, patting his belly. "Delicious."

"Mine is better," Veben said and snapped her fingers. "Coffee?"

"I would love a cup," Pol said.

"Denman, love?" Veben asked Sno, who was busy staring out at the lake as the sun dipped below the horizon.

"What was that?" Sno asked, slowly returning his attention to the dinner table. "Oh, yes, I have been to Jafla Base many times."

"That was not the question, love," Veben said with exaggerated pity in her voice. "Poor thing. Nearly worked into a stupor."

"My apologies, V," Sno said, giving her a small smile before turning his gaze to Pol. "I was trying to figure out how to get this man to GF headquarters safely, securely, and without incident."

"I appreciate the mental effort," Pol said.

"Yet, the question still stands, love," Veben said to Sno. "Would you care for dessert?"

"No. Thank you," Sno said and pushed his chair back. He stood and snapped his fingers. A bot appeared with a tray holding a cigar box, lighter, and snifter of brandy. "I'll have this and my thoughts."

"Your thoughts are hardly as good as my cheesecake, love," Veben said.

"I am quite aware of that," Sno said. He took a cigar, pocketed the lighter, lifted the snifter of brandy, and glared hard at Pol. "Cigar by the railing, Mr. Hammon?"

"Pol, please," Pol said. "No need to be formal if I am partaking in your personal supply of cigars. I can smell Blaveon tobacco a kilometer away. Not exactly legal, Sno."

"Family stock," Sno said and handed Pol a cigar as the old man got to his feet.

"Are you two leaving me to eat my dessert alone?" Veben asked, feigning offense. "Oh, the shame of it."

"Go ahead and cut me a slice, V," Sno said. "I'll have it later before bed."

"And ruin that physique? I think not, love," Veben replied. "You can have it for breakfast."

"That's better how?" Sno laughed.

"Science, love," Veben said.

"I would still like a slice," Pol said, rolling the cigar in his fingers. "And some more of that brandy, if it is not too much trouble."

"That is why servant bots were invented," Veben said. She stood up and gave an elegant curtsey. "I'll let you two talk while I freshen up. Then cheesecake as we watch the twilight on the lake. I truly love this time of evening."

Sno waited for Veben to leave then lit his cigar and walked to the veranda railing. The sun setting over the lake was brilliant, an explosion of colors from all parts of the spectrum. He watched as the light faded and the many, many moons of Nab began to rise, filling the night sky with orbs like jewels.

"A true paradise," Pol said as he smoked his cigar. "Must have been a great place to grow up in."

"What's the tech?" Sno asked. He puffed on his cigar, bringing the end to a glowing bright red. "How badly do the Skrang want it?"

"I can answer that second question," Pol said. "They want it bad enough that they're risking destroying the peace the War Treaty has brought us for so many years. They will plunge the galaxy back into violent chaos for this tech."

"What is it?" Sno asked again.

"Does it matter?"

"Would I ask if it didn't?"

"I don't know you well enough to answer that question."

Sno finished off his second glass of after-dinner brandy. A bot rolled up to pour him more and he shook his head, placing the empty glass on the tray instead.

Pol began to open his mouth, but Sno took the man's empty glass and set it next to the first one on the tray. The bot waited a half-second then turned and rolled off.

"Ah. We are back to business," Pol said, watching wistfully as the brandy was whisked away by the bot.

"We never left business, Mr. Hammon," Sno said. "What is the tech?"

"I cannot say," Pol replied. "I am sorry. But the terms of my protection are contingent upon my silence."

Sno didn't have to ask the question that hung there, "How will the GF know if Pol doesn't stay silent?" He knew the answer and frowned as he kept himself from grinding his teeth in frustration.

"Who put the lock on?" Sno asked.

"That I can answer," Pol said and smiled. "A wonderful doctor by the name of Klejg. She was able to isolate the plans to the tech inside my mind. I am still in awe at her abilities."

"If you try to tell me what the tech is, all traces of it will be wiped from your mind," Sno stated. "Making you worthless to the GF."

"And worthless to everyone else," Pol said, tapping his temple. "I believe I will hang onto this bit of information until the lock is removed at GF headquarters."

"Where you will build the tech for the GF? And then what?" Sno asked.

"The lock cannot be circumvented, Sno," Pol said. "You cannot come at it from a different angle. The entire subject is isolated."

"I guessed as much," Sno said, puffing on his cigar. "Klejg is very good at her job."

"That she is," Pol replied. "I was fascinated by her techniques. Once this ordeal is over, I may have to look her up and study her work more."

"By look her up, you mean you'll hack her systems and spy on her work," Sno stated.

Pol shrugged. "Hard to unlearn a lifetime of behavior."

Pol puffed on his cigar then turned to face Sno. Sno continued to watch the fading light play across the lake. Pleasure boats were out for night cruises and running lights began to pop up here and there all over the lake.

"Speaking of unlearning a lifetime of behavior. How do you propose we travel?" Pol asked. "We cannot take your ship. The Skrang have already tagged you."

"And if there's a spy in the Division, then even switching ships will be an issue," Sno said. "Any official vessel will be spotted. Same with any of my personal vessels. We have to log those into the Division mainframe when becoming Special Agents."

"Public transport is not an option," Pol added.

"Neither is hiring a ship. We have no idea who can be trusted. Even sources and contacts I know would never betray me may have already been compromised without their knowing," Sno said. "This is a galactic cluster fuck, to be blunt."

"Then we are stuck," Pol said.

"Do you have anyone you trust? A contact that can arrange transport?" Sno asked.

"No," Pol replied flatly. "I haven't had anyone in my life that I can trust like that in a very long time. Otherwise, I wouldn't be in the position I'm in."

"I needed to ask," Sno said.

Pol returned his attention to the lake and the two men watched the pleasure boats tack back and forth, leaving brilliant trails of light behind them. Some of the boats had set up holo effects so that images danced in their wakes. Sno loved the evening show that the lake became. It had always been a favorite part of his childhood.

"Dessert," Veben announced.

Sno turned away from the view and smiled as he watched the woman place three plates of cheesecake onto the table.

"Too good for you to refuse," Veben stated.

Sno wasn't going to argue. He knew he'd lose.

He put out his cigar and returned to the table. Pol was already in his seat, having nearly sprinted to the table, his eyes drooling over the slice of cheesecake before him.

"I remember the first time I ever tried TLonga Squid cheesecake," Veben said. "This had to be half a century ago."

"Couldn't be," Pol said around a mouthful of dessert. "You weren't even born then."

"Points to you, Mr. Hammon," Veben said.

"Pol."

"*Pol.*"

Sno rolled his eyes.

"Stop that, love," Veben said, swatting at Sno. "Let an old woman have her moment."

"You were saying something about the first time you had TLonga Squid cheesecake…?" Sno prompted.

"Oh, yes, of course," Veben said and cleared her throat. "I was on a luxury liner, I believe we were heading to the Havlov System to view the gas planets."

"Oh, the Havlov System is magical when the planets align," Pol said.

"So very true," Veben said and giggled like a teenager. She shot Sno a look before he could roll his eyes again. "As I was saying, we were on a luxury liner and it was our night to dine with the captain. He insisted that the dessert be TLonga Squid cheesecake that night. Now, mind you, I was well educated on fine dining by that point in my life, but I had never heard of TLonga Squid being used for anything other than savory dishes. I was a little afraid."

"Which luxury liner?" Sno asked suddenly, giving Veben a start.

"Which? Oh, love, I cannot remember that detail. All those liners run together in my memory. Only reason this one stands out is because that TLonga Squid cheesecake was divine. I ended up loving it so much that I insisted on thanking the captain personally for bringing such a dessert into my life." She leaned conspiratorially towards Pol. "I thanked him for the rest of the night and most of the next morning."

"I am sure you did," Pol said. "How lucky for that captain."

"What do you know about luxury liners today?" Sno asked.

Veben and Pol blinked at him a few times.

"I'm serious," Sno continued. "Luxury liners. I've never been on one."

"Denman's family owned their own fleet of luxury vessels at one point in time," Veben explained to Pol. "Traveling with the public would have been inconvenient."

"V, stop making me sound spoiled. You and I both know my childhood was the complete opposite," Sno said curtly. "So, enough with the commentary and answer my question. What do you know of today's luxury liners?"

"Most are a complete waste of credits," Veben said after a couple of seconds' hesitation. "But there are some that are worth every last credit. A couple that go above and beyond. Why do you ask?"

"Any that you know of that may cater to a clientele that insists on discretion, and shall we say, complete and total security?" Sno asked.

Understanding dawned on Veben's face. "Yes. There are three of those that come to mind. Two of them will fit perfectly with what you are thinking."

"I believe you have found our transportation solution," Pol said. "Hide in plain sight, is it?"

"It is," Sno said. "Even the Skrang won't attack a civilian luxury liner."

"Are you sure about that?" Veben asked with disgust. "Skrang do not have limits when it comes to brutality."

"Neither do I," Sno said. "But the Skrang won't try an overt attack on a luxury liner, especially if it's carrying clientele that even the Skrang must rely on to function in the galaxy."

"Masters and mistresses of industry make their own rules," Pol said.

"Something like that," Sno said. He waved his hand across his wrist. "Ledora?"

"Yes, Agent Prime?" Ledora replied.

"We're going on a trip," Sno said as he stood up. "I'm going to need two tickets—"

"Three," Veben said.

Sno paused and stared at the woman. Veben sighed.

"A young man, that many in the galaxy know as Agent Prime, arrives on a luxury liner with an old man, however charming that old man may be, will attract attention and build suspicion," Veben said.

"Then we book separately," Sno said. Veben shook her head. "Why not?"

"Pol will need to be watched around the clock, even on a luxury liner with top of the galaxy security," Veben said. "Were you planning on watching him all by yourself? You'd need to stay locked in your cabin the entire time to do that. Which will attract even more attention and suspicion. Especially from the crew. And they will be the weak link in the security. I am sure they are paid well, but someone out there will pay more for good intel."

"What are you proposing, V?" Sno asked.

"That I accompany you both," Veben said. "Better yet, that Pol and I pretend to be a couple on our anniversary trip. You can book separately and keep an eye on our safety, but I will be the one to make sure Pol is watched day and night."

"How kind of you," Pol said, placing his hand on Veben's.

She enveloped his hand with her other and gave him an innocent smile.

"It is the least I can do," Veben said.

Sno's eye roll could have been seen from orbit.

15.

It took two days to book passage on a luxury liner that fit Sno's needs.

"Ledora?" Sno called.

"Yes, Agent Prime?" Ledora responded over the comm.

"Triple check the aliases," Sno ordered. "I want them as tight as possible."

"I have tripled checked them, Agent Prime," Ledora replied. "It would take a considerable amount of effort to breach the false identities the three of you will be traveling under. However, I highly doubt that the identities will hold up once you are amongst other beings. The reality is, Agent Prime, one of you will be recognized."

"We only need them to board," Sno replied. "I'll handle things once we are on the liner."

"Do you want me to still—?"

"Triple check again," Sno said.

"I have."

"Humor me," Sno insisted as he finished packing his bags.

"The identities have been checked again," Ledora replied almost immediately. "Facial recognition protocols will connect to your new identities. The only way you can be recognized, as I have said, is by an in-person meeting with someone that knows your face."

"And what about Pol Hammon?" Sno asked as he closed and locked his luggage then began the task of securing weapons to his person.

Luxury liners had a very strict no weapons policy. But, unlike a planet such as Egthak, enforcement was lax. Telling a gajillionaire that they can't bring their favorite plasma pistol or laser blaster on board a galactic cruise where the tickets cost more than most galactic beings make in their lifetimes, presents certain customer relations issues.

Simply put: the grotesquely rich make their own rules in the galaxy, as they always have throughout every single civilizations' histories.

Sno strapped the Defta Stinger in a holster on his right calf. The holster instantly formed to the shape of his calf then smoothed out so there was no visible bulge in the trouser leg. He strapped a Keplar knife, a weapon that used energy instead of steel alloy for its blade, to the back of his belt, setting it sideways so it was easier to grab and also so it had less of an outline. Then he took a sharpened piece of metal he called his "In Case Blade" and slid that inside a specially concealed slit in the back of his waistband. Someone could take his Keplar off him, but they'd miss the In Case Blade.

Sno thought about additional weapons, perhaps a Blorta 22 laser pistol or a T&G blunt, but he didn't want to alarm security if they decided he was targeted for a good frisk. Sno was used to being targeted for frisks. He carried himself a certain way that made security nervous, no matter how much he tried to act casual. Unlike his Defta Stinger, Sno's lifetime worth of training was impossible for him to conceal.

"Ship service is here, love," Veben said as Sno's bedroom doors slid aside and she came walking in, looking incredibly elegant.

Sno smiled and glanced down at his white shirt, cuffs rolled up, and black trousers. It was a classic look, but no one was going to turn their head to watch him go by. Veben, on the other hand, was going to draw a good amount of attention with the plunging neckline of her blouse and the form-fitting cut of her ankle-length skirt.

"Not very subtle," Sno said.

"Love, you grew up in this world," Veben said. "And I have lived inside, as well as adjacent, to the scene for a good part of my life. We both know that if you do not make a proper entrance, then you will be spending most of your social time in a dreary stateroom."

"I highly doubt any of the staterooms on this liner are dreary," Sno said. "The GS M'illi'ped, correct?"

"Correct," Veben said. "Do you know its reputation?"

"Does it have one?" Sno asked.

"Oh, love, we need to get you out more," Veben said and laughed. "This job of yours is sheltering you. The GS M'illi'ped is known for its amazing ability to match singles into lifelong pairings. Marriage, permanent affairs, relationships of convenience, the M'illi'ped is where the rich go to find that special someone."

"You booked us on a singles cruise?" Sno asked.

"Oh, all the Heavens no," Veben said, shocked. "How droll. There will be plenty of couples aboard, as well as singles not looking for romantic entanglements. It just so happens that the M'illi'ped has a knack for bringing together those that want to be brought together. Convenient, yes?"

"Convenient? How so?" Sno asked.

"Once your true identity is discovered, which it will be, as we both know," Veben said.

Sno nodded reluctantly.

"Yes, once that occurs, there will be female beings lining up to meet the infamous Agent Prime," Veben continued. "But the crew of the M'illi'ped will be prepared to make sure that only those with true intentions make it to your table. The thrill-seekers will be weeded out immediately."

"I fail to see how this is convenient," Sno said.

Veben sighed. "How you do your job sometimes, I wonder."

"V," Sno grumbled.

"Counter agents will be part of the group that makes it to your table, love," Veben said in a voice that made condescending an understatement. "The enemy will be delivered to you, love. They will not be waiting in the shadows of your stateroom, but seated at your elbow during dinner. Perhaps across from you in the lounge for drinks. Maybe in the spa after a massage. No need to look over your shoulder, love. The threat will be in sight almost from the moment you step on board."

"We hope," Sno said. "A good operative won't want to make themselves known."

"A better operative will," Veben said. "Trust me, love. I have a lot more experience in this galaxy than you do."

"We'll see," Sno said.

"A friendly wager?" Veben's eyebrows raised. Sno chuckled.

"I know better than to make a wager with you, V," he replied. "If you feel confident enough to bet on it, then I'll trust your judgment."

"Always wise, love," Veben said. Her wrist chimed. "The ship is waiting. Are you ready?"

"I am," Sno said and snapped his fingers as he waved his wrist over his luggage. Carry bots appeared from hatches in the walls and fetched the bags. "Pol?"

"Is already on the ship, I suspect," Veben said. "He was very eager this morning to get going."

She gave Sno a knowing smile and he didn't press for details.

Veben was right, Pol was already onboard the ship that was waiting on the landing pad. He had a drink in his hand, his seat tilted back, and his feet up on a small table set before him. He raised his glass at Sno and gave Veben a wink as they were shown to their seats by an attendant bot.

"Refreshments?" the bot asked.

"No, thank you," Sno said. "A little early for me."

"I'll have a Bloody Mary," Veben said. "Juice, not real blood, please."

"Yes, ma'am," the bot said and whirred off to a small wet bar set in the back of the ship.

Sno looked around and shook his head.

"Does the ostentation make you uncomfortable, Sno?" Pol asked. "I thought you'd feel at home."

"Denman Sno has never felt at home with his heritage," Veben said as the bot returned with her Bloody Mary. "The man has enough wealth to never work a day in his life yet he chooses to be a..." She feigned a sickened cough. "A...civil servant."

"We all have our duties to fulfill, V," Sno said, his voice sounding bored with a topic that Veben never tired of bringing up.

"Well, it leaves your home unoccupied for most of the year, so I guess I should thank you," she said as she sipped her Bloody Mary again. "This is not juice." She shrugged, but didn't stop sipping at the drink.

"Identities," Sno said and waved his hand across his wrist as the ship took off and angled steeply for the orbital exit. Grav dampeners kicked in as the ship accelerated, and Sno only swayed a little as a holo was projected from his wrist.

"Not a very good picture of me, is it?" Pol said as his new identity was listed and the holo of him turned a full 360 degrees. "Mahjul Talpic? From...Bax? Bax? The swamp planet?"

"You created technology that harvests the swamp gases and concentrates them into portable fuel pellets that can be used by almost any vehicle in the galaxy, if needed," Sno said as he scrolled through Pol's identity. "Your tech was used covertly during the War and made you more money than ten generations of ancestors can spend."

"Do I have ancestors?" Pol asked.

"Sadly, no," Veben said as she aimed her wrist at Sno and took the holo from him. Her new identity came up. "Vertuna C'alpescue. Widow and heiress. I inherited a God's fortune when my parents passed then another God's fortune when my wife passed a decade later."

"C'alpescue?" Sno asked. "That's a real family, V. They have an estate on the other side of Nab. Near the Triangle Barrier Lakes. People will know that name."

"And I know the family," Veben said. "Intimately, love. They have thousands of cousins spread across the galaxy. No one will bat an orb at another C'alpescue showing up on a luxury liner. I'll slip through almost unnoticed."

"Oh, I doubt that," Pol said and raised his glass to her.

"Differ Shaw," Sno said as his identity came up. "Several trillion credits made at the end of the War when surplus needed to be offloaded fast so that accounting irregularities on the GF's books wouldn't raise any red flags. Funds that may have been allocated to unofficial channels during the War were returned, no questions asked. Shaw took his piece of those funds and was set for life."

"How long do you expect the identity to hold?" Pol asked.

"For the majority of passengers, it will hold for the entire trip," Sno said. "Only those specifically on the lookout for me will see through the guise."

"And if they are looking for you that means they are looking for me," Pol said. "So, how long do we have?"

"A galactic day, maybe two," Sno said. "It'll take a week to arrive at the destination then another three days before the liner drops some of its passengers off in Bal'stuan System. The new GF main headquarters sits next to the Bal'stuan Nebula. That is our final destination."

"Ten galactic days?" Pol asked, shocked. "That is a long time for me to be exposed, Sno. I could have us there within..."

Pol trailed off. Veben raised an eyebrow, but Sno only shook his head.

"None of that," Sno ordered. "No tech superiority bragging while we are traveling."

"Isn't my identity someone that would have a massive ego due to the tech that I developed?" Pol asked. "You cannot expect me to stop being me only because I have a new name."

"What I expect is for you to keep a low profile," Sno said. "Veben will be at your side to ensure you maintain that low profile. Two galactic elders on a luxury cruise, both hoping to bring back that romantic spark that they've each been missing in their lives."

The glares Sno received from Veben and Pol made him laugh.

"The story is part of the cover," Sno said. "Don't blame me."

"Galactic elders indeed," Veben said and downed her drink. She held up the glass. Within a second, the bot arrived with a fresh drink and took the empty away. "And, Mr. Differ Shaw, what are your romantic goals for the cruise? No one steps onto the GS M'illi'ped with solitary intentions, love. Even if you are found out to be Agent Prime, you'll need to still blend in for the rubes. Blending in means romance, love."

"I can handle the burden of the cover," Sno said, a smirk playing at the corner of his mouth.

"Oh, I am sure you can, love," Veben said, holding her drink up. "Cheers."

"Cheers," Pol said and clinked his glass to hers.

Sno nodded and smiled then eased back into his seat. He closed his eyes and prepared himself for the mission ahead.

16.

The GS M'illi'ped was the size of a small moon. Sno had been on stations that were smaller than the luxury liner. Yet Sno knew that the occupancy of the M'illi'ped would be a fraction of a typical galactic cruise. Exclusivity made sure of that.

Ships of various makes and models swarmed the M'illi'ped as passengers were dropped off by their travel services and private pilots. Sno had to tamp down his annoyance and anger at the show of wealth that zipped in and out of each other's flight paths. A good fifty percent of the ships were worth more than Sno's GF pension. Even with his inherited wealth, it was hard for Sno not to be disgusted at the gaudy displays that most of the ships were meant to be.

Then a ship caught his eye. A swift ship, needle-shaped and fast, threaded through the clogged spaceways and found an open port to dock in. Sno knew that swift ship.

"Ledora? Log that ship now," Sno ordered.

"I am afraid I cannot, Agent Prime," Ledora replied. "While I can maintain comms with you during your journey to the GS M'illi'ped, I cannot access mainframe capabilities due to the security on this ship and the security on the GS M'illi'ped."

"No one wants an AI protocol snooping about while they are on vacation," Pol said. "I checked. Once we board, Ledora will disconnect from you."

"No AIs at all?" Sno asked, surprised.

"It's a new trend," Veben said, looking bored. "Traveling raw, is what it's called. Only the captain and his command crew have access to AIs. The passengers are on their own. Other than comms and wrist holos, all implants will be made inoperative as well."

"And you're only telling me this now because...?" Sno wasn't mad, simply puzzled.

"I thought perhaps I could find an end around," Pol said and shrugged. "I can, but if anyone takes a look, they'll find the code and track the source to me. The M'illi'ped is a contained system, in and of itself. The AIs that actually run the ship for the captain and command crew are top of the line. I am impressed. And it takes a lot to impress me."

"I would think this is good news, love," Veben said. "I thought it was. Even playing field is the expression, yes?"

"You two have already discussed this topic," Sno stated.

"You can't call it pillow talk unless you have something to talk about," Veben said with a smile.

"Of course," Sno replied as the ship angled sharply for its approach to an open port in the belly of the GS M'illi'ped. "Looks like we're docking now."

"Delightful," Veben said and stood up. "If you'll excuse me, I am going to freshen up for our entrance."

Sno and Pol watched her make her way to the lavatory. Then they fixed eyes with each other.

"You are worried I'll make this journey difficult for you," Pol stated and held up a hand. "Don't deny it. I can see the worry all over your face."

"Good," Sno said. "Because I'm not denying it. In fact, Pol, I want you to know that my instincts are not happy with this mission. Too many issues that scream danger."

"You have a dangerous job, Sno," Pol said. "I would think this is routine for you by now."

"For me, yes," Sno said and pointed his chin at the lavatory. "For Veben? No. She is not an agent, Pol."

"She has more experience with these matters than you think, Sno," Pol said. "Give the woman some credit."

"I give her plenty," Sno said. "But my problem is not how experienced she is. My problem is that I do not know who I will choose if a situation presents itself where both of you are in danger at the same time. My mission is you, my loyalty is to the SSD, but my life and personal feelings are wrapped up with Veben."

"You'll do what you need to do when you need to do it, Agent Prime," Pol said, his voice losing the nonchalance that had been present since Sno met the man. "What I am worth to the Galactic Fleet is more valuable than all of our lives combined. I'm not one to pick sides, but if the Skrang get ahold of the tech I have developed, then this galaxy will not only be plunged back into war, that war will be over within days, not decades. And the Skrang will rule everything. I'd be lying if I said I was a GF patriot through and through. But being a forced subject of the Skrang Alliance would be considerably worse."

Sno took a deep breath and nodded. The ship was almost inside the docking port and a vast shadow had enveloped them. Sno's guts clenched as he felt like he was being swallowed whole. There was more than metaphor to that feeling.

"Goodbye, Agent Prime," Ledora said over the comm. "Good luck. I will be available once your journey has ended."

There was no physical sensation to Ledora's departure, but Sno felt the emptiness anyway.

"Docked," the pilot's voice announced. "Thank you for flying with me. It was my honor."

"The honor was ours," Veben said as she returned from the lavatory. "Gentlemen? Shall we disembark?"

"We shall," Pol said, standing and taking her hand.

"Love?" Veben asked Sno.

"I exit first," Sno said. "Make sure our trip doesn't start off with a bang."

"Here's hoping it ends with one," Veben said and gave Pol's butt a hard pinch.

He jumped and swatted her butt. Sno groaned as he stood and walked to the exit hatch.

The hatch opened and instead of the ship's stairs descending, an elaborately carved set of wood stairs were waiting outside the ship. Sno knew with one glance that the wood was real and not synthetic, having been carved from a species that was more than a millennia extinct.

"Mr. Shaw. Welcome," a uniformed porter said from the bottom of the stairs. He was human with a bright purple complexion. "I believe you traveled with a Ms. C'alpescue and a Mr. Talpic, yes?"

"They're behind me," Sno said as he walked down the stairs and shook the porter's offered hand.

"Hello!" Veben announced as she walked out of the ship with Pol. "Oh, aren't you cute as a button."

"My name is Osol," the porter said, bowing at the waist until Veben and Pol were down the stairs and standing next to Sno. "I have been assigned to assist you with any needs that you may have. Please, do not hesitate to ask. I am here to make your travels with us as pleasant as can be."

"Only one porter?" Pol snapped. "Mr. Shaw isn't living with us, you know. We only traveled together because of convenience."

"Oh, dear one, I believe Mr. Osol will be sufficient," Veben said. "I mean, how much assistance will we need while in bed?"

"Osol, ma'am," Osol said. "No need to add the mister. That is a prefix for our guests, not for the ship's crew."

"How humble," Veben said and leaned in to give Osol a kiss on his cheek. The man blushed brightly, surprised by the gesture. "Osol, I hereby decree that you shall attend to Mr. Shaw's needs for this trip. That is your priority. If Mr. Talpic and I find ourselves in need of assistance, we will call you. How does that sound?"

"If those are your wishes, Ms. C'alpescue, then that sounds perfect," Osol replied. He gestured to a small roller that was being loaded with their luggage by several bots. "The ship is vast, so we will need to take a roller, if that is alright with the three of you. If not, then I can arrange moltrans delivery directly into your respective staterooms."

"Oh, I'd love to see your moltrans tech," Pol said.

"The roller is fine," Sno interjected as Osol began to respond to Pol. "Moltrans within a vessel like this makes me nervous."

"Oh, there is nothing to be nervous about, sir," Osol said. "Our systems are state of the art. If it is cutting edge, and deemed one hundred percent safe, then the GS M'illi'ped is outfitted with it."

"Is that so?" Pol asked.

Sno gave him a side look that could only be interpreted as, "Shut the Hells up."

Osol showed Veben to her seat in the roller then waited for Pol and Sno to take their seats before he sat down in the driver's seat and piloted the roller away from the service ship and onto a laneway that cut through the network of docking ports that filled the underbelly of the GS M'illi'ped.

"May I give you a history of the GS M'illi'ped while we make our way to your staterooms?" Osol asked.

Another roller came up beside them, the driver giving a quick beep of the horn, then swerved off away on a different path. Sno studied the roller's occupants carefully, but the Spilfleck couple in the back gave Sno zero notice. A lizard race with large neck frills that extended when excited, the Spilflecks were too busy being amorous to pay attention to their surroundings.

"How cute," Veben said as the roller disappeared through a large hatch.

"Public displays are common on the GS M'illi'ped," Osol said. "However, decorum does suggest that they be kept discrete. Some beings are not comfortable with outward showings of affection."

"Their loss," Veben said and patted Osol on the shoulder. "Please continue with our history lesson, Osol."

"Of course, Ms. C'alpescue," Osol said. "The GS M'illi'ped is four kilometers long by one kilometer wide and two high. Certainly not the largest luxury liner in use today, but we like to think that service, not size, is what distinguishes the Mip."

"The Mip?" Veben asked.

"That is our nickname for the ship, ma'am," Osol said.

Sno didn't pay attention to the rest of the history lesson that Osol gave as they traveled towards a massive lift set against the far wall of the docking port bay. Osol stated a litany of names that Sno didn't care about, something to do with the rich history of travelers that the Mip had catered to over the centuries. Sno's attention was on the faces of the guests that filled the backs of rollers heading in the same direction as theirs.

He was looking for a very specific face. A face that would go with the swift ship he watched dock earlier. But all Sno saw were beings whose faces had had more repairs and work done than the ships they had disembarked from. Sno was quickly reminded why he ran from the world he grew up in the second he was old enough to leave. The beings filling the backseats of the various rollers moving about the docking port bay turned his stomach.

"And then our beloved Mip was purchased by the Doq Corporation where it was refurbished and turned into the elegant vehicle it is today," Osol said.

"Isn't that lovely," Veben said. "Mr. Shaw? Don't you think that is a lovely history? So full of adventure and intrigue. Who knew a luxury liner could have such a storied past?"

Everyone waited. Sno slowly made eye contact with Veben and realized she'd addressed him.

"Yes. Fascinating," Sno replied.

The roller entered the large lift and waited as three others joined it. The lift doors closed and soft music began to play as the lift ascended to each roller's deck of destination. Sno studied and logged the faces of the beings in the other rollers, but didn't attempt to greet or communicate with any of them.

On the other hand, Veben was Veben and struck up a conversation with nearly every other passenger. Pol simply sat back and let Veben work, his face beaming at her with affection and desire. Sno realized the look on Pol's face was not part of the act. Veben had worked her magic and the master of dark tech was smitten.

Veben had been right, Sno needed her on the trip if for that reason alone. Cover or not, Veben was an asset when it came to handling Pol. She would make sure he was watched every hour of every day while also keeping him from being Pol Hammon instead of Mahjul Talpic.

Their roller was the last to leave the lift.

"Your staterooms are adjoining," Osol said with a hint of hesitation in his voice. "I do hope that is not a problem for you. It was our understanding here on the Mip that you were traveling together. If we were mistaken, then I am sure other accommodations can be arranged."

"We have mutual business interests," Veben said. "Being in close proximity will allow us to conduct business efficiently which then allows us time for more...pleasurable endeavors."

"Always with the business," Pol said.

"Adjoining staterooms is fine as long as they can be individually secured," Sno said.

"Oh, of course, Mr. Shaw," Osol said as he drove the roller down a wide corridor and stopped directly in front of two doors facing each other. "As you can see, the staterooms are on opposite sides of the corridor with a service hall as the connector between. The hatches to the service hall can be biometrically locked so only the guest of each stateroom may open their respective hatch."

"You have thought of everything, Osol," Veben said.

"Thank you, ma'am, we try," Osol replied as he stepped out of the roller and offered Veben his hand.

She took the offered hand and was helped from the vehicle with Pol next followed by Sno. Bots appeared from small hatches in the walls and fetched the luggage, dividing the bags according to which stateroom they were for.

"Our service automatons are at your beck and call," Osol said. "As am I."

He waved his wrist in front of all three and their wrists chimed as his personal comm signature was registered.

"Say my name and I will answer promptly," Osol said.

"What? Don't you sleep?" Pol asked.

"Only when I'm not on duty, sir," Osol said with a short bow. He straightened and gestured to each door as they were opened by the bots. "Please enjoy your stay. You will have several hours to freshen up, rest, and explore the ship before dinner service begins."

He swiped at his wrist and a holo was projected into the air.

"Let's see here," Osol said as he manipulated the holo image. "Here we are. Oh, you are scheduled to dine with the captain tomorrow evening. That is perfect. I always feel sorry for guests that dine the first evening. The captain is so busy the first day that those guests do not always get to hear his best stories. And the captain has so many great stories to tell."

"We look forward to hearing them all," Veben said and took Pol by the arm. "Darling? Shall we?"

"We shall," Pol said and the two followed the last service bot into their stateroom.

Veben gave Sno a quick wave before the doors slid closed, leaving Sno alone with Osol in the corridor.

"How much access to other guests do you have, Osol?" Sno asked.

"Access, sir?" Osol replied, trying to look confused. Sno saw through the rouse.

"Access, Osol," Sno said. "If I were looking for the pilot of a swift ship, how would I go about finding her or him?"

"Does this pilot have a name, sir?"

"Velly Tarcorf," Sno said.

"Hmm," Osol responded as he brought up a new holo. "I do not see that name in the manifest, but I can do some research and get back to you within the hour. Will that be acceptable, sir?"

"I'd appreciate that," Sno said.

Sno began to open his mouth to say more, but Osol waved him off.

"No explanation needed, sir," Osol said. "Far from the first time this has been asked of me. I will do my best to obtain the information you desire, sir. Is there anything else I can do for you?"

"No, Osol, thank you," Sno said. He reached into his pocket and pulled out five shiny chits. "For your trouble."

"I cannot take those, sir," Osol said, his eyes studying the chits. "Against policy. All gratuities are split amongst the crew and staff at the end of each cruise, sir. You are welcome to place those in the appropriate envelope which you will find in the top left drawer of your room's desk."

"I could do that," Sno said and took Osol's hand, placing the chits in his palm. "Or I can give these to you now. That way we understand our relationship the rest of this trip."

"It is good to understand relationships, sir," Osol said without a word of further protest. The chits disappeared into his pants pocket. "If you need any additional help beyond what you have already requested, do not hesitate to ask."

"I won't, Osol," Sno said and nodded at the porter. "If you could write down what you find out about Ms. Tarcorf and deliver it to me directly, that would be great. I do not trust internal comms like you have on this ship."

"Wise, sir," Osol said and bowed once more before climbing into the roller. "I'll return with the handwritten information within the hour, sir."

Osol turned the roller around with a deftness of skill that impressed Sno. Sno watched the roller move down the corridor and waited until it was back on the lift and gone before he walked into his stateroom.

The punch to the side of his head came the second he stepped over the threshold.

17.

Dazed, Sno went for the Keplar knife on the back of his belt, but a second blow, this time to the throat, took Sno's mind off retrieving a weapon and instantly on how to continue breathing.

Sno gasped and choked, but managed to jump back as a third strike came for him. It was instinct that told him where the third strike would be aimed for, not a visual confirmation. As far as Sno could see, there was no one else in the stateroom.

His attacker was invisible.

Still struggling to take in a full breath, Sno let his focus relax. He concentrated on watching for visual anomalies using the edge of his vision instead of trying to see the attacker straight on. If the person was using cloaking tech, then there would be a tell-tale shimmer to the air. Nothing and no one could be perfectly invisible. Physics had a lot to say on that subject.

Pain exploded in Sno's left side and he looked down to see the barest outline of a fist being pulled away from his body. Sno followed that fist and struck high, aiming for a spot about half a meter up and to the right. Someone grunted and Sno smiled internally with satisfaction. Then his head rocked back as his nose was shattered.

Sno stumbled a few feet then scrambled over a chair that was set in the center of the room as part of a sitting ensemble meant for entertaining guests. Knowing what he knew of luxury liners, the furniture was for non-important guests. A more intimate space was reserved behind one of the many doors that lined the main entry of the stateroom.

Where there was a chair, there was a footstool. Sno grabbed that up and threw it at where he thought the attacker would be next. There was a grunt and the footstool's flight was stopped midair.

With distance and time on his side, Sno was able to retrieve his Keplar knife. Instead of using it as a weapon, Sno glanced at the ceiling, found what he was looking for, and set the energy blade to high. It glowed a brilliant red and Sno threw it straight up as he dove to the side to avoid the next attack he knew was coming.

Air whooshed past Sno's scalp as the next attack barely missed taking his head off. Then a sting and a burn told Sno that he hadn't fully avoided the attack. Blood began to pour down his forehead from his scalp, dripping over his eyebrows and into his eyes.

Before Sno could recover from the dive to the ground and slash to his scalp, his left shoulder exploded with pain. Something razor sharp dug deep into his flesh, tearing through muscle and scraping across his bone. He roared with agony and grabbed whatever was embedded in his shoulder. His hands found that it was connected to a foot and that foot was connected to a leg. And the leg began to twist. Sno screamed.

Before the leg could twist too much farther, an alarm began to sound. Everyone in the galaxy, even the Skrang Alliance, would know instantly what the alarm meant: fire. Emergency lights in the stateroom extended from the wall and began to flash. Then what Sno hoped would happen, did happen.

The heat from the Keplar knife embedded in the ceiling triggered the fire retardant system. A thick, white foam cascaded from a thousand nozzles tastefully concealed in the ceiling's tiles. The attacker was suddenly a ghostly silhouette and Sno had a target to go for.

The ghost's leg was attached to something that was still stabbed into Sno's shoulder. But with the outlining of form came dawning realization for Sno. He hadn't been stabbed by a weapon, but by a talon. And he wasn't fighting an attacker outfitted with cloaking tech. He was fighting a Tcherian.

Tcherians were another of the galaxy's many lizard-like races. Humanoid, with a similar size and build as humans, Tcherians' skin could camouflage and adjust to the beings' surroundings. If they were naked, they could become nearly invisible. The beings also sported a nasty, several-inch-long talon on each foot. It was sharp enough, and strong enough, to disembowel even a stone-skinned Gwreq.

One of those talons was still inside Sno's shoulder.

Sno pulled his Defta Stinger and took aim up at his attacker, but the being yanked his foot back, causing Sno to almost drop the small pistol, and took a swipe at Sno's head with the other foot as the attacker jumped backward out of arm's reach.

Sno ducked his head and rolled several times to his right until he was pressed up against a couch. The foam-coated Tcherian turned and ran towards the stateroom's doors, but Sno put three flechettes into the beings back before he could get to the entryway.

The being cried out and Sno knew he was dealing with a male Tcherian. That presented a problem. With proper training, and years of conditioning, Tcherian males could redirect hormonal excretions into their foot talons. Not all males had the ability, just like not all male humans had the same physical abilities as other male humans.

As Sno felt the wound in his shoulder go numb, and his vision begin to swirl, he had a fairly good idea that the Tcherian that attacked him did have the capability. Sno guessed he had maybe five minutes before either unconsciousness, which was preferable, or possible mind-destroying insanity kicked in. The latter being less than preferable.

Sno shoved up to his feet, crying out when his shoulder briefly awoke from its numb slumber to alert him to the flesh tearing around the wound. He needed to get to the attacker before the poison flechettes did their job. Three flechettes meant it was a race between Sno staying sane, or at least awake, and the attacker staying alive.

The attacker must have heard Sno coming because he leapt half a meter into the air and spun around, his left leg whipping out in a solid roundhouse kick aimed for Sno's head. Sno barely ducked back, the foot talon missing his chin by only a centimeter. The move threw Sno off balance and he slipped on the foam that covered every square millimeter of the floor.

Landing hard on his ass, Sno grabbed whatever was at hand and threw it at the attacker's chest. He'd managed to grab a piece of foam-coated art that was probably worth more than Sno wanted to guess at. The piece of art hit the Tcherian squarely in the crotch, dropping the being to his knees fast. The Tcherian vomited over and over as Sno scrambled to get to his feet.

"I have the antidote," Sno said, lying.

He never kept the antidote to the flechettes on him. He didn't want the option. He also didn't want to deal with an inquiry in front of a GF review board asking him why he did not use the antidote when he had it on his person. To solve that bureaucratic dilemma, Sno simply stopped keeping it with him. But the Tcherian didn't know that.

Wounded, poisoned, and still coated in foam, the Tcherian's camouflage ability was spent. His skin returned to its normal scaly iridescence and he struggled to stand upright and continue the fight.

"Stay down," Sno warned, getting back to his feet. He wobbled, but willed himself to stay standing and took the few short steps to the Tcherian, towering over the struggling attacker. Sno slammed a fist into the being's face, crushing bone and sending bits of teeth flying everywhere and skidding across the room in the foam. "I said to stay down!"

The Tcherian stayed down, his shaking hands trying to staunch the blood that poured from his mouth.

"Who were you sent to kill?" Sno demanded.

The Tcherian's eyes looked everywhere but at Sno. Sno hit him again.

"Who were you sent to kill?" Sno shouted.

"You," the Tcherian hissed, the man's voice weak and fading.

"Me? What's my name?" Sno asked.

The Tcherian blinked a few times in confusion.

"Tell me the name you were given," Sno said, raising a fist again. It took all his willpower not to sway before the Tcherian. That toxin was kicking in hard. "The name of your target. Give it to me."

"Denman Sno," the Tcherian whispered, his body slumping to the ground. "Agent...Prime..."

The Tcherian's eyes rolled up in his head as pink froth spilled from between the being's lips. Sno slowly lowered himself into a crouch, careful not to fall over onto the body, and checked for a pulse. The Tcherian was gone. Sno tried not gag as the being's body voided itself of all digestive waste.

With complete and total deliberation, Sno stood back up and limped to the foam-coated couch. He fell into the cushions, launching clouds of foam high into the air. He activated his comm and waited.

"Hello, love. Everything alright over there?" Veben asked.

"No," Sno said, his voice weak in his throat, but ragingly loud in his ears. He winced and took a slow breath. "Bit of an intruder problem."

"Yes, well, we've had our own intruder problem," Veben said. "Was yours a naked Tcherian?"

"Yes," Sno said, but wasn't sure he actually formed and uttered the word. "May have caught... A talon in the..."

"Denman? Love? Are you wounded?" Veben asked.

"Probably..."

"I'll be right there, love. Try not to die on me."

There was banging at the doors as Sno's comm went silent. Then the doors burst open and in raced several uniformed crew members, their faces hidden by environmental hazard masks and rebreathers. Half of the crew members scanned the room for the fire while the other half raced over to Sno. Half of those crew members skidded to a halt when they saw the Tcherian corpse amongst the fire retardant foam.

"Hello," Sno said, unfamiliar faces swimming in his vision. "Tcherian...talon..."

A crew member nodded and stepped forward. She leaned over Sno and checked his pulse, lifted his eyelids, then smiled behind her mask as she opened a pouch on her belt and withdrew a pencil. She jammed the pencil into Sno's talon wound and he screamed at the top of his lungs. The pain in the wound began to subside and some focus returned to Sno's sight. He glanced down at his shoulder and realized it wasn't a pencil, but an injector.

"Thanks for that," he mumbled.

"Are you hurt anywhere else?" the woman asked.

Masked crew members were milling about behind her, most arguing about how best to clean up the mess, with the remainder arguing about who was going to alert the command crew about the Tcherian corpse. The woman, a medic Sno had to assume, purposely put herself in Sno's line of sight.

"Ignore them and answer my questions," the woman said. "Are you injured anywhere else?"

"Everywhere," Sno said.

The woman's eyes were a dazzling emerald green which matched beautifully with her pitch-black skin. Ebony couldn't even describe the woman's skin. It was as if he was staring into the center of oblivion. And he liked it.

"Oblivion?" the woman asked as she pulled off her mask. She gave Sno a smirk. "I've never been compared to oblivion before."

Sno frowned right before realization hit him. "Was that out loud?"

"It was," the woman replied, amused. "Should I start asking you about your bank account codes now?"

"Better hurry," Sno said as he tried to stand up. "I'm feeling much better."

He collapsed before he got more than a few centimeters off the couch, sending more foam clouds flying up into the air. The woman batted them away and put a hand gently on Sno's chest.

"Stay put, sir," she said. "I'm going to fix your nose."

Sno didn't have a chance to protest before the woman jammed a small hose into each of his nostrils and pressed a button on a canister the hoses were attached to. Sno's nose was fixed almost instantly. And with that speed came an excruciating amount of pain.

"Thanks," Sno said with a hint of sarcasm.

"My pleasure," the medic replied.

"Where is the fire?" a crew member snapped. "The system is registering a fire, but I don't see it!"

"Knife," Sno said and pointed up at the ceiling without taking his eyes off the woman bent over him, her hand still keeping him in place. "Keplar knife."

"You threw a Keplar knife into the ceiling?" the crew member shouted. The way the others deferred to him, Sno guessed he was a supervisor. "Are you mad?"

Sno blinked a couple times then shook his head. "I do not believe I am. Might have something to do with a Tcherian assassin waiting to kill me the second I stepped into my stateroom."

Sno looked about.

"I'm going to need a new stateroom."

"Do not fret on that issue, love," Veben said as she pushed past the crew members. The supervisor tried to stand in her way, but thought better of it after only a glance from Veben. "You'll room with us."

Veben hooked a thumb over her shoulder.

"Had a bit of my own Tcherian assassin issue and I believe it is safer if we stay together for the rest of this trip," Veben said. "Don't you, love?"

"No one is going anywhere until I have some answers," a massively tall Leforian growled as she entered the stateroom. All of the crew members, even the supervisor and the medic, instantly stood at attention. "Relax, people. You don't work for me."

The Leforian scanned the room quickly then snapped her fingers. The supervisor moved to her side.

"Is the fire out?" the Leforian asked.

"There was no fire, ma'am," the supervisor replied.

"That so?"

"Keplar knife in the ceiling set off the sensors." The supervisor gave Sno a quick glare.

"Smart thinking," the Leforian said, confusing the supervisor. She sighed. "I was talking to Mr.... Shaw, is it?"

"That would be me," Sno said.

"We should talk," the Leforian said. "Everyone out."

"I'll be staying," Veben stated.

"I wouldn't argue," Sno said. "She has her own dead Tcherian in her stateroom."

Realization hit Sno and he flashed a look of panic at Veben. She smiled and waved him off telling him his alarm was not warranted. Pol was safe.

"Can he be moved?" the Leforian asked the medic.

"I'd rather he wasn't," the medic said.

"I feel like I could die," Sno said, placing a hand on the medic's arm. "You may need to stay close."

"Eight Million Gods," the Leforian grumbled. "Fine. Everyone but the old woman and Medic Woqua needs to get out. Now!"

The crew members left at once.

"Old woman?" Veben growled.

"No offense," the Leforian said.

"We'll see," Veben replied and turned her back on the being.

The Leforian grimaced then shook her head. She eyed the medic then focused on Sno.

"Before we begin, I need to know if you would prefer the use of a med pod," the Leforian said as if reading from a card. "If you succumb to your injuries during this interview, then it must be stated that you refused use of a med pod."

"I refuse use of a med pod," Sno said. "For the moment. Can we get on with this?"

The Leforian found a chair, wiped off as much foam as she could, then sat down and glared at Sno. The medic went about patching his wounds and tending to the cuts and scrapes on his face and neck. Sno grinned the entire time.

"Talk," the Leforian demanded.

18.

Once Sno had finished relaying the events, the Leforian sat there, her quad-jawed mandibles clicking in obvious irritation.

"Mr. Shaw," the Leforian said. "You have no idea why a Tcherian assassin would be hiding in your stateroom to try to kill you? That's what you are telling me?"

"I'm telling you what happened," Sno replied. The medic handed him a steaming mug and he smiled. "Thank you. Tea?"

"Hot caff," the medic said.

"Tea would be better," Sno said in a playful tone.

"Whiskey would trump both, but I'm not allowed to serve you that," the medic said.

"Maybe I can buy you some later? Say, after dinner? I bet you know a wonderful bar we could sit in," Sno said.

"Excuse me!" the Leforian snapped. "There is a Tcherian corpse on the floor, flame-retardant foam everywhere, and a second Tcherian corpse in the stateroom next door. Can you two refrain from flirting for the moment so I can get all the information and prepare a report for the captain?"

"Oh, my Tcherian isn't dead," Veben said.

All eyes fell on Veben, but she seemed nonplussed and only stood there, her arms crossed.

"I never said I killed the Tcherian," Veben said when everyone continued to stare at her. "I said I had a similar problem. Except I managed to keep my attacker alive. Mr. Talpic is watching over him now."

"You left P… You left Mr. Talpic in your stateroom with a living Tcherian assassin?" Sno growled.

"The man is quite restrained," Veben said with a wicked grin. "I do know my bondage techniques, love. That young man is not getting loose unless I allow him to get loose."

"I'll have security take him to the brig," the Leforian said with a sigh as he activated his comm and gave quick orders.

"I thought you were security," Sno said.

"Like I said before, my name is Investigator J'gorla," the Leforian said. "I am the ship's investigator, separate from security."

"Let me guess," Sno said. "Your job tends to be more about finding lost necklaces and responding to complaints of passengers harassing each other. Maybe make a bust or two when contraband is found. Dead Tcherian assassins are not part of your daily workload."

"You'd be surprised," J'gorla said. "With some of the high profile clientele we attract here on the Mip, I have dealt with more than a few murder attempts. Not to mention the crimes of passion that are inevitable when dealing with the privileged class."

"We've all had to deal with the aftermath of those incidents," the medic said.

"I'm sorry, but I never caught your name," Sno said.

"Zan Woqua," the medic said.

"Pleased to meet you, Ms. Woqua," Sno said.

"Zan, please," Zan replied.

"Medic Woqua, is Mr. Shaw stable enough now that perhaps we can move this conversation to somewhere less...foamy?" J'gorla asked.

"If Mr. Shaw feels up to it," Zan replied.

"I certainly feel up to it," Sno said.

Veben snickered then covered her mouth with her hand and coughed. "Tickle in my throat."

"I'll come by and check on you later, Mr. Shaw," Zan said.

"I'll be in the stateroom next door," Sno said.

"No, you will not," J'gorla said. "That room, as well as this one, are now part of an active investigation. I will have Osol arrange for new accommodations."

"Joint accommodations," Sno said. "I feel it's best I stay with my friends. Easier to maintain proper security."

"Osol can take care of all of that," J'gorla said. "Until then, how about we move to my office so we can finish our conversation for the official record?"

"I'll find you," Zan said as she gave Sno's arm a pat then scooped up her gear and left.

"Delightful woman," Sno said. "Cannot wait for our...conversation later."

"I'll bet," Veben said.

"Shall we?" J'gorla asked, standing up and gesturing to the door. "We'll fetch Mr. Talpic on the way."

Sno stood, made sure his legs weren't going to betray him, then smiled and walked confidently to the stateroom doors. Veben was at his side immediately, an arm ready to steady him if he stumbled or slipped. But Sno made it out of the stateroom and into the corridor without assistance.

Osol was waiting there with a small roller with Pol already seated in back.

"Hello," Pol said warmly. "How are you? It sounds like you didn't fare as well as we did. Caught a talon to the shoulder."

"Are you well, Mr. Shaw?" Osol asked, his face pale and wan. "I am so sorry this happened. If we weren't already moving through trans-space, I am sure the captain would have postponed the trip so the GF could come—"

"That's enough, Osol," J'gorla said. "Please transport Mr. Shaw, Ms. C'alpescue, and Mr. Talpic to my office. Do not stop along the way and do not engage in conversation with our...guests. Drive the roller."

"Yes, ma'am," Osol said, looking thoroughly chastised.

"You aren't riding with us?" Sno asked.

"I'm going to look at the other stateroom first," J'gorla replied. "I'll meet you there."

"Please be gentle with my delicates, Investigator," Veben said. "Try not to mix them up. I have an ordered system for my underthings."

J'gorla did not laugh or smile.

"Well, that fell flat," Veben said as Osol spun the roller around and headed for the lift. "She's not one for breaking tension with some light humor, is she?"

"Investigator J'gorla doesn't like jokes, ma'am," Osol said. He drove the roller into the lift and stared at the rear facing doors.

"It's fine, Osol," Sno said. "We won't tell the investigator that you disobeyed and started speaking to us. In fact, I believe you may be able to answer a few questions I have."

"I would love to, Mr. Shaw, but Investigator J'gorla could have me fired," Osol said. The lift dinged and Osol waited for the rear doors to slide open. He drove the roller out into a sterile-looking corridor. Completely different than the elaborate decor of the other corridors. "It would be better if I did as told and simply drove you to her offices."

"I can see why she lacks a sense of humor," Veben said, studying the drab corridor. "I'd never laugh again if this was where I had to work."

"The crew and personnel areas are not decorated like the rest of the ship," Osol said. "Beauty is reserved for our guests, as the captain says."

"The captain," Sno mused. "Experienced fellow?"

"Captain Loch? Oh, he has been the Mip's captain for over two decades now, I believe," Osol said.

"Captain Look?" Sno asked.

"Yes, but spelled with a CH," Osol stated. "One O. More like lock, but pronounced look."

"Of course," Sno said.

He'd grown up around beings that stood at the periphery of the wealthy elite. They tried their hardest to fit in, but they never would.

Even if they insisted on the most pretentious pronunciation of their name. Look, indeed.

The roller continued down the corridor and Sno glanced over at Pol.

"Tcherians?" Sno asked.

"Yes," Pol replied.

"And...?" Sno pressed.

"And...what?" Pol responded.

"Why specifically would two Tcherian assassins be after us? Why use them?" Sno asked.

"How should I know? You're the professional here, Sn—"

"Shaw," Sno interrupted.

"Shaw. I was going to say that. I know your name," Pol replied. "As for why Tcherians were used, I do not know. No reason that I can think of."

"One killer is as good as another, love," Veben said. "Does it matter?"

"It matters when they aren't very good at their jobs," Sno said. "Those were amateurs."

"One nearly killed you, love," Veben said.

"Not hardly," Sno replied. "A lucky talon strike is all. If the Tcherians were professionals, they would have remained hidden and observed us for a while before striking. Mine came at me as soon as I stepped through the doors. That's a nervous attack born of fear. He wanted the job done fast so he could escape."

"The ship had already moved to enter the wormhole portal, sir," Osol said. "Where would they escape to?"

"That, Osol, is an excellent question," Sno said. "It would make me believe that the attempted killers have co-conspirators still on this ship. Most likely members of the crew."

Sno watched Osol's body language carefully. The young man appeared upset by that theory, but he didn't twitch and fidget like half of the guilty do when found out. He also didn't go rigid like the other half of guilty parties do. Sno assumed for the moment that Osol wasn't part of the conspiracy to kill him and the other two. Which brought up an interesting thought.

"Why kill you?" Sno asked, looking at Veben and Pol. "Killing me, sure. Killing you?" Sno's eyes focused on Pol. "Defeats the purpose, doesn't it?"

"Perhaps," Pol said and glanced at Osol.

"A conversation for another time," Veben said.

"Of course," Sno agreed.

"Here we are," Osol said, sounding relieved as he brought the roller to a stop in front of a set of plain, office doors. "Investigator J'gorla will be with you shortly. I am sure you will hear from Captain Loch soon, as well. Again, on behalf of the GS M'illi'ped, I apologize for the incident. I will have a new stateroom ready for you as soon as Investigator J'gorla is finished with her questions."

"Thank you, Osol, much appreciated," Veben said as Sno helped her from the roller. "Oh, and Osol?"

"Yes, ma'am?"

"Will you make sure our new stateroom has a security guard in place the entire time we are gone? I'd hate for a repeat attempt to be made because of simple opportunity."

"I will protect the room myself, if I have to, ma'am," Osol said.

"You are too kind," Veben said and gave him a little wave as he reversed the roller, turned, and headed back to the lift. "A lovely boy. I do hope that he isn't harmed during our travel."

"Harmed? Why would he be harmed?" Pol asked.

"Veben is referring to the fact that those around me tend to come to harm at some point in their lives," Sno said. "Isn't that what you are saying, V?"

"Not everyone is cut out for the excitement, Agent Prime," Veben said and nodded at the office doors. "Will someone open those for me or must I open them myself? Murder attempts do not strip us of manners, gentlemen."

Sno opened the doors.

The office was as stark as the corridor outside. The entry room was small, with two nice, but certainly not expensive, chairs against the wall. A single desk sat against the opposite wall just enough room for a chair behind it. The chair was unoccupied, so Sno gestured for Veben and Pol to take a seat. Sno positioned himself close to the doors and leaned back against the wall.

There was only one other door in the room and Sno's eyes locked onto it. If he concentrated, he thought he could hear movement coming from the other side of the door. He wasn't surprised when it finally opened and who he assumed was the receptionist, or possibly J'gorla's assistant, came into the entry room.

What Sno was surprised by was the receptionist/assistant was neither human nor any other galactic being.

"What?" the android snapped as electronic eyes turned to regard Sno. "You one of those bigots that hate AIs?"

"Not at all," Sno said with a smile. "Just wasn't expecting an android on a luxury liner. Not one that obviously was a battle model back in the War."

"You think you can judge the book inside me by my cover, that it, pal?" the android said as it took a seat behind the desk. "Get over yourself, will ya? You don't know me, so keep your opinions bottled up inside that meat locker of a skull."

The android was humanoid with two arms, two legs, and a basic body structure. Its synthetic skin was as generic beige as beige could get. The lighting in the office gave the skin a sickly, tacky look to it.

"Plucky," Veben said. "Are you a he or she? Your voice pattern sounds male, but I hate to assume."

"I'm sure that's something you don't hate at all," the android replied. "And I'm an it. A machine. I don't have a dongle or a woohoo, none of that reproductive crap, so assigning me a gender only makes your life easier. I have no interest in making your life easier, lady. So, how about you sit there quietly while I work and we wait for Investigator J'gorla to return? Can you handle that? Or do I need to fetch you some tea and scones to occupy that trap of yours?"

Veben stared at the android for a second then turned and looked at Sno.

"I think you've met your match, V," Sno said.

"It appears so," Veben responded then smoothed her blouse and returned her gaze to the android. "Tea and scones would be lovely. Thank you."

"What?" the android asked.

"You offered to get us tea and scones," Veben said matter-of-factly. "I could do with some refreshment after our ordeals. Any tea would will be fine, but please, no fruit scones. I never know what fruit the cooks will use and most make me gassy."

"Are you kidding me with this shit?" the android asked. "I was being sarcastic."

"Well, then maybe you should be more careful with your wit, Mr....?"

"Ested. And no mister to it. I'm an android, lady. The GF barely allows us to exist. They sure as shit don't allow us to be misters or misses or anything like that. You can call me Ested and leave it at that, alright? We clear on names here? Or do I need to make tags we can wear on our chests like salesbeings at a fucking business convention?"

"Ested is now my favorite crew member," Veben said. "I would like to state that for the record."

"Still not getting you tea or Eight Million Gods damn scones, lady."

"I'd think less of you if you did."

"Any idea when J'gorla will be here?" Sno asked, waving his hand over his wrist to check his chrono. "I'd like to be able to take a steam before dinner."

"You'll get to clean up, pretty boy," Ested said. "Don't get your ten million credit boxers in a twist."

"I should be recording this," Veben said.

"Don't you fucking dare," Ested snapped.

"XN-357, yes?" Pol asked.

All eyes turned to him.

"Grandpa speaks," Ested said. "And yeah, that's my original model number. Had a few upgrades along the way, so not exactly stock anymore."

"Surveillance and extraction were your primary duties, if I am not mistaken," Pol continued.

"Oooh, someone's read a book," Ested said.

"I designed your power cells," Pol said.

Ested's face was blank, but its lack of response told everyone that statement had struck a chord.

"Have you upgraded your power cells since manufacture?" Pol asked. "If you have, then that might explain the surly personality."

"Suck a B'clo'no's vent," Ested replied.

"Yes, well, a simple adjustment can take care of—"

"I haven't touched my power cells," Ested said. "Have you stuck your hand inside your ribcage, old man, and messed with your heart and lungs?"

"As a matter of fact, yes," Pol said. "But I would not recommend it."

Ested blinked dramatically. Androids didn't need to blink. Sno wondered why they even had eyelids at all. Probably to simulate sleep and not freak out living beings.

"So the winning personality is normal," Sno said. "You must be great at crew parties."

"I end up mixing the drinks at crew parties," Ested said. "Because that's what androids are good for."

"How many missions did you complete in the War?" Pol asked.

"What?" Ested responded, raising a synthetic eyebrow and looking at Sno. "Is this guy for real?"

"Unfortunately," Sno said.

"Seven hundred and fourteen," Ested said. "Not that the GF cared when the War was done. All combat experience was stripped from my database and any memories I may have had from those missions was wiped once uploaded to the GF mainframe. Ask anything you want, I can't tell you shit about what I specifically did in the War. Nothing like having a black hole in the middle of your memory. Fun shit."

"I can fix that issue for you," Pol said.

"Mr. Talpic," Sno said firmly. "That is not why we are here."

"Can you fix it so I don't have to listen to any of you speak? Or do I need to take a spandriver and jam it into my aural pathways?" Ested asked.

The doors opened before anyone could respond. Sno's stance immediately went into a defensive posture then relaxed as Investigator J'gorla walked into the office.

"Uh oh," Ested said. "Our guest has training."

J'gorla glanced at Sno for a moment then she shook her head and waved towards the door next to Ested's desk.

"Come on," she said. "I hope Ested didn't offend you too much. Can't find a tech to fix its personality glitch."

"That's because it's not a glitch," Pol and Ested said at the same time. Except Ested added "asshole" to the end of its sentence.

J'gorla ignored the statement.

"Come on," she insisted. "I want to finish the interview before Captain Loch arrives. He'll whisk you away and try to dazzle you with tours of the bridge and promises of preferential treatment for the rest of your journey. Once he takes you away from me, our interactions will pretty much come to an end."

"Had this happen before, have you?" Sno asked as he followed J'gorla into her office.

"Not quite this same issue, obviously, but close enough that I know the captain has already been briefed by Legal on how much to spend in order to keep this from getting out to the rest of the passengers," J'gorla replied.

"It was a pleasure to meet you, Ested," Veben said as she and Pol followed Sno into J'gorla's office.

"Eat my spent lubricant, lady," Ested said just before the office doors closed.

19.

Investigator J'gorla went through the motions of having Sno repeat his ordeal for the official record. She took notes which amused Sno since he was positive she was also recording the interviews. She nodded at the right times then leaned back in her chair and frowned once Sno finished.

"On behalf of the GS M'illi'ped, I humbly apologize for this matter. We can assure you that it will not occur again and all security measures are in place to protect all three of you while you journey with us on the GS M'illi'ped," J'gorla stated. "My professional assessment is two amateur thieves were caught in the act and you stopped them. If there are more aboard, I will find them."

"Thieves?" Sno laughed. "Stealing from staterooms where occupants haven't finished unpacking? They jumped the gun a bit, even for amateurs."

"It is an opinion and can change as new facts come to light," J'gorla said sourly.

"Of course," Sno said.

"Is that all?" Veben asked.

"That is all," J'gorla said.

"You do not want to hear what happened to myself and Mr. Talpic?" Veben pressed.

"Is there anything you care to add beyond what you have already stated?" J'gorla responded. Veben shook her head. "Then our time here is done. I'll be looking into the matter on my end, but there is no reason any of this should concern you further."

"I'd like to speak with the Tcherian in the brig," Sno said.

"No," J'gorla replied.

The two beings stared hard at each other then Sno nodded.

"Of course," Sno said. "We'll leave you to it then."

"Again, my apologies," J'gorla said.

"Apologies accepted," Sno said and gestured to Veben and Pol. "Time to go, folks."

Veben and Pol stood up and walked out of the office. Ested could be heard sighing with exasperation when they stepped through the office door and into the entry room. Sno didn't follow right away. He paused and eyed J'gorla.

"I get it," Sno said.

"What's that?" J'gorla asked.

"On a ship like this, with the clientele that you have, investigations are not high priorities," Sno said. "Security, yes, but investigations, no. Those tend to turn up answers to questions best not asked. I have no idea how you got this job, but you have my sympathies, Investigator J'gorla."

J'gorla blinked a few times then nodded. "Thank you, Mr. Shaw. I appreciate that."

"Before I go, can you tell me who is in charge of security for the Mip?" Sno asked. "I'd like to have a word with him or her."

"I'm afraid I cannot do that," J'gorla said, looking honestly sorry. "You are welcome to ask the captain; answering that question is up to his discretion. But our Head of Security remains anonymous so that he or she can do his or her job effectively without passenger interference."

"Of course," Sno said and gave a quick bow of his head. "If you have any more questions, you know where to find me."

J'gorla didn't offer the same courtesy in return so Sno smiled and left.

"Ested, a pleasure," Sno said as he walked to the doors.

"You wish," Ested said.

Sno chuckled as he exited the offices and joined Veben and Pol in the corridor. The lift doors at the end of the corridor were opening, and Sno could see Osol and the roller about to disembark.

"We're not going to get any answers out of that show back there. J'gorla has been shut down," Sno said. "Which tells me that either someone in security or someone in the command crew is in on this. I plan on finding the answer to that before the night is out."

"That would be lovely," Veben said. "A week of uncertainty will not be good for my complexion."

"You didn't have to come, V," Sno said.

"Lovely boy," Veben said and patted Sno on the cheek as Osol pulled up with the roller.

"I do hope that experience was not too taxing," Osol said when the three stepped onto the roller and sat down. "The captain has requested a meeting with all of you."

"Once I can get cleaned up," Sno said.

Osol gulped with embarrassment. "He has insisted it be immediate."

"Is that so?" Sno responded.

Sno knew the tactic. The captain was trying to assert command over them. Either that or he knew exactly who Sno was and wanted to establish his authority on the luxury liner. Sno had dealt with the behavior before on too many occasions. Captains of ships always forgot that they were small cogs in a much larger machine. They saw their ships as the one and only machine and acted accordingly.

"Then let's not keep the captain waiting," Sno said. "Drive on, Osol, drive on."

As the roller moved through the ship, Sno came to the realization that a key element was missing from the ordeal. How did they get made so fast? Sno expected to be discovered eventually, but not within the first day of being on board the Mip. And certainly not before he even had a chance to unpack. The Tcherians had been waiting and knew their targets.

That meant the tickets Veben purchased were compromised from the start. Which meant Sno's residence was bugged. There was no other explanation. Except that didn't fit. Sno knew the tech he used stopped anyone from eavesdropping, even with a quantum microphone set up across the lake. The estate house couldn't be hacked. Sno hired a different security agency twice a year to try and none could crack his house's mainframe. He even bet a tech at Division to try and the woman had failed.

So where was the leak? Where was the weak point where their trip went from covert to overt? When did the crack in Sno's armor happen?

There was one answer and Sno didn't like it. Not at all.

"V?" Sno asked.

"Yes, love?" Veben replied, tearing her eyes from the magnificent view of one of the luxurious lounges they were passing over. Apparently, rollers had their own plastiglass enclosed tramways above many of the lounges and dining halls. It made moving from one area of the ship to another rather entertaining. "What is on your mind?"

"Have you been using Ledora?" Sno asked. Veben hesitated and that was all Sno needed to know. "That solves that."

"Her capacity is so vast and you hardly use her to her full potential," Veben said.

"How did you get her to serve you?" Sno asked.

"Promise not to be angry, love?"

"I make no such promise."

"I must insist."

"V…"

"Very well, you little ball of anger you." Veben sighed. "I may have overheard your use of the master code one evening and memorized it in case I was in need of assistance at some point."

"Do you not have an AI assistant of your own?" Pol asked. "Quality AIs are quite affordable these days."

"Yes, well, I may have been banned from purchasing AIs at some point in my life," Veben said quietly. "A romance gone wrong, a horrible breakup, my threatening a major galactic corporate executive with blackmail. You know how it goes. I was younger then and didn't see the future repercussions."

"How long?" Sno asked.

"Hmmm?" Veben replied.

"Answer the question, V," Sno said.

"A year, maybe longer," Veben said. Sno didn't reply, only stared at her. Hard. "Possibly a decade."

"A decade?" Sno exclaimed. Guests riding in a roller passing in the opposite were startled by the force of his voice. Sno took a deep breath and got himself under control. "Do you know what you've done?"

There it was. Plain as the swirling vortex of trans-space outside the Mip. A decade of possible SSD security breaches all because of Sno's careless trusting of Veben. He clenched his fists and tried not to explode.

"At some point, your hacking of Ledora was hacked, V," Sno said as calmly as he could. He thought back on the improbable outcomes of several missions. The majority he was able to salvage, but more than a couple failed miserably, nearly killing him and other agents. "You have no idea what you've done."

"I was under the impression that Ledora was not a tactical AI," Veben replied, defensive anger in her voice. "If she had access to sensitive information, then that is on you, love."

"Oh, the house AI didn't need to have access to sensitive or classified information," Pol said. "Any operative worth their weight can extrapolate quite a lot simply by studying Mr. Sno's life patterns. While exact details may not be gained, it would not be that hard to deduce where and when Mr. Sno might be working."

Sno glared at Pol.

"What?" the old man asked.

Osol was squirming in the driver's seat, failing at pretending he didn't hear the revelation of Sno's real surname.

"Hardly a secret now," Veben said. "Perhaps we should do away with the pretense completely."

"You do not get a say in this, V," Sno responded. "You lost that right a decade ago."

"Oh, love, don't be cross with me," Veben said. "I am a single, older woman, living on my own while my closest friend and neighbor travels about the galaxy saving the GF from bad guys."

Sno groaned in response.

"You know," Pol said. "This is actually a good thing."

"Oh, I cannot wait to hear why," Sno said.

"If your house AI's security was breached, then there will be breadcrumbs left behind," Pol said. "I can follow those breadcrumbs and trace them back to the person that discovered our travel plans."

Osol cleared his throat and waited.

"No, please, Osol," Sno said. "You might as well chime in."

"I am sorry, sir," Osol said. "I do not want to add to your anxiety, but house AIs cannot be accessed while we travel in trans-space."

"I knew they were severed from service, but no access at all?" Sno asked. "Not even a remote uplink?"

"I'm afraid not, sir," Osol replied.

"Why is that?" Pol asked, intrigued.

"It is a privacy measure to ensure that any of the...press that might be aboard do not report on guests' activities," Osol said.

"And once we are out of trans-space?" Sno asked.

"Then you will need the captain's permission to access your house AI, sir," Osol answered.

"Good thing we're on our way to see the captain now then," Sno replied. "And Osol?"

"No need to ask, sir," Osol said. "I will keep your confidence. It is obvious you are doing good in the galaxy and I certainly do not want to be one to get in your way, sir."

"Thank you, Osol," Sno said. "You might be the one person I trust on this ship."

"Oh, for all the Heavens' sakes," Veben said with disgust. "No need to be quite that melodramatic, love."

Sno did not reply as Osol drove the roller into another lift and gave the command to ascend to the bridge. The occupants of the roller remained quiet for the rest of their journey to meet with the captain of the GS M'illi'ped.

20.

Captain Rane Loch barely came up to Pol Hammon's shoulder.

Short, pudgy, pinch-faced. A halfer that obviously had Ferg in him for one half, but an unknown race for the other. Fergs looked like a mix between a beaver and a praying mantis and were rarely more than a meter tall. Loch's height and features were easily recognizable as Ferg, but his fur was a bright orange which certainly wasn't Fergian.

"Ah, Mr. Shaw," Loch said with an exaggerated wink. "I am so sorry for your ordeal. And you, Ms. C'alpescue, how dreadful this all must be. As for you, Mr. Talpic, there is no excuse I can make to explain the horrible breach in security we have faced. I promise all of you that I will do my best to make up for this incident. I assure you that the remainder of your trip will be nothing but luxurious now that all the dirty business is over with."

"I'm afraid the dirty business, as you call it, is far from over, Captain," Sno said. "We will be needing your most secure stateroom as well as a shadow guard."

"Shadow guard? I do not follow," Loch replied, looking confused.

Sno could tell it was an act instantly. The captain was obviously desperate to maintain the Mip's reputation of pure luxury and refinement. Sno suggesting that more trouble may occur was messing with the captain's sense of order and how things "should" be. Sno had run into many a man and woman that acted the same way when presented with reality.

"A shadow guard," Sno said. "We will need at least three of your best security officers to be on hand at all times in order to maintain our safety."

Sno looked about the bridge. It was elaborate and ornate. More gilded curves and edges than actual working consoles. The truth was that several pilot AIs were running the ship, not the bridge crew present. Sno knew luxury liners like the GS M'illi'ped were almost totally automated. It allowed the captain to play the part of a privileged host as opposed to the part of glorified galactic servant hiding behind the facade of importance while those that were truly privileged lounged and luxuriated around him.

"Is your Head of Security available?" Sno asked. "I would like to speak with him or her so we may establish a protocol that will keep myself and my friends safe."

The captain looked about the bridge too as if the being would be standing right there. Sno struggled not to roll his eyes. Dealing with the captain was going to be a test of patience.

"Captain Loch?" Sno insisted.

"Yes, well, I am not sure if Investigator J'gorla explained to you that our Head of Security remains anonymous?" Loch asked. When Sno didn't respond, Loch cleared his throat and continued. "We have that policy in order to avoid any conflicts of interest. By remaining anonymous, our Head of Security cannot be targeted for…gifts that might damage his or her impartiality."

"Without a name, guests don't know who to bribe," Veben said. "Got it."

"V…" Sno warned. He smiled broadly at the captain. "I'm afraid I will have to insist."

"I am afraid that your insistence is of no consequence, Mr. Shaw," the captain said, emphasizing Sno's alias. "But, I will send a message to our Head of Security about providing additional guards for your protection. Will that do?"

"No, it will not," Sno stated. He looked down at the state he was in and shook his head. "I'll tell you what, Captain Loch, I am going to go get cleaned up and make myself presentable. Then I'll return to speak with you further on this matter. When I do return, I am hoping you'll have had time to rethink your position. I would hate for an official record of your refusal to be logged with the Galactic Fleet. You have a very comfortable job here, Captain. I am sure there are many highly qualified officers looking to fill this position the second it becomes free."

"There is no need for threats, Mr. Shaw," Loch said quietly. He tried to sound menacing, but only managed to sound like a whisper had gone wrong. "I am sure we can come to some sort of arrangement."

"I am sure we can," Sno said. "Now, is our new stateroom ready?"

Loch glanced behind him and an ensign nodded. "Your assigned porter, whoever that may be, will show you to your new stateroom."

"You don't know which porter has been assigned to us?" Sno asked, unable to decide if he should be shocked or amused.

"There are capable crew members in charge of those assignments, Mr. Shaw," Loch replied, offended. "And since every one of our porters is more than qualified, I do not worry who is assigned since I know you will receive the best service no matter what."

"We certainly have so far," Pol said. "Great chap."

"Thank you for the meeting, Captain," Sno said.

"Such a pleasure, Captain Loch," Veben said, offering her hand. Loch took it and kissed the back, giving Veben a half-hearted smile. "Will we be dining with you tomorrow evening?"

"This evening," Loch said.

"This evening?" Sno asked.

"Yes," Loch said. "I believe you will be. It will help smooth over any rumors that may be moving through my ship. Rumors are worse than fire, in my opinion."

"That says much about your opinion," Sno said. "Until tonight, Captain."

"Is that all?" Pol asked. "Aren't we going to discus—?"

"Perhaps over dinner," Veben said, cutting him off as she took Pol by the arm and swung him around to face the bridge's doors. "For now, we rest after our ordeal."

The bridge doors slid apart and Sno led them down the short corridor to the lift. The lift doors opened and Sno, Veben, and Pol stepped on, their backs to the captain until the doors closed. Then Sno turned around and nearly punched the control console.

"He's useless," Veben said before Sno could.

"The Head of Security is who really runs this ship," Sno said. "I need to speak with that man or woman."

"Unless that man or woman is a part of the danger," Pol said.

"Especially if the man or woman is a part of the danger," Sno said. "I speak with him or her and I'll know."

The lift descended for a couple of decks then stopped smoothly. The doors opened and Osol was waiting there for them in the small roller. He was smiling from ear to ear. The smile faded as Sno, Veben, and Pol climbed aboard the roller.

"The captain was not helpful," Osol said. "I am sorry."

"Head of Security," Sno stated. "I need a meeting."

Osol concentrated on navigating the roller down the ornate corridor, avoiding even the hint of encroachment upon guests strolling on their own two, sometimes four, feet. Sno let the man have his silent moment.

"I may be able to assist you, Mr. Shaw," Osol said as he turned a corner and stopped the roller to allow a throng of already thoroughly intoxicated guests move from one lounge to another lounge across the corridor. "But I will need something in return."

"Which is?" Sno asked.

"Your real names," Osol said with a tone like he'd just asked for a first-born child to be bled out and served as the holiday roast. "I apologize, sir. But the Head of Security will not even entertain the idea of meeting with you unless he or she knows your actual identities."

"The Head of Security already knows our identities," Sno said. "If not, then he or she is crap at his or her job."

"I believe the revelation would be for confirmation, sir," Osol said. "That way, any confusion can be avoided up front."

"Let me think on that, Osol," Sno said. "You are asking a lot."

"Especially for a porter," Veben said. "No offense, Osol, but we have had a trying day so far and trust is hard to come by."

"I like the kid," Pol said. "He's certainly been helpful. Don't see why we can't trust him."

"Which is why you are in this roller with me," Sno said. "So I can decide who we can and cannot trust."

Sno rubbed at his cheeks then placed a hand on Osol's shoulder.

"How soon can you arrange a meeting?" he asked the porter.

"Almost immediately, sir," Osol replied. "The Head of Security and I share a special relationship."

"Is that so?" Veben asked, leaning forward. "Do tell, love. I adore hearing about on-ship romances."

"No, not that kind of relationship," Osol said.

"Oh. How disappointing," Veben said and sat back, occupying her attention with a small chip in her right index fingernail.

"Let me get cleaned up first," Sno said. "Then we can discuss any ground-shaking revelations."

"Thank you, sir," Osol said. "The Head of Security will appreciate your trust and I promise her or she will do anything and everything to maintain your safety for the rest of your journey."

Sno nodded then focused on studying the layout of the ship as the roller took turn after turn. Three lift rides and two kilometers worth of travel later, Osol brought them to a set of massive stateroom doors.

"This is the best we have to offer," Osol said. "I do hope it will suit your needs."

Osol led them into the vast foyer then on to the huge sitting room beyond. Luxurious was an understatement.

"I could go blind from all the shiny," Pol said, actually shielding his eyes as he followed Sno and Veben into the stateroom.

"Oh, this will do nicely," Veben said. "How many bedrooms?"

"Eight, ma'am," Osol said. "Choose any of them for yourself and the bots will bring you your personal affects."

"Which one has the best steam shower?" Sno asked.

"All rooms have top of the line steam—"

"The best one, Osol," Sno said.

"Third room on the left, sir," Osol replied. "The middle jet has perfect pressure."

"Thank you, Osol," Sno said. "One more favor, Osol—"

"There are six trusted security guards posted outside your stateroom doors," Osol said. He waved a hand over his wrist and a holo of the outside corridor came up, showing six very large guards of various races setting up a security station halfway between the lift and the stateroom doors. "I know them all and you can trust them to keep you safe for the remainder of your journey."

"Again, thank you, Osol," Sno said. "I'll have your answer when I'm finished with a steam and feel like a person again."

Osol bowed then looked to Veben and Pol.

"Will you need additional assistance?"

"No, Osol, thank you," Veben said. "We will call you when needed."

"Until then," Osol said and left.

Veben turned to Sno.

"Are you sure we can be left out of your sight while you steam?" she said with a sly grin. "Seems like an awful risk until we have the assurance that the Head of Security is taking our problem seriously."

"He is, V," Sno said. "And I believe that while we are in our stateroom, we are perfectly safe. Once we leave these doors, Pol is to remain by my side at all times."

"That doesn't sound like much fun," Pol said from inside the room he chose. He came walking out in a plush robe. "By your side at all times? What if we disagree on entertainment choices?"

Sno looked the old man up and down, blinked a few times, then shook his head as he turned and walked into his room.

"I'm going to be a while," Sno called over his shoulder. "Call me only if you are dying."

"Enjoy, love," Sno heard Veben call as he closed his doors and began to strip his soiled clothes off. He headed straight for the lavatory and steam shower.

21.

"Food," Pol said, his mouth stuffed with something red and fluffy as Sno came out of his stateroom. "You should try this."

"I'll wait until dinner," Sno said, adjusting his suit jacket.

Black jacket, black trousers, and crisp white shirt. No tie, which would probably irritate Captain Loch considerably. It was custom to wear a tie when asked to dine with the captain of a ship, especially on a ship like the Mip. It was the little things that kept Sno sane sometimes when faced with dealing with imbeciles like Loch.

Sno looked Pol up and down and realized that Sno's intentional irritant would be overshadowed by Pol's complete lack of decorum. The old man was dressed in ratty trousers, a worn work shirt, and a visor that was more holes than actual material.

"No," Sno said. "You cannot go to dinner dressed like that. You have clothes that are appropriate. Go put them on."

"They're quite uncomfortable," Pol complained.

"This entire mission is quite uncomfortable," Sno said. "Would you prefer I ditch you and go gambling down on deck thirty-four?"

"Only if I can go with you," Pol said then scrunched up his face. "Which would defeat the purpose of ditching me. I see that."

"They are only clothes, Pol," Sno said. "Endure them during dinner then you are free to change when we return."

"Oh, my," Veben said as she came out of her room, dressed from neck to knee in a shimmering gown of emerald green jewels. "Pol, love, do as Denman asks and get changed. I cannot have a ragamuffin escort me to the Captain's Table."

"For you, darling, anything," Pol said and bowed so low his forehead touched the carpet.

"Eight Million Gods," Sno muttered as Pol left. Then he studied Veben and grinned. "I only hope I have half your charisma when I am your age."

"Oh, love, you do not want to reach my age," Veben said, waving off the compliment. "Too much work. Go out in a blaze of glory like so many in your profession do. Die a young patriot and be happy with that."

"I doubt I'll be happy, V," Sno said with a laugh. "I'll be dead."

Veben shrugged. "One can be happy no matter the circumstances if one tries hard enough."

There was a light knock at the door.

"That must be Osol," Sno said. "He'll be pleased to hear I've decided to share our true identities with him. Even though he already knows them."

"He does?" Veben asked as Sno headed off a servant bot and opened the door himself.

"Osol," Sno said and gestured for the man to enter the stateroom. "Come in."

"Thank you," Osol said.

There was a complete lack of servitude in Osol's stride as he walked past Sno, through the foyer, and into the main room.

"You look ravishing, ma'am," Osol said to Veben. "You will be wasted on Captain Loch. Although he will not think so. Be sure to watch his right hand, ma'am. It can get...aggressive."

"Oh, well, thank you, Osol," Veben said, giving Sno a side-eyed glance. "That is good information to have. Although, I can handle myself."

"No doubt, ma'am," Osol said and nodded politely. "But I felt you should be warned."

Osol took a seat without being asked to and Veben gave Sno a full-on look, ditching the side glance for direct eye contact.

"I should make the introductions," Sno said. "I am Agent Prime. My given name is Denman Sno. This is Ms. Veben Doab. The man still changing in his room is Pol Hammon. But all of this you already know."

"I do," Osol said curtly. "But it is good to hear you say it, Sno. Showing trust in me is a key step to me being able to keep all of you safe. I have to apologize up and down for the Tcherian incident. Sometimes amateurs are harder to deal with than professionals. I expected an assassination attempt on your life, followed by the kidnapping of Mr. Hammon, but not the moment you stepped into your rooms."

"Has Investigator J'gorla discovered the Tcherians' identities?" Sno asked.

"I'm sorry, but I have to interrupt," Veben said. Her eyes narrowed and she stared hard at Osol. "Who are you?"

"Osol Clemov," Osol said. "Head of Security for the GS M'illi'ped. Did Sno not inform you?"

"No, Sno did not inform me," Veben snapped. "And Sno will be hearing several words on that subject later."

"I needed a proper steam, V," Sno said. "Let a man have his small pleasures, please."

"Unfortunately, love, one of your small pleasures includes playing me for a fool," Veben said.

"I am fairly certain that is a game that you are well matched in, V," Sno said.

"This," Osol said, waving a hand back and forth between Sno and Veben. "This is cute. You two have known each other for a long time. I can tell. Does your mother always accompany you on missions, Sno?"

"For Head of Security, you have just made a tactical error, sir," Veben said in a calm, deadly voice.

"I am playing, Ms. Doab," Osol said. "No offense meant. The barb was intended for Agent Prime, not you."

"How about we try for no barbs and focus only on compliments, Osol?" Veben said then frowned. "Or do I call you Mr. Clemov?"

"Osol is fine," Osol said. "When we leave this stateroom, and are out amongst the guests, calling me Osol will retain my cover."

"Is this how you operate?" Sno asked. "Pretend to be a porter?"

"Or waiter, or server," Osol said. "I once had to keep an eye on a couple that were gambling addicts. I learned to deal every card and tile game imaginable. They never left the tables which meant I could never leave the tables. It came to a point where I had their cocktails spiked so I could get some sleep while they were unconscious. Otherwise, they would have continued to inject stim and play tiles the entire week-long journey, non-stop."

"Stim gives me such a headache," Veben said.

"Investigator J'gorla," Sno mused. "Trustworthy?"

"Is anyone?" Osol countered.

"Oh, Osol, good," Pol said as he came out in trousers too long and a shirt only halfway tucked in. "This pudding that was delivered. I have to know the origin so I can get some on my own. Can you send me the name of it?"

"I'll have one of my people send you the name," Osol said. "I have no idea what the pudding is. I only know it was tested thoroughly before being allowed into your room. Wouldn't do to have you all poisoned before we could talk."

"I have missed something here," Pol said. "Anyone feel like filling me in?"

"Later, darling," Veben said, taking Pol by the shoulders and turning him around to face his room. "Let's finish getting you properly dressed. Apparently, it is not a task you are capable of handling on your own."

Veben pushed Pol into the room then turned and closed the doors, giving both Sno and Osol a wink.

"Game plan," Sno said as he went and fetched a drink from the wet bar. He glanced at Osol, but the man shook his head. "The invite to dine with the captain tonight is an obvious panic decision by Loch. He is nervous that someone else will attempt to kill me and take Pol away before whoever has paid him gets a chance."

Sno turned and leaned against the wet bar. He sipped his drink, but kept his eyes on Osol over the rim.

"Maybe I should have one," Osol said. "Not too strong. Have to keep my wits about me."

"Condition yourself, Osol," Sno said as he faced the wet bar once again and poured a stiff drink for the man. He turned and crossed to Osol, offering the drink as he took a seat in the chair across. "One of my greatest talents is to drink my target under the table without losing my edge."

"Something to be proud of," Osol said and raised his glass.

Sno returned the gesture and waited. Osol sipped his drink then shook his head.

"I'm not sure you are right about Captain Loch," Osol said.

"I am," Sno stated.

"I have known the captain for a long while," Osol said. "I believe what you are mistaking for duplicity is simple incompetence."

"Could be, but I do not think so," Sno said as he leaned back in his chair. He crossed one leg over the other and drank deeply then set his almost finished drink onto a side table. "Were you observing our interaction via surveillance?"

"I was," Osol said.

"And his body language didn't alarm you?" Sno asked.

"That is Captain Loch," Osol said with a sigh. He set his drink on the side table next to his chair then leaned forward, fingers steepled as he rested his elbows on his knees. "The man no more knows who I am than anyone else on this ship. Other than Investigator J'gorla, and my guards, your little party are the only ones that know my true identity."

"I find it hard to believe that the captain of this ship is in the dark," Sno said.

"Yet he is," Osol replied. "And that would explain his body language and entire attitude when you asked him to reveal my name. The moron doesn't know. How embarrassing for the captain of a luxury liner to have to admit he doesn't even know who his Head of Security is."

"Is this a general policy or a specific one because of Loch?" Sno asked.

"Specific to Loch and those in power that are like him," Osol said. "They work perfectly as hosts, but lack a certain moral compass that can truly ensure guests' security and privacy. Give a man like Loch my name and soon half the ship will know it because he can't help but brag."

"Ah, yes, those beings," Sno said and nodded. "I have worked for men and women like him before. Eventually, someone dies because of their idiocy."

"Precisely," Osol said. "If the guests under my protection die, then hundreds, thousands, sometimes millions of beings across the galaxy are affected. Corporations go under, fortunes are lost, entire industries are dissolved overnight. I know my job and my duties, Sno. They are much larger than this silly ship."

Sno grinned. He had liked Osol when he was a porter. He liked the man even more as a Head of Security. Osol understood the true currents of how power flowed in the galaxy.

"Pol Hammon," Sno said.

"Yes. Him," Osol replied. "I could retire forever, leaving enough for six generations of Clemovs, if I sold his whereabouts to half a dozen interested organizations. And before you worry about my integrity, I am paid handsomely. Enough that I cannot be bought. It would be more trouble than those credits would be worth."

Sno nodded and Osol continued.

"The problem with Hammon is I don't know specifically why he's so valuable. His reputation as the galaxy's premiere dark tech expert notwithstanding, the buzz is he has something that could change the balance of power forever. I don't know what."

"You keep your ear to the right buzz," Sno agreed. "And I am in the dark as much as you are. My superiors have not educated me as to what this new tech might be." He held up his hands to take in the massive room. "All I know is it has landed me here and my only priority is to get Pol to GF main headquarters alive."

"And there we might have a problem," Osol said.

"I was afraid you'd have bad news once we were on the level with each other," Sno said. "Out with it?"

"We are not going anywhere near GF headquarters," Osol said.

"Right. The ship's destination is—"

"No, the original destination was changed just prior to your boarding," Osol said. "We are headed for a new destination."

"Which is?"

"We are going to the Bgreete System."

"Bgreete? There's nothing to see there," Sno said. "And guests are alright with this?"

"The guests do not know," Osol said. "They will be informed, and I am sure Captain Loch has some brilliant excuse already that he can tell everyone, but until then, the guests are oblivious. Not that they care much. You do know the Mip's reputation, yes?"

"As a singles cruise?" Sno chuckled. "I was informed."

"It is so much more than that," Osol said. "I've watched disinterested heirs become infatuated with each other, bringing together fortunes that neither of us can even conceive of. The GS M'illi'ped is probably more responsible for the consolidation of wealth in the galaxy than any corporate merger can take credit for. This ship could be headed for the center of the black hole in the Mlo System and the guests wouldn't let that reality spoil their matchmaking."

"I'd be lying if I said that didn't make me somewhat nauseous," Sno admitted.

"And I work with it daily," Osol said.

"Bgreete has two suns," Sno stated. "Two suns that create an energy flux, making it hard for ships to leave the system without special shielding on their engines."

Osol nodded and raised an eyebrow.

"The outside attack will come then," Sno said. Osol nodded again. "When do we arrive?"

"Three days," Osol said.

"They moved the timetable up as well," Sno said.

"That they did. Which means we have three days to watch for the internal attack," Osol said. "There will be at least one more attempt to wrest Pol from you before we arrive in Bgreete."

"To your knowledge, how many factions are after Pol?" Sno asked. "What does your buzz say?"

"I would think the SSD would have already given you that information," Osol said.

"The SSD is flying blind with a lot of this operation," Sno replied, picking at the arm of his chair. "That's why I'm here. Intel was shady or unconfirmed. At least to SSD standards. I will have to rely on those working the field to get me usable information."

"Six. Maybe seven," Osol said and shrugged. "Could be more. And that doesn't count the Skrang."

"It never does," Sno said and rubbed his face. "Six or seven? Maybe more? I'm thinking SSD knew of my house AI issue and is punishing me by putting Pol into my hands."

"Strange punishment since they want Pol Hammon delivered alive," Osol said.

"He'll be there alive," Sno said. "That isn't the point. The point is I'm being tortured. You have to love bureaucracies and their perverted sense of internal justice."

"Which is why I work in the private sector," Osol said.

"Yes. Good on you," Sno said and sighed. "So, what is the plan for the evening?"

"I'll deliver you to Captain Loch," Osol explained. "You'll endure dinner with him while I have a minimum of eight guards stationed throughout the dining room, their sole jobs to keep eyes on Pol Hammon. Another eight will be watching the guests at other tables for signs of interest beyond simply wishing they were at the Captain's Table for the attention that brings."

"Sixteen guards. Seems adequate," Sno said.

"Too few, in my opinion," Osol responded. "As you know, Pol Hammon's true security rests in your hands, Sno."

"I am gravely aware," Sno said as Pol's room doors opened.

"Much better, yes?" Veben asked as she escorted Pol out.

He was dressed in a mini version of Sno's outfit. That wasn't a problem since the majority of the beings in the main dining room would be dressed similarly.

"A prison in cloth," Pol muttered.

"Shall we?" Osol asked as he stood up and gestured to the foyer. "Please know that when we leave these rooms, I am Osol, the porter that is here to serve you. Act accordingly. Your lives do depend on it."

"Role playing," Veben said, clapping her hands together. "Such a turn on."

"Before we go," Sno said to Osol. "I will need a weapon."

"There will be one waiting for you at your assigned seat," Osol said. "Feel under the table. I didn't want to risk you having one that can be scanned as we travel from here to the dining room. Will that do?"

"It will have to," Sno said reluctantly.

22.

The dining room was slightly disappointing to Sno. Yes, it was superbly decorated, and the smell of the many appetizers and cocktails being served was tantalizing, but the Captain's Table was considerably less intimate than Sno had thought it would be. Of course, with what Osol had said, less intimate was probably a good thing considering the captain's lack of intellectual prowess.

However, there was one pleasant surprise and Sno had to struggle to maintain a neutral look on his face.

Seated at a table four over from the Captain's Table, with her back to Sno, was the swift ship pilot, Velly Tarcorf. That bright orange skin was unmistakable. She was dressed elegantly, a nice switch from her flight suit, in an off-the-shoulder dress made of a material that looked to change colors depending on the light, but always matched perfectly with her skin tone. Her hair was a short bob of ebony curls.

"Ah, she is lovely," Veben whispered to Sno as they were shown their seats at the Captain's Table. "Do you know her, love?"

"We met briefly," Sno replied. "Under very different circumstances."

"I am sure," Veben said. "Too bad you won't have time for socializing, love. Gotta keep me safe."

"I'm here to keep Pol safe," Sno said.

"And I don't intend to leave his side for the rest of the trip, so you'll be keeping me safe as well," Veben said as Sno pulled her seat out for her. "I have become fond of the little troublemaker."

"Speaking of me, are we?" Pol asked as he took the seat Sno had pulled out for himself. "Thank you, Mr. Shaw."

"Of course," Sno growled as all seats facing Velly's table became occupied. He thought about asking someone to move, but decided against it when he realized he'd have the best view of Pol's seat. Velly Tarcorf was not a priority no matter how lovely she looked.

"Mr. Shaw," Loch said, leaning forward so Sno could see the exaggerated wink. "I trust that your new accommodations are satisfactory?"

All eyes fell on Sno. He would have reached under the table, taken the pistol waiting for him, and shot the idiot, but Pol was seated where Sno was supposed to be. Lucky for Loch, the pistol was out of reach. Sno would have to remedy that situation shortly. Not the shooting of Loch, but the retrieval of the pistol so Sno could protect Pol better if a move was made in the loud, bustling dining room.

"The new accommodations are perfect, Captain Loch," Sno said. "Thank you for your hospitality."

"I don't know if any of you heard, but Mr. Shaw's first stateroom caught fire," Loch said. There were several gasps. Fires were for the lesser mortals, not the galactic elite. "I know! Not sure what you did, sir, but please don't let us have a repeat performance in your new rooms."

There was polite, and not so polite, laughter from the diners. A few of the beings seated jokingly chided Sno for allowing such a thing to happen. Others nodded sympathetically, assuredly thinking to themselves horrible thoughts of belongings damaged.

"What is it you do, Mr. Shaw?" the woman seated to Sno's right asked.

The woman was a Groshnel, an eight-armed, boneless race that must constantly gulp air in order to keep their bodies inflated and solid. Sno regarded her politely, an eyebrow raised.

"Ms....?" Sno asked.

The woman looked taken aback by the question. She obviously assumed Sno would know her. While Sno was born into the galactic elite, he hadn't kept up on the social hierarchy that dominated that class. The woman could have been queen of her own system and Sno wouldn't have known. Unless that system was vitally important to SSD matters.

Instead of offering her name, the woman turned from Sno and began a conversation with the gentleman on her other side. Sno wasn't exactly heartbroken over the snub.

Conversation rose as everyone waited for the first course to be served. Sno endured more questions, dodged them expertly then tried to block out the conversation the captain was having with an ancient-looking Spilfleck. The man was so old that his neck frill was almost shriveled up to nothing, barely a band of skin showing over his collarbones.

But, before Sno could completely ignore the conversation, the Spilfleck said, "I do hope I have enough funds available. I asked my secretary to combine six different accounts, but when you look about at who has joined us, there is no doubt that some financial heavyweights were clued in, as well. I am surprised given the short notice and scramble for tickets, but then we hardly have to wait, do we, Captain Loch?"

Loch's eyes flitted towards Sno briefly then looked away just as fast. The captain and the old Spilfleck had Sno's undivided attention.

But Sno played it cool and pretended to be listening to a conversation between a Klav and Halgon two seats down from him.

"You know how much we try to accommodate everyone," Loch said to the Spilfleck. "It was inconvenient, yes, but we managed to get everyone aboard that needed to be."

"Quite right. Quite right," the Spilfleck said. "Do we have a schedule yet?"

"When we reach the…system," Loch said.

"The Bg—" the Spilfleck began to say, but the rest of his statement was drowned out by Loch coughing loudly.

"Are you alright, Captain?" Veben asked. "Can you hear me?"

"How does his hearing you matter?" Pol asked. "Beings choke when their airways are blocked, not when their aural pathways are blocked. He could certainly hear you all the way up until he died."

"I am hardly near death," Loch said as he stopped coughing and gave the table a warm smile. "Fit and fine."

There was polite applause and Sno had to tamp down his rising disgust with the captain.

"Ladies and gentlemen," a soft voice said over the dining room's speakers. "On behalf of the GS M'illi'ped and Captain Loch, we are proud to present a live broadcast of the unbelievably talented, Ms. X X!"

A space at the front of the dining room became illuminated with bright yellow light which quickly dissolved into a shimmering holo image. The image solidified and a tall woman, apparently of almost every race in the galaxy, appeared in a flowing, sheer dress that looked like it was made up of stars, not cloth.

The dining room erupted into excited applause and heads bent towards each other as guests whispered with anticipation. Even Sno knew who the galactic megastar was. There wasn't a singer better known than Ms. X X. Veben caught his eye and gave him a wide smile.

Sno returned the smile, but it was a front. As the lights in the dining room dimmed to nothing, he knew if anyone was going to take a chance at snatching Pol, it would be during the performance. Sno twisted in his chair and casually looked about the dining room, ready to spot the being or beings that weren't there for the dessert course.

Velly Tarcorf was smiling at him. Sno returned the smile and gave her a nod. She smirked as the first few notes of quite possibly the most popular song in the galaxy began. When Ms. X X belted out the lyrics with her signature bombastic enthusiasm, Velly pretended to be gagging into her handkerchief. Until half the guests at her table gave her a look of such reproach that Sno wondered if they wouldn't murder her right there and then.

Velly tilted her head quickly to her right, indicating for Sno to meet her away from the tables. Sno shrugged and shook his head slowly. Velly frowned, narrowed her eyes then glanced at Captain Loch. The captain was staring straight at Sno instead of watching the performance. Sno met the man's gaze and nodded politely. Loch seemed startled by the response and smoothed the orange fur down on his cheeks before twisting in his seat to watch Ms. X X start in on her second song.

Sno's attention returned to scanning the dining room, but he couldn't help glancing back at Velly several times during the third and fourth songs. The woman was facing the holo of the famous singer, but her eyes darted towards Sno continuously as if she knew when he was watching her. A smile played at the corner of her mouth. Sno suddenly wanted nothing more than to kiss that smile.

But, despite his rising amor for the swift ship pilot, Sno's work brain was in control. His romantic brain would have to take a seat and wait its turn. Sno listened politely to a too sweet, too sappy ballad about a man crying over his lost loves as he was sucked into the burning hot heart of a sun about to go supernova. The metaphor was a little overplayed for Sno's taste, but the audience seemed to love it as there wasn't a dry eye in the dining room.

Then he saw her. A waitress moving about the edge of the room, a tray of dirty glasses and plates in one hand. Her other hand was hidden inside her uniform jacket. There could be any number of reasons she had a hand in her jacket, but Sno knew from years on the job that she was hiding a weapon. The unmistakable outline of a muzzle poked at her jacket's material as she threaded her way through the dining tables in Pol's direction instead of heading to the kitchen doors in the complete opposite direction.

"Excuse me," Sno said, standing up. He wiped his mouth, folded his napkin, and set it next to his drink. "I'll be right back."

No one paid him any attention. All eyes were on the performance. Except for Veben and Pol's. They each gave Sno a quizzical look. Sno only grinned slightly as he walked the length of the Captain's Table, came around the other side, and headed straight for the oncoming waitress.

It took the woman a couple seconds before she realized she'd been spotted. In that time, Sno was more than halfway to her. The waitress's eyes widened in panic and she froze in place. Sno did not stop his progress and closed the distance between them.

Guests hissed and spat at Sno, depending on their cultural custom, as he briefly blocked their views of Ms. X X. He tried to ignore them, but some were rather enthusiastic with their shows of annoyance. One man, a wizened Klav that had only two of his many, many eyes not clouded over with cataracts, whipped out a tentacle and snapped Sno across the backs of the thighs as he passed.

Sno glared at the old Klav, but he didn't stop his progress. The waitress was panicked and hunting for the fastest way out of the maze of tables and guests. Sno adjusted his direction and moved to cut off the waitress from one avenue of escape. The waitress set her tray down on a table, startling the guests, and spun about. She nearly sprinted towards the kitchen doors. Sno ignored the hisses and spittle that flew his way as he shoved through gaps between chairs and increased his speed of pursuit.

The doors had barely closed when Sno reached them. His hands were about to shove them wide when a shot rang out in the dining room. The shot was the energized blast of a plasma pistol and Sno spun around, his hand going for his Defta Stinger. But the Stinger wasn't there. Investigator J'gorla had taken it as evidence. Instinct gave way to surprise which gave way to reticence as Sno remembered the only weapon he had was back under the Captain's Table.

Guests were shouting and screaming, all up on their feet and racing to the nearest exit. The visual part of the broadcast holo of Ms. X X had been cut off, but the singer's voice was still playing at full volume, providing a soundtrack to the panic that had enveloped the room. Sno shoved guests out of his way as he raced back to the Captain's Table.

There was another blast then another and Sno became the only being in the room to not duck at the sounds. He stayed upright and could see plainly the terrified look on Veben's face as she stood next to Pol, a pistol in her hand and aimed down at something at her feet. Sno couldn't tell what or who she'd shot until he was only two tables away.

Security guards were closing in on Veben and Sno held up his hands, shouting at them to back off. They ignored his protests as they rushed to apprehend what they saw as the threat to the guests and the ship.

"It's not her!" Sno yelled, but a moment too late as Veben was tackled around the waist by an overzealous guard.

Veben screamed as she was taken down and the pistol flew from her grip. Sno jumped and slid across the last dining table, coming down on his feet only a meter from Veben and the guard. He held out his hand, snagged the falling pistol, brought it back up, and pressed the hot muzzle to the guard's temple.

"Let her go," Sno said calmly. The guard let Veben go. "Good."

"Drop the weapon!" another guard shouted.

"Listen to your comms, people!" Sno yelled as he slowly moved back from the guard and lowered the pistol.

Before the guard could regroup and get to his feet, Veben slapped him so hard across his left cheek that the sound of the vertebrae in his neck cracking echoed throughout the dining room, even over the continuing vocalizations of Ms. X X belting out some new song from her latest album.

"Identity confirmed," a guard stated, pointing to Sno. "Apologies, Mr. Shaw."

"Help her up," Sno snapped at the struck guard.

The guard seemed conflicted, but finally offered a hand to Veben, helping her up off the floor. Sno gave her a questioning look and she nodded that she was fine. Pol was standing next to the Captain's Table, eyes wide with fear, and looking like he wanted to bolt with the rest of the guests.

"He came at me so fast," Pol said. He looked down at the floor. "How did he move so quickly?"

Pol was staring at a scorched corpse. It was a man, a human, in a server's uniform. Veben had placed the shots perfectly in the man's chest.

"Do not let that corpse out of your sight," Sno ordered the guard as others approached. "And watch him! Veben?"

"I'm fine, love," Veben said, glaring daggers at the guard that had assaulted her. "And I will make sure that Mr. Talpic is watched very closely."

"Good," Sno said and turned to face the kitchen doors. "Return to our stateroom as soon as Osol comes to retrieve you. Stay there and do not let anyone in except for me."

"Go," Veben said.

Sno went. He sprinted across the dining room, which was nearly empty of all guests, and burst through the kitchen doors. Stunned staff stood around, mouths agape, dishes going unwashed, food burning on the range, water running freely from the taps. No one moved to stop Sno, but no one moved to help him either.

When he shouted, "Which way did she go?" Sno only received confused stares.

"Useless."

Sno pushed cooks and prep staff out of his way and hurried through the massive kitchen until he found a short corridor in the back. With pistol up and at the ready, Sno moved cautiously to the first door in the corridor. He listened, heard nothing, then yanked the door open and covered the room beyond with his pistol.

Storage. Boxes of supplies at the ready. Sno ignored the stacks and instead studied the floor of the room. He was looking for scuff marks from the boxes being moved, but the floor showed no signs that someone had tried hiding behind the stacks. They were pressed evenly up against the room's walls.

Sno retreated and continued to the next door. He yanked that open to find an insanely long corridor. It was dimly lit and must have stretched for nearly the entire length of the ship. Quick access corridor for kitchen staff to deliver food on that deck to the many lounges, bars, snack stands, specialty eateries, and cafes.

The view down the corridor was unobstructed, and Sno knew his pursuit was at an end when he counted the dozens and dozens of doors that lined one side. The waitress could have gone through any one of those doors. Sno would have to backtrack and bring up the ship's security surveillance to track her further. If she used the long corridor, and was still on the ship, he'd find out where.

Sno ducked back into the short kitchen corridor and regarded the last door. It was slightly ajar and there was a sound coming from inside. Sno carefully approached it, listened, grew puzzled then ripped the door all the way open, his pistol leading his way inside.

Another storage room, but not unoccupied like the last one. On the floor was a dazed Velly Tarcorf. Bright red blood had started to dry across the orange skin of her nose and face. Her eyes swam in her head as she struggled to remain conscious.

"Shit," Sno said, tucking his pistol in his pocket as he knelt by Velly and checked her pulse. Erratic. He scooped her up in his arms and hurried back through the kitchen. "Hang on. We'll get you to a med pod."

23.

It took Osol over two hours before he arrived at Sno's stateroom.

"Anything?" Sno asked.

"No," Osol replied. "No identification on the man killed and no identification on the woman that escaped. We ran all vid surveillance of her over the past couple of days through every database at our disposal. She doesn't exist. He doesn't exist."

"Grid ghosts," Veben said from the couch, a very large tumbler of brown liquor held in both hands. "They happen."

"Ignore her," Sno said quietly to Osol. "That's her fourth and she's still coming down from the rush of the incident."

"I can hear you, love," Veben said, drinking liberally from the tumbler. "Do not speak as if I am of a diminished capacity. Certainly not the first, second, or third corpse I have seen in my lifetime."

"Then perhaps that should be your last tumbler," Sno suggested.

"Would you like some, love?" Veben asked, offering the tumbler. "I could cram it up your arse for you."

"Yes, that's the last one," Sno said and waved a hand over his wrist and brought up the protocol for the servant bots. "No more alcohol for Ms. C'alpescue."

"I'll simply serve myself," Veben said and attempted to stand. She made it approximately three centimeters before collapsing back into the couch. "Later. I am good for now."

"Any ships leave the Mip?" Sno asked, turning his attention back to Osol.

"No," Osol said. "And no sign of the woman escaping the dining room. If she went through the kitchen, then she must have used moltrans tech to get out because there is no vid evidence of her leaving."

"Did someone say moltrans?" Pol asked as he came into the sitting room, a towel wrapped around his head and one wrapped around his waist. The man's chest was shrunken in and his arms looked like toothpicks. "I have a way to track moltrans use. If the attempted assassins are using that kind of tech, then I will be able to not only find residual traces, I might be able to track that energetic residue to the destination."

"That would be helpful," Sno said. "But you are not leaving this stateroom for the remainder of the trip. I thought a luxury liner would be the perfect cover, but I was wrong. A public transport would be more secure."

"Excuse me," Osol said angrily.

"No offense," Sno replied. "But you have too many privileged guests onboard and that privilege is a wild card that I did not anticipate. Beings are able to buy their way around the security protocols. I'm not saying you are bought and paid for, Osol, of course, but some of your people surely are. You said you had the dining room covered?"

"It was covered," Osol insisted.

"Yet a potential killer or kidnapper dressed as a waiter was able to get close to Pol," Sno countered. "And a second one was on her way. That is not covered, Osol. That is neglectful."

"Are you expecting another apology?" Osol asked. "You will not be getting one. The neglect I am seeing is on your part. You chose this mode of transportation when you could have used a private ship to get to your destination."

"Not with the Skrang out there," Veben interrupted. "Those nasty Skrang bastards! Always trying to kill, kill, kill."

Sno sighed as Veben kept muttering about kill, kill, kill, then tilted to her left, and in almost perfect slow motion, fell over onto her side on the couch. Her eyes closed and she began to snore.

"There we are," Sno said. He thought for a moment then shook his head. "In the end, and the beginning, I suppose, yes, the responsibility is all on me. I accept that. But with the information I had been given, I could not risk using one of my ships or using a GF ship. I suspected that a luxury liner such as the Mip, with its clientele and need for absolute perfect security, would be the safest avenue of transport. The only reason I was wrong is that we are looking at several unknown factions all trying to get at Pol and no idea how many may have gotten aboard."

"Break your thoughts down for me," Osol said.

"The Tcherians were amateurs," Sno explained. "That is one faction. The two servers in the dining room were more experienced, so they're from a different faction. They escaped too easily to be on the low level as the Tcherians."

"That's two factions," Osol said. "We thought there were more."

"There's at least one more," Sno said. "Whatever faction has bought Captain Loch. That would make three. The rest of the factions are waiting for their chance to snatch Pol."

The subject of that statement still stood in the sitting room dressed only in two towels. He looked from Sno to Osol and back before he cleared his throat and said, "Did neither of you hear me when I said I can track the moltrans residue?"

"Did you not hear me when I said you aren't leaving this stateroom?" Sno replied.

"I do not need to," Pol said. "All I need to do is load a bot with the protocol and that bot can handle the investigation for me. I'll be safely here in this stateroom while data is transmitted to my implants."

He waved both wrists and a series of complex protocols streamed across a drab green holo vid then faded back out to nothing.

"Those are not supposed to work," Osol said.

"Please," Pol replied.

"You can track moltrans?" Sno asked. "Seriously?"

"Get me a bot and we can go from there," Pol said.

"I can do that," Osol said.

"Oh, better yet!" Pol exclaimed. He was loud enough to elicit a snort and grumble from the sleeping Veben. Pol smiled over at her then returned to his excitement. "The android! The one that works for J'gorla. Yes. Get me..."

Pol snapped his fingers over and over.

"Ested," Sno responded.

"Ested! Yes! Get me Ested!" Pol said. "The android will be much better suited to an investigation such as this."

"I'll ask J'gorla," Osol said.

"Tell her," Sno insisted. "This isn't a choice."

"I'll ask," Osol said and waved his wrist. "Give me a moment to comm her."

"Take your moment," Sno said. He pointed at Pol. "Go get dressed, please."

"Sno, get the android," Pol said as he walked to his room.

The towels fell before he reached the doors and Sno turned his eyes up to the ceiling in exasperation. Sno waited for the doors to close then caught Osol's eye before glancing at his own room's doors. Osol nodded at Sno to go ahead while he conversed with J'gorla on the comm.

With Pol getting dressed, Veben asleep on the couch, and Osol in a heated discussion with J'gorla, Sno opened the doors to his room and grinned at the sight he saw.

The med pod he'd insisted be installed in his room was occupied by Velly. Her eyes were blinking at him and she looked more than a bit confused. Sno closed the room doors, crossed to the med pod and unlatched the lid, letting it rise quickly so Velly could sit upright.

"A blanket or towel would be nice," Velly said, her body completely naked. "Or even clothes."

"Here you go," Sno said, handing her a pile of fresh clothing.

Velly studied the clothes and pursed her lips. "You went into my quarters?"

"Not personally," Sno replied. "One of the guards fetched these for you. We're on lockdown in this stateroom until we reach our destination."

"Is that so?" Velly asked as she slid out of the med pod and began to get dressed. "What if I want to leave this ship now? Are you going to stop me?"

"I'll stop you from leaving this stateroom," Sno said. "If you manage to get past me, then leaving the ship will be your problem, not mine. I'd think you'd want to stay after your bit of heroics back there."

Sno watched her get dressed. Her body was incredibly tone, orange skin taut against well-formed muscles. Velly raised an eyebrow as she pulled her shirt down over her head. Sno did not look away as she then pulled on trousers, buckled them then looked around the stateroom.

"Boots?" she asked.

"Here," Sno said and found a pair sitting by the closed doors. He handed her the boots and took a couple of steps back. "Why'd you do it?"

"I'm sorry?" Velly replied as she sealed her boots up over her ankles. "Do what, friend?"

"Chase after the woman," Sno asked. "For that matter, why are you on this ship?"

"Our mutual friend thought you might need the help," Velly said. "Which you do, friend. Yeah, you do."

"Trel'ali? He sent you here?" Sno asked.

Velly didn't answer that question except for a slight shrug. She finished with her boots and stood straight, facing Sno. Then she looked beyond him to the room's doors.

"Can I at least leave this room?" Velly asked.

"Do you want to?" Sno countered.

Velly looked confused then a grin spread across her face.

"Agent Prime, are you hitting on me?" she asked.

"It's Mr. Shaw," Sno said. "And, yes. Hard to get the image of you in that dress out of my head."

Velly stepped closer and stroked Sno's cheek. Then she gave it a hard pat.

"Maybe later," she said. "Although, a couple hours in a med pod does tend to get the juices flowing."

"And you can't leave the stateroom anyway," Sno said.

"And I can't leave the stateroom anyway," Velly echoed. "Which doesn't make this scenario creepy at all."

Sno laughed. "I guess it's not the best time. A raincheck when we can both enjoy each other at a more relaxed pace."

He stepped aside and gestured to the doors.

"Are you giving up that quickly, friend?" Velly said and shook her head. "Disappointing."

"I'm sorry…?" Sno said.

"Why would you be sorry?" Velly asked as she grabbed Sno by the buckle of his belt and pulled him to her. "Do you want to be sorry?"

Sno didn't know how to respond to that, so he did what came naturally and put his hand on the back of Velly's head, bringing their mouths close to each other. But he paused just before their lips met.

"You sure?" he whispered.

"Shut up," Velly whispered back and kissed him hard.

The new clothes she'd just put on came off fast. As did Sno's clothes. The two beings, arms wrapped about each other, lips embraced, stumbled their way around the med pod to Sno's bed. They fell across the bedclothes and their passion built quickly. There was no need to pull back the covers; Velly and Sno did not have the patience for that.

There, on top of the bed, they took each other, tasted each other, satisfied each other. Twenty minutes, thirty, an hour passed before they were sated and came up for enough air to realize they were probably being missed. Their chests rising up and down, up and down, sweat-covered bodies entwined, Sno sighed.

"Osol is probably pissed he had to stay out there and babysit Pol," Sno said. "And who knows what Pol has done to that android."

"Android?" Velly asked, tracing a finger up and across one of Sno's many scars.

"Long story," Sno said. "What can you tell me about the woman you chased into the kitchen?"

"Business already?" Velly chuckled and sat up. She ran a hand down the inside of Sno's thigh, but dodged his hand as he reached to pull her back to him. "The fun never lasts."

"I think we lasted fairly long considering," Sno said as he watched Velly get dressed for the second time. She didn't hurry and was obviously angling herself to give Sno the best show possible. He licked his lips and realized he was starving. "Food?"

"Would love some," Velly said. "But I'll eat when I get to my quarters. I want to go check on my ship just in case it has been tampered with. If we need to leave this ship quickly, I want to be able to do that without exploding in the docking bay."

Sno laughed and began to get dressed too. "Funny."

"My ship exploding with me in it is funny to you?" Velly asked.

"What? No. You leaving this stateroom is funny," Sno said. "I already told you that you aren't leaving. We're here for the long haul."

Velly opened her mouth to respond, closed it, opened it again then busied herself with putting her boots back on. Once they were on, she marched to the room's doors and tried to open them. When they didn't open, she spun about and glared.

"Sno," she snarled. "Let me out of here."

There was a knock at the doors.

"Hold on," Sno called then focused on Velly. "Listen to me. You are safer here than out in the ship. Leave if you want, but I'd rather you didn't."

"So I can leave?" Velly asked.

"Yes," Sno said. "But if you do leave the stateroom, then your name will be added to the suspect list. Hard for me to trust you if I don't know what you are up to."

"Trust me? How about me trusting you?" Velly said.

There was another knock.

"Fine," Sno said and swiped across his wrist. The doors unlocked. "I tried."

"You did," Velly said as she squeezed by an irritated-looking Osol.

"What in the Hells, Sno," Osol snapped. "Is this really the time for romance?"

"I take it when I can get it," Sno said. "In my line of work—"

"Do not care," Osol said. "We have bigger issues. J'gorla is dead. Ested is missing. My people have been hunting for the android for the past hour. No trace."

"Shit," Sno said.

24.

"Get your hands off me!"

Sno was about to ask Osol a string of questions, but a shout stole his attention. He looked passed Osol to see a wobbling Veben grabbing ahold of an alarmed and enraged Velly.

"You ain't going nowhere, chicky!" Veben yelled. "You think I don't know what you are? Huh? You think I can't smell you? I knew it! I knew it back in the dining room!"

"Let go of me, you drunk old cow!" Velly shouted and tried again to wrench free of Veben's grip. "You've lost your mind!"

"Hey!" Sno roared. "What is going on?"

"This woman has gone insane!" Velly shouted, still unable to pry Veben's fingers from her arm. "Let me the fuck go!"

"V? What are you doing?" Sno asked, his hands working to free Velly as well. "Eight Million Gods dammit, V! Let her arm go!"

"No!" Veben shouted back. "I will not let this skintaker walk out of here without explaining herself!"

Veben pulled Velly close to her, their noses almost touching.

"If you are a she," Veben hissed. "Or are you one of those that likes to mix genders? That it? You playing my Denman for a fool? You playing us all for fools? Who are you?"

"V? What is going on?" Sno asked. He shoved himself between the women and finally got Veben's grip loose. "Talk to me."

"Your Denman?" Velly asked. "Are you putting a claim on Agent Prime?"

"No one is claiming anybody," Sno said.

He put a hand on Velly's chest and eased her back a few steps. He started to do the same to Veben, but without Velly to grab onto for support, Veben almost toppled over onto her ass. Sno caught her and moved her back to the couch. He slowly lowered her into the cushions then stood back and shook his head.

"She's gone—" Velly started.

"No," Sno snapped and jabbed a finger at Velly. "She hasn't gone anything. She's drunk. I know her when she's drunk. It's when the honesty comes out. V? Can you tell me what you are talking about?"

"Ask her, love," Veben said, as she sunk deep into the cushions, the back of her hand to her forehead like a melodramatic actress in the holo vids. "She is the one with the secrets to be plied. Or did you already ply them, love? Did you and your little Jirk girlfriend whisper to each other after your poorly timed rendezvous? Pol is in need of protection, love, and you get it on with the lying Jirk swift pilot. How many seats does her ship have? How many people can she really save? What is her worth to us, love? Banish her, I say. Banish her from... Banish her from... Banish...from... Snnnnnkkkkkkgggggrrrr..."

Veben's eyes closed and she began to snore.

"And she's out," Sno said. He slowly turned to Velly, one eyebrow raised.

"I don't know what she's talking about," Velly said.

"I don't care," Osol said, punching a fist into an open palm to get everyone's attention. "This little play of yours is over. We have real problems to deal with."

"Hold up," Sno said and took a step closer to Velly. "This is a real problem if it's true."

"And what if it is, friend?" Velly asked, defensive and close to enraged. Her eyes were wide and her skin had begun to take on a brownish tint, making the natural orange look muddied. "What if I am a Jirk? How is that a problem, Sno?"

She pointed angrily at the snoring Veben.

"She's a Jirk and I'm watching you defend her like she was a lover."

"Not a lover, Velly. She is as close to a parent as I have left," Sno snapped. "She is a dear, trusted friend. A friend that would give her life for me and a friend I would give my life for."

"A Jirk friend," Velly insisted.

Sno didn't respond.

"But you knew that," Velly continued with a short, harsh laugh. "You come after me because I may be a Jirk, but you ignore the fact she is."

"First, I didn't come at you. V did. Second, are you a Jirk? I don't need maybes right now, Velly. Third, I have known Veben Doab my entire life and she has been this person the entire time. Is she a Jirk? Probably, but I have never asked and she has never told me. That is her business."

"Jirks do have to kill to take a being's skin," Osol interrupted. "More than her business, Sno."

"Shut. Up," Sno said, raising a finger towards Osol. "I am aware of how Jirks take on their new identities. But Veben has had this one for decades, possibly much, much longer. One skin taken a long time ago." He cocked his head and stared at Velly. "How long ago did you assume this persona?"

"I'm not answering that," Velly said. "I'm leaving."

"No," Osol said. "You stay right here. Having Jirks aboard changes things immensely. We're going to have a talk before I even think of letting you go."

"I'm leaving," Velly stated. "I'm taking my ship and getting the Hells away from the Mip the second we are out of trans-space."

"Again, no," Osol said. "Sit down." He faced Sno. "You. We need to talk. Now. This ship is falling apart and it is happening at a rate that I do not understand. Something else is going on here. My guards are reporting very odd behavior by the guests. I'd say we're in for a coup if this was some small asteroid station or planetary outpost. But this is the GS M'illi'ped. A coup would accomplish nothing. We're going to lay our tiles on the table and figure this shit out, Sno. Now."

"Yes, you keep saying now," Sno said. "I get it. Velly? Would you mind giving us a moment?"

"What? You want me to leave?" Velly asked.

"I do," Sno said. "Would you mind? Veben's room is free. Freshen up. Take a steam. Order new clothes on V."

"These are new, friend," Velly said, waving her hands over her body. "Or have you forgotten you gave them to me earlier tonight?"

"I haven't forgotten. I do apologize for all of this," Sno said. "I truly do and I will make it up to you."

"She is still a Jirk, Sno," Osol said with obvious disgust. "Never owe a skintaker."

"Thank you for your galactic wisdom," Sno snapped. "Velly? Please?"

"New clothes and a steam," Velly said, giving both Sno and Osol her middle fingers. A galactic symbol no one had an issue interpreting. "Just what a girl wants, right? Fucking assholes…"

Sno and Osol waited until Velly had closed the doors to Veben's room before they both glanced at the passed-out woman on the couch.

"She'll be out for hours," Sno said. "Trust me."

"I'd like to, Sno," Osol said. "But trust is hard to come by tonight. Wouldn't you say?"

"I decided to trust you, didn't I?" Sno replied. "I have my reservations, but I'm usually very good at seeing who is and who isn't my ally."

"Reservations?" Osol asked as he sat down in a chair across the room from Veben and her sleeping couch.

"I'd be an idiot not to," Sno said, taking a chair across from Osol. "But there have been more than a few opportunities to kill me and take Pol this evening. You have ignored all of those and remained here to help. That says something."

"Was you going into your room with Ms. Tarcorf a test, Sno? Leaving me alone out here with your friends to see if I'd make a move?" Osol chuckled. "Were you watching a holo while also romancing Ms. Tarcorf?"

"I can multi-task, but not that well," Sno said. "I placed a tracker on Pol as well as a simple alert on his doors. Basic protocol considering." Sno nodded at the doors to Pol's room. "He has stayed in there since we returned and those doors haven't opened."

Sno brought up a holo of his tracking protocol which showed a large schematic of the ship. The image zoomed in to the stateroom they sat in then centered on Pol's room. A flashing icon showed Pol to be in his bed.

"The old man must be exhausted," Sno said. "And I'm surprised V lasted as long as she did. Field work like this is trying even on trained agents."

"Trying on us all," Osol said and spread his hands out. "So, where does this leave us?"

"This leaves us with what we know," Sno said. "The SSD suspected a mole. I believe the breach was on my end with the corruption of my house AI. However, I cannot be for certain of that. I am rarely assigned a mission by the Head of Fleet Intelligence himself. I met Velly Tarcorf on Egthak during a mission that went very wrong. There is a freelancer by the name of Trel'ali that is involved, as well."

"A friend?" Osol asked with obvious sarcasm.

"Colleague that I know when to trust and when not to," Sno said with a shrug. "I have no reason not to trust him now."

"Pol Hammon? What is this tech he created?" Osol asked.

"I do not know," Sno replied.

"Sno…"

"I don't," Sno insisted. "My job does not require knowing that information. My job requires safe delivery of Pol Hammon to the Galactic Fleet main headquarters. Pure and simple."

"Hardly simple," Osol grumbled.

"True," Sno said. "It has been mostly painful so far. But Pol still lives and I still have a mission to complete. Which makes our travel to Bgreete a problem. That will add several days onto the trip and poses a serious security threat."

"Because of the energy vortex the Bgreete System's suns create," Osol said, rubbing at his face. "I know. But the captain will not deviate from the new destination."

"And the guests have no problem with this?" Sno asked.

Osol leaned forward, frowning. "Surprisingly, no. These are a class of people that do not enjoy surprises nor do they enjoy changes of plans. But I haven't heard a single complaint from those that have become aware of our changed destination."

"I overheard a guest at the Captain's Table sound almost excited to get to Bgreete," Sno said. "Which is odd considering Bgreete is nothing special."

"Other than the energy vortex."

"Yes, other than that. Would the captain intentionally take us to Bgreete to trap the ship in the vortex?"

"That would put everyone at risk, including himself," Osol replied. "Captain Loch is many things, but brave is not one of them."

"Yes, I did not get the heroic vibe off the man," Sno said with a smirk. "I do get the self-serving, profit-off-others vibe, though."

"That is Loch in a nutshell," Osol said. "Which means there is something waiting for us in the Bgreete System."

"We need to find out what," Sno said. A thought hit Sno. "J'gorla. When did she die? You were on the comm with her when I was in my room with Velly."

"No, I was on the comm with Ested and put the android in touch with Pol via the comm," Osol said. "I never spoke to J'gorla directly. She was indisposed. Which only added to my irritation."

"Holo of J'gorla's office?" Sno asked.

"Wiped."

"Not easy to do. Unless you're an android."

"Or Head of Security," Osol added. "I can wipe any holos I want, but my ID would leave a trail a mile wide."

"J'gorla found something out," Sno said. "And Ested killed her for it. We need to see that holo. We need to see if there was a confrontation between the two and if possibly J'gorla, or Ested, revealed any pertinent intel."

"Good luck with that," Osol said. "I've had techs working on it, but the holo is gone."

"The recorder was damaged?"

"No, I had that checked. Perfect working order."

"Then the holo is not gone. It can be recovered."

Sno stood up and walked to Pol's doors. He knocked loudly.

"Pol? Time to get to work," Sno said. There was no answer. "Pol? Wake up, old man, you're needed."

Still no answer. Sno brought up his holo and the protocol showed Pol securely in his room. Sno tried the doors, but they were locked. He stepped aside and glanced at Osol.

Osol stood and crossed to the doors. He popped open a panel on the wall and presented his wrist to a hidden scanner. The light under the scanner flashed green then flashed red. Osol frowned and tried again. Same result.

"Someone doesn't want to be disturbed," Osol said.

"Dammit," Sno said. "That little SOB better be in there. If I find out he's hacked my tracker and he's left this stateroom, then I swear I might kill him myself."

"We'll have to take the doors off," Osol said and activated his comm. "I need an extraction bot on me now."

"This trip could have been a breeze," Sno said, looking about the stateroom. "It could have been nice."

"You're from this class, Sno," Osol said when he was done with his comm call. "Is there anything nice or breezy when these people are involved?"

"Far from it," Sno said and moved to the wet bar. "Drink while we wait?"

"Might as well," Osol said with a sigh.

25.

It took the extraction bot more than an hour to remove the doors to Pol's room. No matter how much Osol yelled at the bot to simply tear the doors out of their tracks, the bot continued in a slow, methodical manner, all the while apologizing. The bot's directives prevented it from destroying ship property and even Osol's security overrides didn't work against the very basics of its programming.

Sno wavered back and forth between intense frustration and ironic amusement as the bot worked at the doors while Osol spat a string of profanities at the slow machine. Then the doors were off their tracks and the room was wide open. Both the amusement and frustration were gone in an instant and Sno sprinted past the bot and the still fuming Osol, and into Pol's room.

The old tech sat upright in his bed, his back resting against a mound of pillows. His eyes were closed and chest was moving up and down in a slow, constant rhythm. Sno rushed to the old man's side and checked his pulse. Strong, even.

"Pol? Wake up," Sno ordered.

The old man sat perfectly still other than the rising of his chest.

"Pol!" Sno shouted. "Wake up!"

The old man did not wake up. He didn't even twitch as Sno shouted in his ear.

"What's wrong with him?" Osol asked.

"Call a medic," Sno said.

He lifted one of Pol's eyelids and saw nothing but white. Sno brought up a holo and swiped through a short menu before finding the simple protocol he needed. He waved his wrist up and down and back and forth across Pol's body.

"Son of a bitch," Sno said. "He's connected."

"Connected? To what?" Osol asked. Osol brought up his own holo and studied it. "Not to the ship's mainframe. I'd see that connection here."

"He's piloting," Velly said from the doorway.

She was leaning against the frame, ignoring the extraction bot's protestations for her to move so it could repair the tracks it damaged getting the doors off. She'd received her new clothes and had opted for her usual flight suit. Velly sneered at Sno then returned her attention to Pol.

"Yep. He's piloting," she said.

"Piloting?" Sno asked. "Piloting what? And how do you know?"

"Been in that technotrance many times in my career," Velly said. "Remote piloting. Sometimes I'm hired to go into environments that even my ship cannot protect me from. I get as close as possible then remotely pilot my ship from there."

"Pol is not a pilot," Sno said. "I know that for certain."

"Ships are not the only machines that can be piloted," Velly said.

"Can he be disconnected?" Sno asked.

"Not from here. Not unless you want to kill him," Velly said. "The connection can be severed from the other side. It's a failsafe protocol in case the piloted machine is destroyed. Keeps the remote pilot from having their brain annihilated."

"He did this to himself," Osol said. "He has a reason."

"What is that reason?" Sno asked. He pressed the heel of his hand to his forehead. "This mission has been out of control since we arrived. I can't get a handle on it."

"Sometimes even Agent Prime gets confused," Velly said, amused. "Welcome to how the rest of us feel."

"I don't need your shit," Sno said and pointed at Velly. "What I need is your help. How do we trace this connection? How do we find out which machine he is piloting?"

Velly glared.

"Sorry," Sno said. "I am. How do we find out which machine he is piloting?"

"You don't," Velly stated. "Not unless you want to jack directly into his mind."

"I do not want to, but we have to," Sno said.

"Then you're gonna need a medic," Velly said. "And a pilot that's been through trances like this. You have one of those two."

Velly pushed away from the frame and stood with her hands on her hips.

"Got a medic you trust?" she asked Osol.

"I do," Osol said. "I'll call her now."

Osol stepped out of the room. Velly stepped fully in and walked to Sno's side, her eyes on Pol.

"This takes prep," she said. "Even for a tech like Pol, remote piloting anything takes prep."

"I do not doubt it," Sno said. "I've had this feeling that I have only seen a glimpse of the entire picture ever since I met the man. I chalked it up to the SSD and Fleet Intelligence playing the need to know card. But this here, this trance, is more than that. That is what you're saying, yes? That Pol has possibly been playing us all from the beginning."

"He's Pol Hammon," Velly said and shrugged. "The greatest manipulator in the galaxy."

"I doubt he's the greatest," Sno said.

"Have you met a man named Roak?" Velly asked.

"I know of his reputation, of course," Sno said. "But I have never met the bounty hunter."

"Roak was hired to rescue Pol from Razer Station," Velly said. "Or that is the rumor. The station ended up being destroyed and Roak was left empty-handed when Pol disappeared on him."

"From what I know of the man's reputation, he is not one to anger that way," Sno said. "I hear even the syndicates are afraid of Roak."

"Yet Pol played him and everyone else," Velly said.

"According to the rumor," Sno said. "I doubt reality lines up so perfectly."

"I don't know," Velly said, gesturing to Pol's still form. "Look at him. To do this, he'd have to know he would be protected. I could stab him right now and he wouldn't be able to do a thing about it."

Sno snapped a harsh look at Velly. She sighed.

"I'm not going to stab him," she said. "I'm saying that Pol knew he'd have you looking after him. He knew security would be good enough that he could take a risk and remote pilot…something."

"That is quite a risk," Sno said. "Relying on only me."

"Except he isn't relying on only you, friend, is he?" Velly asked. "There are more than a dozen guards assigned to keep this stateroom safe. That beats hiding in a dank cave to stay safe, which I've done before. Look at the guy. He's not exactly suffering."

"He saw his chance and took it," Sno said.

"He did."

"Medic will be here shortly," Osol said.

"You trust him?" Sno asked.

"Her. I trust Zan with my own life," Osol said.

"Zan?" Sno asked with a smile. "She helped me when I was attacked by the Tcherians. Very competent medic. Attractive, too."

"Good for Zan," Velly said. "How soon will she be here?"

"Seconds," Osol said. "I had her standing by just in case anyway. Dealing with this wasn't what I had in mind, but she'll handle it fine."

"With my help," Velly said.

"I hope so," Osol replied.

"Good," Sno said. "As soon as Zan arrives, you and I are going to find the other end of this tether."

"You're leaving me here with Pol alone?" Velly asked.

"Not alone," Sno said. "You'll have Zan here, a dozen security guards, and V."

"She is still snoring on the couch," Velly said.

"I'll wake her up," Sno said. "She'll stay out of your way, but be close enough to keep an eye on everything."

"You really trust her that much?" Velly asked. "Are you sure?"

"Not up for debate," Sno said.

There was a commotion in the foyer and Zan appeared, flanked by two guards. Osol waved them off and waved Zan in.

"Zan Woqua meet Velly Tarcorf. You two are going to get inside Pol's head and figure out what is going on from this end," Osol said.

"While we hunt for the other end and ensure Pol is not making an already out of hand situation worse," Sno said.

"I'm telling you he has this all planned out," Velly insisted.

"We'll see," Sno said. "Osol? I'm going to need a pistol."

"I can make that happen," Osol said then faced Zan who was looking perplexed. "Listen to Velly, but remember that your primary job is to keep Pol alive and safe."

"I'm a medic, Osol," Zan said. "My job is to keep everyone alive. Safe, however, is your job. And you're leaving?"

"Alright. I like her," Velly said.

"Get in that man's head," Osol said to Zan.

"Comm us if you need to," Sno said. "But be vague when we speak. No doubt the comms system is monitored by Captain Loch."

"Guaranteed," Osol said. "Let's get geared up."

"I need to wake V first," Sno said as he left Pol's room and marched over to the couch where Veben was still passed out.

He watched her for a moment then went into her room and searched her bags. He found what he needed and returned to Veben's side.

"Sorry, love," he said as he stabbed the injector into the side of her neck. "Has to be done."

Veben came awake with a scream and flailing arms. Sno jumped out of striking distance as Veben lurched up from the couch, eyes wide and confused.

"Good. You're awake," Sno said when Veben was able to focus on him. "Got a job for you, V. Can we pretend water is under the bridge for a bit until all of this over?"

"You know I can't refuse you, love," Veben said, her voice a harsh croak. "But we will have words at some point."

"Of course," Sno said and explained everything she had missed.

26.

"I'm sorry, you want to go where first?" Osol asked as the lift descended at express speed, ignoring calls from the many decks they passed. Osol overrode the controls to get them to their destination as fast as possible. "Why?"

"Because I need to check something," Sno said. "I have a hunch."

"Oh, great, a hunch," Osol said. "It all makes sense now."

"Bear with me," Sno said.

The lift stopped and the doors opened to a pair of guards waiting next to a roller.

"Get in," Osol said to Sno. "You two, get back to the search of the ship. If you see any bots acting strangely, report it to me personally. Do not report it to maintenance or any curious techs. To me only."

The two agreed and saluted as Osol drove the roller away from the lift and down the corridor.

"See, that's what is bothering me," Sno said as they took several turns before racing down a straightaway to another lift. "Pol is a good enough tech that he shouldn't have to take over a bot for it to do what he wants."

"Velly is probably a good enough pilot that she could use a tablet to run a ship," Osol said. "But she says she's used remote piloting before."

"Exactly," Sno said. "She needed perfect control of her ship as if she was in the cockpit. By tethering mentally with the controls, the ship reacted to her piloting as if she was handling the controls like normal. A tablet interface will not give you that kind of precision. There is always a small lag. A lag that could end up destroying her ship."

"You think Pol is piloting a ship?" Osol said. "How? Where? I thought we were hunting for a bot."

"No, I don't think he's piloting a ship," Sno said. "I think he is piloting something else. Something that he needs to merge with so he has perfect control."

They entered the lift and Osol leaned back in the roller's seat.

"Tell me what you're thinking, Sno," Osol said. "I'm exhausted and don't have the energy to play guessing games."

"Be patient," Sno said when the lift stopped and the drab corridor of bureaucracy appeared. "Let me check one thing first before I explain. If I'm wrong, then I'm wrong."

Osol sighed and drove the roller down the corridor, stopping before Investigator J'gorla's office. Two guards stood outside and nodded at Osol.

"Has anyone been in here?" Osol asked.

The two guards both looked alarmed.

"No, sir," one said. "You said no one was to enter. We've kept the office secure the entire time."

"Good," Sno said.

"Thank you," Osol said and let him and Sno inside the office.

The place was a mess. Furniture was broken and there were holes in the walls. Fist-sized holes. Sno studied the destruction then looked at J'gorla's office door, which was a bent and broken hunk of metal alloy and faux wood paneling.

"Is the body still in there?" Sno asked.

"Suspended animation bubble," Osol said. "Frozen to the moment she was discovered. I needed the scene to be preserved so I can study it later once we're done with our other mess."

"Undo the suspension," Sno said, walking into the office. J'gorla's huge body was hovering half a meter off the ground, surrounded in a brilliant blue bubble of energy. "I have to check something."

Osol brought up his wrist interface and ended the suspension protocol. J'gorla's body was slowly lowered to the floor before the bubble fizzled out and disappeared.

"Thank you," Sno said as he crouched next to the body. "She was found here?"

"Yes," Osol answered.

Sno looked about the office and frowned.

"Not as destroyed in here," Sno said. "Barely looks like there was even a struggle."

"They must have fought out in the entry area," Osol said. "Either Ested followed J'gorla in here to hand her the killing blow or J'gorla was mortally wounded and made her way in here on her own."

"No, she was struck in here," Sno said. "First. The entry area was destroyed after J'gorla was killed."

"What? How can you know that?" Osol said. "You're making a huge assumption there, Sno."

"I am, true," Sno agreed. "But I'm right. See here?"

Sno carefully turned J'gorla's head to show a crack in the woman's exoskeleton, just behind the upper mandible.

"That's the spot you hit a Leforian when you want to knock them out, not kill them," Sno said.

"I know that, Sno," Osol said. "But look at the rest of her. She was battered to death, not knocked unconscious."

"No, she was killed with one strike," Sno said. "Except that was an accident. You hit this spot too hard and it will kill instead of incapacitate. Someone schooled in subduing others would know the amount of force to use. Someone that has no practical experience can easily end up killing a Leforian if the blow is too hard. And it was too hard."

"Then what are all the other wounds?" Osol asked.

"Camouflage," Sno said. "Meant to divert attention from this one wound. Meant to make you think that Ested lost complete control instead of someone else simply not knowing the amount of control needed."

"And the entry room? Is that camouflage too?" Osol asked.

"Could be," Sno said. "But I think it's different. Here, take a look."

Sno returned to the entry room and pointed at the mess.

"This was a struggle, but a struggle of one," Sno said. "Ested resisted. It didn't want to leave. The android fought as hard as possible to keep from being forced out of this office."

"From being forced...?" Osol's voice faded to nothing as he turned in a slow circle, his eyes taking in the destruction. "Gods... You're right, Sno. The destruction isn't from the corridor into the office, but from the office out to the corridor. Someone killed J'gorla and took Ested since it was a witness."

"Try again," Sno said.

"What?" Osol asked, but didn't argue. Another circle and then he shook his head. "No signs of anyone else. Like I thought from the beginning. Ested killed J'gorla then fought every step out of this office because..."

"Because Ested was fighting inside itself," Sno said. "Pol is the one that killed J'gorla, not Ested. Pol has control over Ested."

"All the Hells," Osol said. "The greatest dark tech in the galaxy is piloting an android on my ship. Do you know how bad this is?"

"If Pol has ill intent? Very bad," Sno answered.

"You don't think he has ill intent?" Osol asked. "He killed J'gorla!"

"Not on purpose," Sno said. "What happened is this. Pol gains access to the android, taking control of Ested. Pol's intention is to knock J'gorla out, but he doesn't know his own strength. Or doesn't know Ested's strength. Pol accidentally kills J'gorla and tries to cover it up by bludgeoning the corpse."

"Okay, then why all of this?" Osol asks, indicating the entry room's destruction.

"I think Ested grew aware during Pol's cover up and was shocked by what Pol had done," Sno said. "Or as shocked as an AI can be. That's when Ested and Pol fought for control of the android body. Pol eventually won, but not without Ested putting up a damn good fight."

"So we are hunting an android body controlled by a tranced-out old man," Osol said. "An old man that also happens to now be able to jack into every single system on this ship. He was dangerous before when he was flesh and blood. Now, he can plug directly into any console he wants and he'll have access to all of the Mip."

"Kind of makes you want to hide in a dark closet, doesn't it?" Sno said. "I'll be honest, I was hoping I was wrong."

"But why?" Osol exclaimed. "What is he up to?"

"That is the question," Sno said. "The surveillance holos are wiped, so we can't see where Ested went."

"But we can see where Ested isn't," Osol said with a grin. "Come on. We're going to my office. I know how to find the old bastard."

"We track the blind spots," Sno said. "Where there isn't surveillance, or the surveillance dropped out briefly, that is where we find Ested."

"Pol Hammon," Osol said.

"At this moment, same thing," Sno said. "Let's go."

They left J'gorla's office and Osol barely had time to shove Sno out of the way as the barrage of plasma blasts tore through the open doorway. Osol cried out and fell to the floor as Sno instinctively used the momentum of the shove to dive behind the roller and pull the Blorta 65 laser pistol Osol had given him back in the stateroom from his belt.

"Osol?" Sno called.

No response.

"Come out, Mr. Sno," someone yelled.

"You shot your boss, so I don't believe I will come out," Sno said.

"Only taking orders, Sno," the guard replied.

"From who?" Sno asked.

"Shut up," the other guard hissed.

"You two have a chance to get out of this alive," Sno said. "Tell me who ordered you to shoot us and I promise not to turn your heads into mist."

"I didn't want to do it, but it's better than being ejected out into space for disobeying the—"

There was a plasma blast and a scream. Sno jumped up and opened fire, tearing into the only guard standing in the corridor. The other one was down on the floor, half of his head missing. The guard Sno shot jumped and shook as plasma ripped through the light armor she wore and mangled the woman's torso. Then she fell across her comrade.

Sno rushed to Osol and was surprised the man was still breathing.

"Hey," Sno said, gently patting Osol on his bloody cheek. "Hey, don't go out this way. You can make it."

Osol's eyes fluttered open and he tried to smile, but only half of his mouth worked and when the lips parted, a good deal of blood came pouring out. Osol managed to lift his arm up and twist his wrist several times until a holo interface appeared.

Sno hesitated only for a moment before pushing his own wrist directly into the holo interface. Sno's interface came up and merged with Osol's. The Head of Security gave one nod then his eyes glazed over and his last breath squeaked out, forming a froth of blood bubbles on his lips. Sno diverted his eyes and stood back up as the froth dropped down Osol's chin.

He studied the holo that was still projected from his wrist, holstered his pistol then marched over to the corpses of the two guards. Sno relived the top guard of her RX31 plasma assault rifle. He slung the weapon over his shoulder and plucked the extra energy magazines from the woman's belt.

He tapped at his comm.

"Velly? You there?" he called. "Come on, come on!"

"No need to shout, friend," Velly replied over the comm. "What's your deal?"

"Osol's dead. Killed by his own guards," Sno said. "How are the guards in the stateroom acting?"

"I don't know," Velly replied, sounding shocked. "Veben insisted that the bot repair the doors to Pol's room. We're the only ones in here. The guards are right outside."

"Good. Keep it that way," Sno said. "If any of them try to come in, drop them. Do not ask questions, do not give them even a moment to suspect you know about Osol. Drop the bastards and lock yourselves in that room. Is the bot still there?"

"Yes," Velly said. "Veben insisted on that too."

Sno closed his eyes and took a deep breath.

"Sno? You there, friend?" Velly asked.

"Yes, I'm here. Have the bot seal the doors now. No reason not to," Sno ordered. "How is it going with Pol?"

"He's locked down," Velly said, exasperated. "Zan has tried everything short of sawing his skull open, but we can't get to the interface."

"He knew we'd try," Sno said.

"What are you going to do?" Velly asked.

"I know exactly what I'm going to do," Sno replied. "Track down an android body and have a nice talk with Mr. Pol Hammon."

"Do what now?"

"No time to explain. I'll call you if I need to. You stay safe in that room and trust absolutely no one."

"Way ahead of you on that, friend."

"Good." He killed the comm and pinched the bridge of his nose as he got his emotions under control.

Sno returned to the roller, made sure it ran and wasn't too shot up, then turned it about and headed back to the lift. He kept the rifle aimed at the lift doors. When they opened, he was ready, but there was no one inside. Sno drove the roller into the lift, checked a schematic on his wrist, and dialed in the deck where Osol's office was housed.

Sno still had a job to do. The first part of which was to track down a rogue android that wasn't really an android any longer.

27.

The first corridor was a shit show. Sno had to fight his way every meter until he got to the next lift he needed. Without Osol as a buffer, Sno was fair game to the guards that had been compromised. And it didn't take a genius to realize who had compromised the guards. The only person that had that kind of command was Captain Loch.

But Sno would deal with that man later.

The second corridor Sno hit was deserted. Not a soul in sight even though the corridor connected with several gaming and entertainment rooms. That nagging suspicion that Sno had since the Captain's Table became less nagging and more demanding. Where were the guests? There should have been guests.

The third corridor did have guests, but as soon as they saw Sno, they scattered and fled. He raced the roller past the panicked groups that pressed themselves to the walls on either side of the corridor. Terrified eyes stared at Sno as he pushed the roller as fast as it would go towards the lift doors at the other end. Then Sno noticed some of the eyes weren't terrified, but simply hostile. With more than a few looking extremely amused.

Sno had the distinct feeling that he was part of a minority on the ship that didn't know what was really going on. Finding Ested and talking with Pol was of even more importance if some of the guests were in on…

Sno didn't even have a clue as to what they were in on. He'd always prided himself on knowing at least some of the end game, but Pol's actions had been too confusing. Everything that had happened to him since boarding the Mip had been confusing. There was no rhyme nor reason to any of it.

Unless…

The roller reached the lift and Sno drove it inside, again making sure it wasn't occupied by guards. He relaxed his grip on his rifle only when the lift doors had closed.

Amateur Tcherian assassins. Random servers attacking during dinner. Both events happened when Sno expected to get a feel for the ship. He was put off balance the second he stepped into his first stateroom. That had put him on the defensive and caused him to distrust the security on the ship. He never intended to fully trust the security in place, but that event sent his mind into overdrive. A constant state of fight.

Then, when security should have been at its peak, an attack came during dinner. Sno hadn't exactly relaxed, but he had expected to get through the meal. He thought if an attack was attempted, it would be en route to or on the return trip from the dining room, not in the room itself. That shook him up enough that he fell back on old habits and took comfort in the arms of Velly the second he had a chance.

Velly.

Everything Sno knew about her raced through his mind. She could be involved, but Sno didn't think so. There was an independence to her that defied corruption. Not that she wasn't above getting paid to do a specific job, but she was a pilot. And Trel'ali had hired her to save his ass back on Egthak. That was real. Sno and Trel'ali had a very complicated past, but at no point did Sno believe that Trel'ali was in on the mess he found himself in. Trel'ali was above what was happening on the Mip.

The lift ride gave Sno time to put Velly in the ally column. Perhaps not one hundred percent, but enough that he figured he didn't need to watch his back around her.

The doors opened and Sno's enemy column grew then shrank as he exchanged fire with the waiting guards in the fourth corridor. A couple of them got some close shots in, but none had the quickness and precision that Sno had. When the last blast's echo died completely, Sno glanced down to see a hole in his shirt. He inspected it with a finger then lifted the shirt and only found a cauterized gouge on his right side, just under his ribcage.

He shrugged and drove the roller half a meter so that the vehicle was keeping the lift's doors from closing. Then he climbed out, put the rifle to his shoulder, and walked carefully around the dead guards until he reached Osol's office.

Sno knocked.

"You cannot enter this room, Mr. Sno," a holo vid of a guard said as the image was projected from a panel next to the door. "Captain Loch asks that you surrender at once. You and your friends will not be harmed if you give yourself up now."

"Is that so?" Sno asked, bringing up the holo protocol he'd been given by Osol. "No harm no foul is official policy on the Mip, is it?"

The guard's holo looked extremely confused. Sno pushed his arm through the image and waved his wrist across the same panel where the projection was coming from.

"Mr. Sno, I am going to ask you one more time," the guard said.

The office doors were already sliding open before the guard's holo had finished the sentence. Sno fired four times, each blast hitting their intended targets perfectly. Four guards dropped dead onto the floor and Sno rushed inside.

"You shouldn't have asked me the first time," Sno said.

He turned, locked the office door with Osol's credentials then set the rifle down on a console. Sno studied the interface equipment until he found the surveillance station. He logged in as Osol and went to work searching the ship for dark areas; places where the surveillance had been compromised. It didn't take long before he found a trail of nothing that told him everything.

"Sno?" Velly's voice called over the comm. "Anything new on your end?"

"Hunting for Ested," Sno said. "I have a lead. Fairly certain I know where Pol is heading."

"Ested? Pol is inside the android?" Velly asked. "Is that what you were talking about before?"

"Yes," Sno said then paused. "What's wrong?"

"Oh, nothing, friend," Velly said. "Only a bunch of security guards not trying to get into the room."

Sno narrowed his eyes and turned away from the surveillance console. "I'm sorry, did you say they aren't trying to get inside?"

"No. They announced to us that we are under house arrest and will be sequestered to this room until we arrive in the Bgreete System," Velly said. "We're now prisoners."

"Alright. At least they are leaving you alone for now," Sno said. "Once I have my chat with the Ested/Pol machine then I'll come get you."

"Gee, thanks," Velly replied.

"I do my best," Sno said. "How is V?"

"She is who she is," Velly replied.

"That's all I can ask," Sno said. "If the situation changes, comm me. You can stop Zan from trying to breach the tether. I have a lead on Ested and I'm heading there now."

Sno swiped the newly found data onto his wrist implant and pushed back from the console.

"Heads up that the captain is involved," Sno said. "He's running the guards now."

"Then why doesn't he send them in to get us?" Velly asked.

"Good question," Sno said. "Velly? Have any of you discussed what we're up against with the guards? Do they know what is happening with Pol?"

"We haven't said anything," Velly replied. "As far as I know, Osol ordered them to keep us secure, but didn't give them any additional information. Why?"

"Don't know yet," Sno said. "But I think that is important. Stay captive and don't speak with the guards."

"Veben has been cursing them out," Velly said.

"Let her," Sno responded with a smile as he stood by the door to the corridor. He placed his rifle back to his shoulder and took a deep breath. "Gotta go. Stay safe."

He killed the comm as he opened the door. No plasma blasts came his way. Sno stepped out into the corridor, the rifle sweeping right then left. Clear. Loch was leaving him alone for the moment. Either that or Loch had no idea how to even handle the situation. The more Sno thought about it, the more he settled on the latter explanation. He had to wonder if Loch hadn't called the remaining guards to the bridge to keep him safe. Smart move considering what short work Sno had made of the guards from J'gorla's office to Osol's.

The lift was still blocked by the roller, but Sno didn't want to go that way. Where he was going had a whole other access route.

Sno walked cautiously down the corridor, eyes watching the few doors that lined each side. He made it to the end without incident and risked setting his rifle down. He needed both hands.

Sno pried an access hatch open then leaned in, seeing the sheer drop down through the ship. All there was to grab onto was a ladder. It was a backup shaft in case the lifts went down and maintenance personnel or bots had to get from one deck to the next. Sno needed to descend twenty decks to reach his destination.

He picked up the rifle, secured it to his back, checked that his pistol had a full charge, secured that in its holster then swung himself into the shaft and began the climb down.

Deck by deck, Sno went. He paused before he reached each deck and took out his pistol, aiming it at the next access hatch. He'd count to thirty then holster the pistol when the hatch didn't pop open to reveal a squad of armed guards. It made the journey slow going, but it kept him from getting ambushed. By the time he reached the deck he needed, his arms were exhausted and his neck was a tense mess from constantly glancing up above him to make sure guards hadn't come through the access hatch he'd used.

Sno realized he was a little soft. Too many hours spent healing in med pods lately. His muscle tone wasn't as strong as he would have liked. He'd have to do something about that when he survived the Mip. If he survived the Mip...

Sno steeled himself for the next part of his plan. With weapons stowed, he had to open the access hatch in front of him. The second he popped it open, he'd be exposed. Sno would have maybe half a second to draw a weapon. Half a second was enough normally, but Sno's arms were not at full strength after the climb down.

No way around the scenario, Sno shoved the hatch open and dove through into a massive corridor beyond. He came up out of the roll with the rifle back at his shoulder, finger hovering close to the trigger. No one was there. No guards waiting, not even mechanics or engineering personnel. Sno counted to thirty, senses tuned for any sound or movement.

When there was still no welcome, violent or not, Sno stood up and walked the length of the massive corridor. It was so wide that Velly could have flown her ship down and still have a meter of space on each side. Sno reached the end and faced a door that was as proportionally massive as the corridor.

Sno waved his wrist across the panel by the door and waited. There were a series of clanks and whirrs before the door began to withdraw up into the ceiling. With the rifle leading, Sno walked into the GS M'illi'ped's main engine room.

And came face to face with the android named Ested.

"Pol," Sno said, making sure he was aiming the rifle for a spot directly below where the android's navel would be. If the android had a navel. It was simply a smooth patch of synthetic skin. "You've been busy."

28.

"Agent Prime," Ested/Pol said. "I shouldn't be surprised you found me."

The fact that Ested wasn't cursing at Sno told him that his hunch had been right. Pol was piloting the android.

"You care to tell me what you are up to, Pol?" Sno demanded. "And don't try to lie or make up a story. I'm done with that crap. Tell me the truth or I put a plasma blast through this android's belly."

"Don't you fucking dare, asshole," Ested snapped.

The android's body shook then stilled.

"I have to say that this AI is quite possessive of its body," Pol said. "I'm working on that issue. Just a little more time to sequester its—"

"You can sequester my ass, you old piece of flesh!" Ested shouted. "I swear, when I get my hands on you, I will squeeze your neck until every single molecule of skin, muscle, and sinew has been torn in half. Then I will laugh and sing over your destroyed vertebrae as I twirl your corpse above my head! It will be glorious!"

"So much for not harming living beings," Pol said.

Sno wasn't quite sure what to do. He should blast the android's guts wide open and expose its main processor. That would put the machine down fast. But the android's mind was still inside and the way it spoke, which was very un-android like, gave Sno pause. It did not sound like a simple AI, but one of the sentient protocols.

"I can see your morals fighting with your training, Agent Prime," Pol said. "Wondering if killing this body will kill the AI's being too. I can say that if you kill this body, you will kill me. My tether to Ested is not a basic override, but a full synthesis of our consciousnesses. Despite the unpleasant personality, Ested is a very remarkable AI. I have much to learn from it."

"How will you learn when you have my foot up your ass, old man?" Ested snarled. "You want to play puppet master? I'll show you fucking puppet master, you tiny shithole."

"Tiny shithole?" Pol replied. "What is that exactly?"

"The hole where my fist goes so I can run your mouth like a sock puppet," Ested yelled. "Keep diving deeper, dickhead. Go for it. See what happens when you reach bottom."

Other than the sound of the Mip's massive drives, the engine room was silent. Sno waited for Pol and Ested to continue their verbal jousting, but the android's body remained quiet. Sno glanced around.

"Where's the engine crew?" Sno asked. "What did you do with the mechanics and engineers?"

"They have been subdued," Pol said.

"Like you subdued J'gorla?" Sno asked. "She was a woman doing her job and no real threat to you, Pol. Why did you have to kill her?"

The android's features scrunched up in rage then slackened completely. Then scrunched back followed by the slack nothing.

"You murderous cocksucking twat sniffer," Ested said so low that Sno almost didn't hear.

"That was an accident," Pol said. "I only wanted to knock her out, but I hadn't gained full control of this body's motor functions. I hit her too hard and I am sorry for that."

"Then you two duked it out for who would be boss," Sno said, jutting his chin towards the android. "Ested wasn't too happy about giving up the driving seat."

"Still not too happy, you fucking moron!" Ested yelled. "Or haven't you been paying attention?"

"What are you doing down here, Pol?" Sno asked.

"Who fucking cares?" Ested roared. "Someone get this old son of a bitch out of my body and out of my head! NOW!"

The android stiffened. Its eyes flashed red, green, red, green, white, then returned to the simulacrum of real eyes. Sno gripped the rifle tighter, his finger only a hair's breadth away from the trigger.

"Pol?" Sno said. "Ested?"

The android relaxed and its head rolled on its neck.

"Pol," Sno said with confidence.

"Yes. Control is complete," Pol said. "I have tucked Ested's conscious mind away in a very safe place. Too valuable a consciousness to delete. I do want to study it thoroughly at some point down the road."

"Pol. What is going on?" Sno asked. "Why are you doing all of this?"

"Doing all of what, Agent Prime?" Pol asked. He spread his arms wide. "Do you see me doing anything?"

"You have been playing me from the beginning," Sno said. "The luxury liner? You set this up."

"What? I believe taking a luxury liner was your idea, Agent Prime," Pol said. "How could I possibly set anything up?"

He took a step closer to Sno and Sno shook his head sharply.

"No. Stop right there," Sno ordered. "I will shoot, Pol."

"And not get answers? I don't think you'll shoot until you've heard me out, Agent Prime," Pol said, taking another step.

Sno shot the floor between Pol's legs and the android body stopped mid-step.

"Try me," Sno said. "The captain? Did you know him before? Or is his involvement improvised?"

"Loch? What is he doing?" Pol asked.

"He has control of the guards," Sno said. "Osol is dead."

"What?" Pol exclaimed. "No. That wasn't supposed to happen." Pol retreated a few steps. "I may need to move the schedule up a tad. Would you mind putting that rifle down so I can get back to work, Agent Prime?"

"You're joking," Sno said. "That was a joke."

"Only if you found it funny," Pol replied. "I didn't intend it to be a joke."

He brought up a holo of the map of the part of the galaxy the Mip was traveling through. The images moved and changed too fast for Sno to track.

"Are you reading trans-space?" Sno asked.

"I am," Pol said with a laugh. "Having the use of an android brain is quite something. I thought my mind was the best in the galaxy, but take my mind and put it in a brain with the processing capabilities of an android? Agent Prime, would it be hubris to call myself a god?"

"I am fairly certain that is the exact definition of hubris, Pol," Sno said.

"I thought as much," Pol said and sighed. "Then let's keep that revelation between you and me, okey dokey? No need for others to worry that perhaps I have lost my marbles when the complete opposite has happened."

"You've acquired extra marbles?" Sno asked.

"Exactly!" Pol crowed. "Now you are getting it!"

"Pol..."

"You are so impatient, Agent Prime."

"Pol...what is going on? Be honest with me. I have been assigned to help you. And that assignment came with the understanding that my help would come at any cost. It wasn't spelled out as such, but the implication was there. Talk to me and let's work this out."

"I can't talk right now," Pol said. "I need to work on moving this ship into position. We were supposed to arrive at the Bgreete System in what? Two days?"

"Three," Sno said.

"You are forgetting that we have been awake and working for a day, Agent Prime," Pol said. "Two days is the new ETA. Going to have to do something about that if Loch is playing games. I suspected he might which is why I needed the android."

Pol's eyes went wide, which was slightly terrifying on an android's face.

"Veben? Is she safe?" Pol asked, alarm evident. "Do not let Loch get ahold of her, Sno. He'll use her against me."

"Veben is secure in your room," Sno said. "She is there with your body, Velly, and Zan."

"Zan? Who is Zan?"

"The medic from before," Sno said.

"Oh, yes, lovely woman," Pol said. "I expect that Zan was called to try to do something about the interface?"

"She was," Sno answered.

"And Velly was talking her through what she knows of remote piloting?"

"Yes. Precisely that."

"Can you comm them?"

"I can."

"Please comm them and have them stop immediately. They'll damage my body and I still have need of it. There is no way to sever the remote piloting tether. At least not with the tech they are using."

"I'd comm them if I could trust you, Pol. But I can't trust you."

"Hmmmm…"

"It's over, Pol. Face that. To get off this ship, you will have to go through me. Are you really going to kill an SSD agent, Pol? You're a tech, not a killer."

"You have no idea who I am, Agent Prime," Pol said quietly. "No one does. They all think they can manipulate me for their ends. They think they can assert control over me by using fear and intimidation. Threats of violence. Threats of imprisonment. Threats against those I care about. Threats, threats, threats!"

Pol's eyes went bright red.

"What I am about to accomplish will end all of those threats. All of them!"

"Pol! Stand down and give yourself up!" Sno shouted as he started to squeeze the trigger.

A blast tore into the floor by Sno's feet and he spun around. Two dozen guards were sprinting towards the wide open entry of the engine room.

"Ah, that should occupy you," Pol said.

Sno didn't dare turn to see where Pol was running off to. He couldn't afford to take his eyes off the guards.

"Put the rifle down!" one of the guards shouted.

Sno did not put the rifle down. Instead, he put two blasts dead center of the guard's chest, knocking the man into the three guards behind him. More guards stumbled and the pile grew as Sno ran to his left, letting loose plasma blast after plasma blast at the guards until he was able to find cover behind a huge turbine.

Sno ejected the rifle's energy mag and slapped in a fresh one. He racked the charge and checked the energy level. The rifle was full and Sno took a deep breath as he came out from behind the turbine, his finger depressed fully on the trigger. Plasma streaked from the rifle and connected with one, two, three guards, dropping them to the ground.

There were still over a dozen guards streaming into the engine room. They split up and Sno knew he was about to be flanked. He ducked back behind the turbine and looked for a new place to hide. Other than the catwalks crisscrossing the ceiling above, there was nowhere else to go. The row of turbines in front of him had too wide of gaps between them to be effective cover. The guards would simply surround him.

Sno looked for the ladders to the catwalks, but they were up against the walls of the engine room. Too far to sprint to without taking serious fire.

"Shit," Sno muttered.

A guard came around the left side of the turbine and Sno put him down. A second followed, but threw herself backward, avoiding the plasma blast Sno sent at her.

"Pol!" Sno shouted. "Help me out of this and I promise I will do whatever I can to help you!"

No reply other than shouts from guards for Sno to give up his weapon and surrender himself.

The scuff of boots caused Sno to turn in time to fend off two guards on his right. He blasted one in the thigh then jammed the rifle barrel into the throat of the second. The first guard got off a lucky shot and Sno felt searing pain across his left shoulder. The pain grew and grew and Sno risked a glance down. The wound was a good four to five centimeters deep and just as wide. Sno was missing a good hunk of shoulder.

More boots and Sno whirled about, firing blindly. He hit one guard in the chest, but missed the next four. They came at him too fast for Sno to get more shots off. He dropped the rifle and came at them swinging. A right hook nearly knocked the helmet off a guard. A left jab sent a guard to her knees, her hands clutching at her throat.

Sno tried for an uppercut on another guard, but his arm was grabbed from behind. Then his other arm was grabbed and Sno found himself restrained as guards sneered and glared at him. None opened fire.

"We have him," a guard said, obviously speaking into her comm. "To the brig?"

The guard waited for an answer then grinned.

"Yeah. We'll take good care of him then bring him right to you, Captain," the guard said. She lowered her rifle, turned it around, and walked towards Sno, the butt of the weapon leading. "This is gonna feel great."

"We should talk this out, folks," Sno said. "I'm an SSD agent. You harm me and you will have to answer directly to Fleet Intelligence."

"We'll take that risk," the guard said as she sent the butt of her rifle flying into Sno's face.

Sno's nose exploded and his sinuses, then throat, filled with blood. The butt hit him again and again. Sno sagged slightly, but he was held up by the guards that had him from behind. Then the rest of the guards started in. Rifle butts nailed him in the stomach, the chest, the knees.

His head rocked back as a butt hit him between the eyes. Lights flashed in his vision and Sno had a hard time keeping focus. He blinked, but the vision grew worse as blood dripped down his forehead and into his eyes. His ribs screamed with pain as two guards went to work on his torso.

"That's good," the one guard said. "Captain wants him to live."

The guard leaned in and snarled.

"But he didn't say he wanted you conscious," the guard said as the last rifle butt connected with Sno's face.

Sno slumped in the guards' grips, nothing but unconscious dead weight.

29.

Sno slowly awoke to a growing pain in his head and arms. The rest of him hurt considerably too, but it was his head and arms that had the loudest voices.

"Agent Prime," Loch said. "Are you awake enough for us to talk?"

Sno struggled to open his eyes, but even the dim light that leaked through the gaps in his eyelids was too much.

"No," Sno rasped.

"You are feeling discomfort," Loch said. To Sno, he sounded somewhere behind and to the left. "Understandable. I had a medic remove your implants. Wouldn't do for you to be able to figure out how to communicate with GF headquarters. Nor could I allow you to fulfill whatever conspiracy you and Pol Hammon have cooked up."

"Conspiracy...?" Sno asked. "With Pol? You have it all wrong, Loch."

"I think not," Loch said.

Sno tried opening his eyes again and managed to lift his lids without screaming. He didn't recognize where he was.

"Antechamber off the bridge," Loch said without Sno asking. "I come here when the stress of the day gets to me. Warm lighting, comfortable furniture, tea, snacks. A delightful way to spend an afternoon or evening."

"Thanks for sharing," Sno said. "Can you put my implants back now?"

"Amusing," Loch said. "Your implants have been shot into trans-space. A risky move considering the slightest of breaches in the ship's hull could kill us all, but over the years, I have developed many methods to jettison contraband that perhaps the GF would not approve of my vaunted passengers of carrying. Not to mention the occasional oopsie moment when an escort winds up dead in someone's stateroom. That would be a bit of a mess to explain when we docked. What is ejected in trans-space stays in trans-space, I always say."

Sno studied his predicament. He was restrained to a simple metal chair in a small, but well-apportioned, room. There was a view window that ran the length of the room, giving Sno a good look at the swirl of trans-space. The swirl hurt his eyes and he turned away to keep from getting nauseous. His forearms had medical sealant running from his wrists to the crooks of his elbows. He had no idea what his head looked like. After the beating he'd taken from the guards, plus the removal of his comm implant, Sno guessed he looked like some mad science project.

"How long was I out?" Sno asked.

"Seventeen hours," Loch replied, seeming miffed. "The guards got a little too enthusiastic. I reprimanded them for you. You are welcome. You spent most of your time in a med pod, but like I said, I had the medic focus on removing your implants more than healing the injuries you sustained from your capture."

"Pol? Where is he?" Sno asked.

"He is in his room," Loch replied. "Apparently, he tried to access the ship's systems and something went very wrong. The medic already on hand says he has no brain activity at all now. For all intents and purposes, Pol Hammon is a vegetable."

"And the others?" Sno asked. "Veben? Velly?"

"Veben and Velly," Loch laughed. "That has a nice ring to it. You know, I have a friend that produces holo vids for broadcast. I should suggest Veben and Velly as a program name. What do you think? Zany comedy? Talk show? It could be any number of things, really."

"Are they alright?" Sno asked.

"They are," Loch said. "The pilot is in the brig and the old woman is locked in her quarters under full guard. Too elegant of a woman to be thrown into the brig with the riffraff. Not that we have riffraff here on the GS M'illi'ped. Gods forbid."

"They are unharmed?"

"What? No, of course I had them harmed. The pilot has been beaten to within a centimeter of her life and the old woman was subjected to a good two hours of nerve stimulation," Loch said with a grin. "She held out for thirty minutes before the pain was too much and then the screams began. When all of this is over, I may make her mine. I could listen to those screams for hours."

"What are you doing, Loch? You've stepped over a line that you can't walk back from. The GF will hunt you down and kill you," Sno said. "There is no way out of this."

"Except there is," Loch said. "All I need is for you to tell me where the plans to Pol Hammon's tech are. Even with Agent Prime assigned to protect and deliver Pol Hammon, which you have failed at, in case you were unaware, even with you by his side, I cannot believe that the SSD would make a deal with the old man unless some assurances were made."

Sno waited for more. When Loch didn't continue, Sno said, "Pol was the assurance. The GF has the plans for his tech, but he's the only one that can reproduce whatever it is those plans are for. If Pol is a vegetable then he's useless to me, to the SSD, to the GF, and to you."

"No!" Loch shouted and slapped Sno hard across the right cheek.

Sno grunted, but didn't cry out even though his head became a nest of Felturean fire ants. Loch slapped him again and again. By the fourth slap, Sno was crying out for Loch to stop.

"No one realizes what kind of trauma the removal of a comm implant can produce," Loch said. "Look at me. I'm barely half your size, yet I am in complete control."

"Take off these restraints and we'll see about that," Sno rasped.

"I think not," Loch said and laughed. "Let's start again."

"More slaps? Aren't you brave," Sno said.

"No, no, I mean I want to try a different way of reasoning with you, Sno," Loch said. "How does fifteen million credits sound?"

"Like the amount I have in my petty cash account," Sno replied. "Bribes won't work, Loch. I'm rich. Family money."

"Right. I forgot," Loch said. "The Sno Fortune. I do plan on rivaling that fortune when this is all over. I could even surpass it."

"Too bad you can't spend it," Sno said. "The GF accountants will hunt that money down and find you, Loch. They find everyone."

"GF? Sno, are you not grasping what is happening here? I plan on selling Pol Hammon's tech. But we both know that the GF will not pay me even half a credit for it. Who else can I sell it to? Edgers? That rebel scum can barely scrape together a single credit to buy soup. Especially after their botched seizing of Razer Station. Oh, the amount of resources those idiots lost. Sad. So sad."

"You have to be kidding," Sno replied, realization dawning in his fuzzy brain. "The Skrang? You plan on selling the tech to the Skrang?"

"They will pay handsomely for it," Loch said. "After all, it is rumored that Pol Hammon developed the tech with their funds to begin with. If they do not end up with the tech in their hands, then their investment is lost. You and I both know that the Skrang never forgive a lost investment. I've heard that a Skrang general once tracked down a ship that had shorted him a single barrel of mealworm skins. A single barrel, Sno. How much does mealworm skin cost? Not as much as it cost to send an entire Skrang ship with full crew after the supplier. Yet that's what the general did and that supplier paid dearly for his mistake."

"Did the Skrang general get his mealworm barrel?" Sno asked.

"What?"

"Did he get the barrel? Or did he simply kill the supplier?"

"He got the barrel."

"Then why do the Skrang need you? You don't have the tech they need, so why should they even deal with you?"

"Because you are going to get me the tech, Sno. You are going to tell me where Pol Hammon has it stored. You will then tell me how to put it together."

"I can't do either of those things, you stupid—"

The slap nearly caused Sno to wet himself. Loch had slammed his palm directly against Sno's left ear. Bright hot pain shot through Sno's head and ricocheted around his skull. He coughed a few times then took slow, even breaths.

"If you listen to me, Loch, I may be able to get you what you want," Sno said. "But I need Veben and Velly to be on a ship and away from here first. I can't have you using them as bargaining chips."

"What if I do, Sno?" Loch asked. "What if I brought Velly into this room and began carving her up in front of you? Would that be motivation enough?"

"Hurt either of them and you get nothing," Sno said. "Bring the ship out of trans-space, let Velly take Veben away on her swift ship, and I can give you Pol Hammon."

"Sno, Pol Hammon is a pile of useless organs," Loch said. "Were you not fully conscious when I mentioned that to you? I have Pol Hammon. He's a brain dead turd."

"His body is, yes," Sno said. "But Pol Hammon's mind is still on this ship and fully aware. You have been played, Loch, and I know how."

The captain stared at Sno for a long while before he shook his head.

"No. I do not think so, Sno," Loch said. "I let the women leave and you'll clam up. I'm not stupid."

He snapped his fingers, his beady little eyes locked onto Sno.

"I may have lied," Loch said as the door to the small room slid open.

Her hands tied behind her back, Velly was shoved inside and forced to her knees by two guards. She looked like she'd been through all the Hells. Sno winced when he saw the state she was in. Velly winced when she looked up and met Sno's gaze. He probably wasn't looking much better.

"Sno," Velly whispered as Loch placed a small plasma pistol to her temple.

"Don't speak," Loch ordered. "Only kneel."

"Sno, listen to me," Velly said, ignoring Loch. "We glimpsed something when Zan was—."

Loch slammed the butt of the pistol down on top of Velly's head, sending her face first to the floor. The two guards grabbed her arms and yanked her back up. Velly screamed as a loud pop echoed through the room. One of her shoulders hung loose. Blood began to pour down her face from the blow to her head.

"Do not speak," Loch snapped, his mouth right next to Velly's ear.

She slammed her head sideways and Loch's nose crunched on impact.

"Bitch!" he shouted then put the pistol back to her temple.

"Stop!" Sno yelled. "I'll tell you!"

"Good," Loch said. "Very good. But if I think you are lying, I will blow her head off. Poof. No more Velly Tarcorf."

"Sno. Don't," Velly said. "Pol has it all—"

"I said to not speak!" Loch roared. He shoved the pistol into Velly's temple, bruising the bright orange skin. Purple began top blossom immediately, he was pressing so hard.

"Sno," Velly said.

"Velly, stop," Sno warned. "The little Ferg will kill you."

"Ferg?" Loch asked, his attention back on Sno. "I'm not a Ferg. Do I look like a Ferg?"

"An orange Ferg," Sno said. "Yeah."

"Don't tell the man a thing," Velly said. "He's going to lose. Tell him and the Skrang will—"

Loch pulled the trigger. Velly's head was vaporized. Only a rough hunk of the bottom of her skull remained attached to her neck. Then that slowly dissolved as the remnants of the plasma energy finished obliterating the flesh. Headless, Velly's corpse remained on its knees for a second then toppled over.

Sno screamed. He screamed with rage and pain and simple confusion. He was going to tell Loch everything and send the captain off chasing Ested. Sno was Agent Prime and he knew how to word the admission so that Loch kept him alive, just in case. Velly didn't need to die. There was no point in her death.

Sno's voice gave out as Loch stood before him, arms crossed and an annoyed look on his face. He glanced over his shoulder at the two guards.

"Get the woman's body out of here and bring me Veben Doab," Loch ordered.

Before the guards could move, a klaxon blared and Loch looked about like he'd never heard one before.

"What is happening? What is that?" Loch shouted then activated his comm. "Talk to me!"

The captain's head swung around to the view window and he gasped as the quantum swirl stopped. The ship had exited trans-space and certainly wasn't in the Bgreete System. It was way worse than that.

"Mlo," Loch whispered. "But how…?"

"I have a pretty good idea," Sno said quietly.

But Loch paid him no mind. The captain raced from his antechamber and onto the bridge. Before the door closed, Sno could hear him shouting orders. Those orders were then repeated and shouted to someone else who began shouting at someone else. Military efficiency was not one of the GS M'illi'ped's strong suits.

30.

Velly's headless corpse wasn't removed from the antechamber. It was left to ooze all over the ornate carpet. Left there in front of Sno as a focus for his rage.

Odds were, Loch was not going to survive whatever Pol had planned. And if Pol didn't plan on killing the captain, Sno swore he would take care of the orange-haired son of a bitch himself.

But, Sno needed to get out of the antechamber before he could think of revenge. He also had to make sure Veben was safe. Once he knew his old friend wasn't going to come to harm, and he crossed his fingers he wasn't too late, Sno then needed to track down Pol and the android body he'd hijacked.

The klaxon continued to blare, making it impossible to hear what was going on outside the antechamber. Although, he suspected the room was soundproofed since it was where Loch came to relax. The thought of Loch made Sno's blood boil.

Sno tested the restraints around his wrists and smiled to himself. The guards hadn't used energy shackles, but plastic ties instead. Not unusual for a ship like the Mip. They weren't expecting a dangerous criminal element to deal with, mostly just drunk passengers that needed a time out now and again.

Sno worked at his waistband. It took him a couple minutes, but he managed to get his "In Case Blade" free from the special slit in his waistband. It was merely a short strip of sharpened metal, but it had come in handy on more than a few missions. Sno angled the blade and went to work on the restraints.

The plastic wasn't cheap. Apparently, on a luxury liner like the Mip, even the restraints had to be top of the line. It wouldn't do to surround guests' wrists with restraints meant for the masses. Add that to the barely healed wounds inflicted upon his arms from the removal of his implants, and Sno wasn't sure he'd cut through the restraints within the hour.

Sno kept at the task, his eyes locked on the antechamber door, waiting for it to slide open and ruin his chance at escape. But the door didn't slide open. The bridge crew, and guards, were obviously still occupied with their sudden arrival near one of the most powerful black holes in the galaxy. With that in mind, Sno doubled his efforts. Free from the restraints or not, if he didn't get off the ship soon, he was going to be sucked into the black hole with the Mip and all aboard.

The pressure was immense, but that was why General Gerber had given him the mission. There was no way the general could have guessed at the exact chaos Sno would face, but Gerber was smart enough to know who to send in case exactly what was happening to Sno happened.

The klaxon continued to blare and Sno thought his head might split open. Having his comm implant removed left his head feeling like he'd gone a couple of rounds with a Chassfornian. And Sno actually knew what that felt like.

The blade slid through half of the restraint on his left wrist then became stuck. No matter how hard Sno tried to move it up and down, the blade refused to budge. His hand slipped and he ended up cutting deep into his right palm. He squeezed his mouth shut and kept the scream from passing his lips. Although, nothing was going to be heard over the sound of the warning klaxon.

Taking a deep breath, Sno pinched the blade between his thumb and forefinger, giving the metal a slight twist so that it would bend just enough to maybe come loose. He twisted then pulled and had the blade free. Sno switched it to his left hand and worked on his right restraint. That was much easier and within a few minutes, the restraint popped free. Sno brought his hands in front of him and worked on a different part of the stubborn restraint and made it through that one in only a few minutes as well.

Arms free, Sno took care of his ankles. Then he stood up, checked his body over, assessed his physical state, realized he'd been in much worse shape, and began to hunt through the antechamber for a weapon. All the while, Sno kept his eyes averted from Velly's corpse. He needed to focus on one task at a time. Velly could be honored later when the mission was done. For the moment, Sno had to consider her a hunk of dead flesh and nothing more.

The antechamber was weapons free. Not even in the hidden panels did Sno find anything. Some weird items that Sno wondered if they might be part of a sexual fetish of Loch's, but no weapons.

Testing his muscles and what was left of his strength by shadow boxing in front of the view window, Sno decided there was no time like the present. He'd go through the antechamber door, burst onto the bridge, surprise the closest guard, and strip that being of his or her weapon. Loch had to have put guards on the antechamber door, so at least one would be within reach as soon as the door opened.

Sno counted to three and activated the door controls. The door slid open and Sno rushed onto the bridge, his fists up and body ready for the first fight. Then he saw what was in front of him and stopped cold. He lowered his fists as he tried to make sense of the scene.

It was brutal, bloody, horrific, and more than a little confusing.

The bridge crew, including four guards, had been butchered. Their bodies were nothing but dismembered and severed limbs strewn everywhere. Offal and skin hung from levers and seat backs. Blood from various races was splashed liberally across the floor, the control consoles, even the ceiling, giving the bridge a disgusting technicolor theme to it.

"What the fuck...?" Sno whispered.

No one was left alive, that was for certain. Even crew members that were of races that could take a beating, a slashing, some serious shredding, they were dead and done. Sno had once watched a maintenance man on his estate put a load of dead wood through a chipper. That was what many of the bodies looked like. Flesh confetti everywhere.

But it wasn't rifle confetti. The guards' weapons were undamaged and simply lying there on the bloody floor. Sno helped himself to an RX31 plasma assault rifle, some extra magazines then he slung the rifle tight to his back and picked up an H16 plasma carbine multi-weapon. It was a Galactic Fleet Marine's standard weapon and with good reason. Sno checked the plasma grenade breach and smiled at the six grenades sitting in the chamber. He picked up a handful of extra magazines for the H16, snagged a combat knife next to the magazines, and turned to face the bridge doors.

He thought about trying to kill the klaxon, but that might attract attention. Attention from whom, he wasn't sure. But someone on board had serious malice in mind, and Sno didn't want to be on their radar unless there was no other option. He activated the bridge door controls then paused and turned back to the gory bridge. No orange fur. Loch had been spared. He'd either escaped or been taken captive. Sno made note then proceeded off the bridge.

The short corridor from the bridge to the lift was as bloody as the bridge, but not covered in flesh confetti. Only blood. Which made the tracks on the floor easy to make out. Several pairs of humanoid footprints surrounded by lines and splotches.

Bots.

Things began to click and the hair on the back of Sno's neck rose as he became certain he was being watched.

"Pol!" Sno yelled. "What are you doing?"

There was no response. Sno continued to the lift and called it to the bridge deck. The doors pulled apart and Sno was relieved that the interior was mostly blood-free. Mostly. He hopped on the lift and placed his wrist to the control panel. Nothing.

"Dammit," he muttered as he manually pressed a button that he hoped was the right level for the brig.

Then he stopped the lift. No need to go to the brig. Velly was dead. Veben was in the stateroom. Zan may be there too. Sno entered a new destination into the control panel and waited as the lift adjusted trajectory and shot towards the new deck.

The klaxon was screeching in the lift as well. Sno thought he'd be bleeding from his ears and eyes soon if it didn't shut up. The noise was drilling into his very soul.

The lift stopped and Sno brought up the H16. The doors opened and four guards were busy fighting off a gang of maintenance bots. Maintenance bots with very deadly blades and welding torches.

One of the guards screamed as her lower leg was severed at the knee. As she fell, a second bot raced to her and jammed a welding torch into her gaping mouth. The woman's head became a grotesque jack-o-lantern for a second then the eyes were burned through and flames flicked out of the empty sockets.

A second guard shot a bot that was swinging a span-hammer at his belly. The bot exploded into a shower of sparks and shrapnel. The guard caught some of the shrapnel and fell to a knee. Another bot jumped onto his chest and drilled up through the underside of his chin. He screamed until the drill bit reached his brain and then his eyes rolled up and he fell over, taking the bot with him. The bot struggled to get free then disengaged from the drill bit completely.

The third guard swatted a small bot against the wall then put four plasma blasts into it, obliterating the machine. Then she saw Sno and started to yell. That moment of distraction cost the woman her life and her head came tumbling from her shoulders as one bot threw another bot at her, two long saw blades extended. Blood geysered up from the headless stump as the body collapsed onto the floor.

The fourth guard swung his H16 around, put the muzzle into his mouth, and fired, just as three bots converged on him. He fell atop the other headless corpse.

Sno did not move a muscle. He stayed frozen in place as the bots poked and prodded the corpses, making sure the guards were well and truly dead. Once finished confirming that the guards were deceased, the bots began to roll off towards the maintenance hatches at the end of the corridor. Then they paused as one, turned and faced Sno. Still, Sno did not move a muscle.

The bots didn't move towards him and Sno barely breathed. A minute, two minutes, five, ten passed before the bots spun back around and left the corridor. Sno sighed with relief then walked carefully through the bloody carnage to the stateroom doors. He knocked when the doors wouldn't open. Sno waited and waited then knocked again.

"Open the damn doors yourselves, you morons!" Veben yelled from the other side.

"V! It's me!" Sno replied. "The guards are dead. Bots killed them, but are gone now."

There was a click and beep then the doors slid wide and Veben stood there, her face a puffy mess of bruises and gashes. Some of the skin just under her chin was loose and hung there like a disgusting dewlap. Veben absentmindedly tucked the skin back in place with her fingers then gestured for Sno to come in.

"Is Zan still here?" Sno asked as soon as he was in the stateroom and the doors were locked and secured behind him. "I could use some medical advice."

"Are you injured beyond the obvious?" Veben asked, heading straight for the bar.

Sno stopped and looked at himself in one of the grand mirrors hanging from the foyer wall. He was a mess. But he did have to admit that he looked worse than he felt. Not that he felt too great, but the booming klaxon had stopped drilling into his brain. That thought brought up the image of the guard being murdered by the bot. Sno shivered.

"Cold, love?" Veben asked, handing him a quadruple whiskey. She had one of her own and downed it in a single gulp. "Go climb in bed with Pol. He's toasty as a fusion reactor. Poor thing has a fever over one hundred and ten degrees Fahrenheit. Or is it Celsius? No, for beings we use Fahrenheit. Measurements are tricky in this galaxy."

She walked away and poured herself more whiskey.

"One hundred and ten?" Sno asked. "He should be dead."

"Oh, he pretty much is," Veben said. "Come see."

Veben led Sno into Pol's room. The old man was still in bed, propped up by several pillows, and his face was beet red with sweat pouring down it. Zan stood next to Pol looking exhausted and scared out of her wits.

"What is going on?" Zan asked, shouting over the klaxon. "Why won't someone turn that off?"

As if her wish had been granted, the klaxon stopped. Then Pol's body convulsed as a seizure tore through him.

"No," Zan said and grabbed a square mat of plastiglass that was half a meter on each side.

She pressed the square to Pol's chest then brought up a holo interface. Swiping like mad, she tried to chase down the electrical impulses that raced through Pol's body. But as soon as she stopped one set, another would start up and be twice as violent as the one Zan had just subdued.

After three minutes, Pol's body went completely rigid then relaxed. Sno didn't need Zan to confirm that the old man was dead. Or his body was, at least.

"That calls for more whiskey," Veben said, holding her glass up high as she left the room. "Who wants drinkies?"

"Have one," Sno said to Zan. He crossed to her, took her by the shoulders, and pointed her towards the doors. "Go. Have a drink or six and rest."

"They took Velly to the brig," Zan said as she allowed herself to be steered out of the room by Sno. "They hurt her bad and took her away. Then they locked us in. How did you get in here?"

"Guards outside are dead. Murdered by maintenance bots," Sno said, letting go of Zan's shoulders. The medic made her way to the closest couch and collapsed into it. "As soon as the guards were dead, the locks must have disengaged."

"So we have murder bots to thank for our freedom," Veben said, another glass down, another glass filled. "Too bad I do not intend to leave this stateroom."

"V?" Sno asked.

"Yes, love?" Veben replied.

"Tell me what's really going on," Sno said.

Veben blinked at Sno a few times then shrugged.

"I fell for a charming gentleman that promised me a galaxy of riches," Veben said honestly. Her eyes shifted towards Pol's room. "So much for that."

"Pol isn't dead," Sno said. "He's moved."

"I'm sorry?" Veben asked.

"What?" Zan asked.

"Pol Hammon is not dead," Sno said. "He moved. He transferred his consciousness into Ested."

"The android?" Veben exclaimed. "No, love, you're wrong. Pol was using the android to try to get us free from Loch. That son of a bitch captain double-crossed us and decided he'd sell us out to the Skrang instead of allowing the auction to go forward."

"Skrang? Are Skrang coming?" Zan asked. "I can't go back. I will not be a slave to the Skrang again."

She stood on wobbly feet then closed her eyes and sat back down.

"There's no place to go," Zan said. "We're in trans-space. I couldn't fly out of here if I wanted to."

"Perhaps Denman's pilot friend could get a ship ready for us," Veben suggested. "Go spring that orange gal and we'll be off this ship as soon as we're out of trans-space."

"I'm going to need another drink," Sno said, holding out his glass. "As strong as before."

"That's your story face, love," Veben said. "Are you sure you want to start a story when you've insisted I tell mine? Narratives could get crossed, plotlines confused, possibly—"

"Stop, V," Sno said. "Velly is dead. Loch killed her. And we are no longer in trans-space. We dropped out and came through the Mlo portal."

"Mlo? The system with the black hole?" Zan exclaimed.

"Do not forget the den of thieves and smugglers that hide at the rim of the system," Veben said. "If we are in Mlo, then they are probably en route to plunder this ship. Boarded by space pirates, how romantic."

"Did you hear me about the Velly part?" Sno asked.

"Yes," Veben said. "But, dear boy, I am not surprised."

"Neither am I," Zan said. "She was beaten badly when they took her away. I expected her to die in the brig."

"Same," Veben agreed.

"Sorry, though," Zan said to Sno. "She meant something to you?"

"She did," Sno replied. "Thank you."

"Hearts and eggshells," Veben said. "Eventually, they are broken wide open."

"What did you and Pol cook up, V?" Sno asked. "During those two days we waited for the M'illi'ped. What did you and Pol plan?"

"I wouldn't call it a plan, so much, love," Veben said. "At least I didn't think it was a plan. Not until we got aboard the Mip. Then I realized that Pol was very serious about carrying out our little flight of fancy."

"You are telling me nothing, V," Sno said. "Details."

"The plan," Veben said, making air quotes with one hand. The other was still occupied by her glass of whiskey. "The plan, love, was to get onboard this ship, have the captain set up a private little auction, and Pol would sell off his tech plans plus a one-time demonstration on how the tech works."

"How?" Sno asked. "The mental lock would stop him." Sno laughed. "The transfer to Ested. That's his loophole. He found one."

"A highly lucrative one. Although I don't expect he wanted the transfer to be permanent," Veben said and shrugged. "We were then supposed to steal away to some remote part of the galaxy to live out the remainder of our years in perfect luxury."

"V, you don't exactly want for anything now," Sno said.

"I don't exactly own anything, either," Veben countered. "Other than my villa, I have nothing, love. I live by your generosity, mostly. Your accounts pay for my food and drink. Your memberships are what I use at the clubs on Nab. Your family still has a great amount of cache, love. I have been remembered as a family friend, so I am still invited to events."

"You have friends, V," Sno said. "People invite you because you are you, not because you are associated with me and my family."

"Oh, love, you are so cute when you ignore reality," Veben said. "Denman, what happens if you die?"

"What?" Sno asked, confused.

"Who gets your fortune? Who gets the estate house?" Veben pressed. "Who takes over the club memberships? Who is left of the Snos?"

Sno hadn't thought of all of that. If he died, there were probably cousins across the galaxy that the fortune would be split amongst. The estate house would probably be sold. Veben wouldn't get anything and she'd be forced to live her days out in her villa, alone.

"I'm sorry, V," Sno said. "I didn't think of leaving it to you. You're so much older than me that I figured you'd go first. To be completely honest."

"Your job is not one for longevity, love," Veben said. "I spend most days wondering if I will be notified of your death. I wonder if anyone would be. Fleet Intelligence has been known to expunge records and disavow agents if a mission goes wrong. You could simply not come home and I would be left without a clue as to your fate."

"Hells, V, I am sorry," Sno said. "But all of this?" He held a palm up and gestured at the room, indicating the entire ship and the events that had unfolded since they'd boarded. "You could have talked to me. I'd gladly put you in my will as the sole beneficiary of my estate. You know I don't care too much for all of it anyway. You should have talked to me, V."

"Should have, could have, would have," Veben replied. "Yet, I did not. I hatched a plan with an old man that has been driven half mad by the dark tech he's worked with during his life." Veben sipped her whiskey and smirked. "I do have to admit that plotting with Pol has been quite exhilarating. All the subterfuge and clandestine chats. Is this what your day-to-day job is like, love?"

Sno pointed at his face. "With a healthy dose of this. Stay out of the espionage business, V. Leave it to the professionals."

"Espionage? Oh, love, neither I nor Pol was committing espionage," Veben said.

"I believe what you are talking about is the definition of espionage," Zan said.

"No one asked you, Dr. Dingus," Veben snapped. She took a breath and smiled. "Sorry. What I mean is that Pol still intends to give the GF the key to his plans. Or he did. Now I am not sure what he intends to do. Mlo certainly wasn't part of our arrangements. We were going to Bgreete where we would conduct the auction then slip away quickly since the ship would be so much slower due to that energy vortex."

"An energy vortex would be welcome about now," Sno said. "I'd trade that for this black hole we're going to eventually be sucked into."

"Attention all guests! Attention all guests! Please proceed to the First Class observation deck at once! Again, all guests please proceed to the First Class observation deck at once!"

"Who is that?" Zan asked, staring up at the ceiling as the announcement was repeated. "That voice sounds familiar."

"That is Ested," Sno said. "But it's not Ested. Pol is in that body and he's using the android's capabilities to take full control of the ship, as well as the bots."

"Is he going through with the auction?" Veben asked. "Doesn't seem like the best timing, if you ask me."

"All guests please proceed to the First Class observation deck! That includes you, Agent Prime. And please bring the lovely Ms. Veben Doab with you."

"You stay here," Sno said, pointing at Zan. "You're crew which means you could be on the bots' kill list. Best you stay in this stateroom until all of this is settled."

"Settled?' Veben laughed. "How do you propose we settle any of this?"

"By going to the First Class observation deck as ordered," Sno said. He offered his arm. "Care to walk with me?"

"If we must," Veben said.

"Good," Sno said and smiled. The smile faded. "But you'll want to prepare for what's in the corridor. It's not pretty."

"Love, I saw the aftermath of the Wendelsohns' couples cosmetic genetic therapy," Veben said. "That was not pretty."

31.

Every step of their journey to the First Class observation deck was watched by bots. Maintenance bots, servant bots, cleaning bots, health bots. Nothing but bots from corridor to lift, from lift to corridor. Sno and Veben couldn't turn around without seeing a bot following close behind.

"We should have brought the booze," Veben said as they waited for the final lift to ascend to the First Class observation deck. The only other being in the lift was a shriveled-up Groshnel that was barely taking in enough breath to stay upright. "She could use a good belt or two."

"My wife was killed," the Groshnel whimpered. "The cleaning bot murdered her."

"I'm sorry to hear that," Sno said.

The lift stopped and the doors opened to show close to every guest standing about on the observation deck. Some were talking to anyone who would listen; many were traumatized like the Groshnel on the lift; all were close to shaking with fear.

Straight ahead, framed by the massive observation window, was the black hole that Mlo was known for. It was several light years away, but that didn't mean much. The ship would eventually be sucked into the maw of the black hole, sooner rather than later. They needed to be hundreds of light years away from the black hole for it to not have influence over the Mip.

From Sno's experience, they had a day, maybe two. Time did not work right when they were that close to a black hole. For millennia, scientists tried to quantify the power and effects that black holes had. While many working theories had been close, most were shot down when practical experience was applied. A black hole would not be physics' bitch.

"Our trajectory shows us to be heading straight for it," Sno said. "The bridge crew tried to get us out of this situation, but they were butchered by bots before they could adjust course."

Several guests close enough to hear Sno gasped in terror. Veben glared at them like they were children afraid of vermin.

There was a stage set up in front of the observation window. A chime sounded, but no one paid any attention. Except for Sno. He watched closely as a hunched-over Loch came limping out onto the stage. His orange fur was matted to his skull with blood. From the technicolor hues, Sno guessed it was the bridge crew's blood. Or bloods, as the case was.

The chime sounded again, yet no one even looked Loch's way. Sno realized that none of them wanted to see the black hole. If they didn't look at the black hole, then maybe it wouldn't exist. The insane wealth of the beings had insulated them from ever dealing with realities they did not want to. Most realities could be bought or sold and tucked away in some closet or hangar or planet. But, a black hole was no gajillionaire's bitch.

The chime grew louder and louder until beings were forced to pay attention. Heads looked all about the deck, hunting for the source. Then Loch cleared his throat and the noise was amplified at a level that no one could ignore.

"Hello," Loch said, his voice tired and lost. "I am your captain, Rane Loch. I have been asked to explain what will be happening next. Please pay attention as I have also been asked to kill anyone that is not focusing on me and my words."

Three dozen bots of various makes and models made themselves known by streaming out of hatches in the walls. The guests were surrounded by machines. The deck went silent. Eyes that had been avoiding looking at the black hole were now pointed in its direction. The new reality of murder bots was too much for the guests. They preferred to stare at the deadly bit of nature over the deadly bit of technology.

"Good," Loch said. "As some of you may know, I had planned a private auction to take place tomorrow when we were supposed to reach Bgreete. Some of you have prepared your accounts so that credits could be transferred instantly. I do hope that those preparations are still in place. They will need to be for you to survive the next few hours."

Loch ran his hand over his face, up across his forehead, then into his fur. He grimaced and yanked his hand back when it got stuck in a thick glob of purple blood. Looking about for something to wipe his hand on, Loch grew slightly alarmed. Then he calmed himself and wiped his hand on his gore-stained uniform.

Veben chuckled.

"What was that?" Loch asked, his head snapping up, beady eyes scanning the crowd. "Who laughed at me? I am still captain. I will have you killed for that."

There were gasps and murmurs, but no one looked over at Veben to give her away. A couple of the bots inched into the crowd, but they did not make a move to go after or harm Veben. Sno leaned in close.

"Try not to get us killed, alright?" he asked.

"No promises, love," Veben replied. "I'm at that nothing-left-to-lose stage."

"I'll get us out of this, V," Sno said. "So let me."

"You are the pro, love," Veben said and raised her hand high.

"V!" Sno snapped, grabbing at her arm.

Veben yanked free and said, "Excuse me? But will we be served refreshments? I'm quite thirsty and could go for some appetizers too. I haven't a clue as to the time, but I am certain we have missed at least two meals. Could some of these bots scurry off and fetch some small bites and drinks?"

Loch stared, wide-eyed. "Wh-wh-wh-what...?"

All eyes fell on Veben.

"Re-fresh-ments," Veben said slowly. "I. Am. Hungry. And. I. Could. Use. A. Drink."

All eyes returned to Loch.

More wide-eyed staring from the captain.

"Refreshments are an excellent idea," a voice said from off stage. Then Pol, in Ested's body, walked to Loch and patted the captain on the shoulder. "Finish what you have been sent up here to say then you can coordinate the serving of refreshments."

"Can't the bots handle that?" Loch asked.

"Do you want to ask that question again, Captain Loch?" Pol replied.

"No, sir," Loch said. "Ladies and gentlemen, I will need you to begin the process of freeing up your fortunes for transfer. Not the entirety of your fortunes, but the majority. I am sorry that it has to be like this..." Loch glanced over his shoulder at the black hole and shivered. "But it has to be like this."

"Why?" someone shouted. "Why would we transfer our fortunes to you?"

"Kill that one," Pol said.

A bot raced through the crowd and speared the man through the abdomen. There was a loud whirring and blood sprayed everywhere as the man's intestines were wound like pasta around a spike and yanked from his navel. The guests started screaming and hurried to get away from the atrocity.

"Quiet!" Pol roared. His voice was amplified over the ship's PA. The crowd went quiet, other than some gagging and a few sobs. "Good. Now, Captain Loch, will you answer the question?"

"Mr. Hammon's tech was to be auctioned off, but that has changed due to my unforgivable duplicity in the matter," Loch said. "Instead, you will transfer funds to an account, the number of which will be provided to you shortly, and those funds will pay for your safety. Everyone that pays will be allowed to remain onboard the M'illi'ped. Those that do not pay will be ejected out into space. You will be shot into the black hole."

Loch took a deep breath.

"I believe paying the funds is a good idea. I have already transferred what credits I possess to the account."

"Extortion?" Sno called out. "You're going to extort these people, Pol?"

"Agent Prime," Pol replied. "I'm giving you a pass, Agent Prime. No death by bot for you. But please do not interrupt these proceedings again. You and I will speak later once the fun is over."

"Fun? Pol, we need to talk now," Sno said.

"Love. Don't," Veben warned.

"Agent Prime, I have great affection for your friend, Veben Doab," Pol said. "But even though she was shown mercy before, that does not mean she is above being harmed. Continue this interruption and I will have her legs hacked off with the dull side of a floor scraper."

One of the bots at the side of the deck lifted the floor scraper up so all could see. One side looked incredibly sharp while the other side looked like it would get stuck slicing butter.

"Continue," Sno said.

"Thank you," Pol replied. "Captain Loch, why is paying a good idea?"

"You stay on the ship," Loch answered.

"And not paying is bad, why?"

"You are ejected into the black hole," Loch said.

"Ah, that is not quite correct," Pol said. He held up a finger. "Let me demonstrate."

The dead man with his bowels hanging out disappeared. Part of the view window became a separate screen, zooming in to show the dead man's corpse being sucked into the black hole. He was there for only a blink of an eye before he was gone for good.

"Moltrans," Pol said. "No, I am sorry, that is a very rudimentary way of putting it. My tech is so much more as many of you know and were prepared to pay for. That was until Captain Loch here sold us out to the Skrang instead for his own profit. Stupid move, Captain Loch."

"Yes, yes, a stupid move," Loch agreed. "I did try to call them off, but—"

"Shhh," Pol said.

"Yes, of course, shhh," Loch replied.

"For those that do not know, what I have invented is a new form of interstellar transportation," Pol said. "No longer will ships need to wait in a queue for their turn through designated wormhole portals in each system. No, that is the old way. With my new tech, ships can go from one point in the galaxy." Pol snapped his android fingers. The synthetic skin made a dull thudding noise, not a crisp snap. He shrugged. "From one point in the galaxy to another just like that. No wormhole portal needed, no relying on each system to maintain said portals. And no more transit charges from the GF. That's a big one there."

Sno raised his hand.

"Now you're learning," Veben said.

"If people pay, what are you going to do?" Sno asked. "Transport this entire ship away from Mlo? Is that what the extortion is paying for?"

"Away from the black hole? That would be quite the reward," Pol said. "But, no, that isn't a great enough threat."

Klaxons began blaring again.

"Ah, the real threat is here now," Pol said. "Who wants to die at the hands of the Skrang? Anyone? No?"

He clapped his hands together.

"Then get those transfers ready, people!"

32.

As the crowd of guests began arguing with each other, their spouses, partners, lovers, companions, servants of convenience, Pol left the stage, his android eyes on Sno. The crowd parted like the red sea, no one wanting to be closer than a meter to the mad tech in the deadly machine.

"Agent Prime," Pol said. "I know this must be confusing and infuriating to you."

"He killed Velly," Sno stated, his rage barely contained. "Loch shot her in the head. She has no head, Pol. I watched it disintegrate in the blink of an eye."

Pol studied Sno for a moment then nodded.

"That is unfortunate," he said. "He should not have done that. I have since straightened out Captain Loch, so I can assure you that will never happen—"

Veben slapped the android across the face then yanked her hand back and tucked it into her body.

"Holy shit!" she yelled. "Ow! Eight Million Gods damn OW!"

"Has my real body expired yet?" Pol asked.

"It has," Sno answered as Veben shook her hand over and over, checking it to make sure it wasn't broken.

"I will miss that body," Pol said. "It served me well for so many years."

He patted himself. "But this body will be so much more appropriate. No need for food or water. No bothersome bodily functions to interrupt important work. Superior strength and speed. Not to mention a brain that has the capacity of the universe."

"Don't start with the God thing again, Pol," Sno said. "You really can't pull it off."

Pol shrugged. The shrug looked humorous on an android; stiff and precise.

"We shall see, Agent Prime, we shall see," Pol said. Then he turned his attention to Veben. "My darling, what can I say to make this better? To make this right with you? We made plans. Those plans can still happen."

"I am not thinking they will ever happen, you little shit," Veben said. "Our plans were simple: you sell your tech to the highest bidder and we disappear with all the riches. This?" She gestured at his android body. "This was not part of the plan. Neither was murdering half the crew and extorting the guests. We get the credits, you said, and live out our lives in luxury and anonymity. That can never happen now, you slime bag. The GF will hunt you until your cybernetic circuits fizzle out and die."

"This brain does not work on cybernetic circuits," Pol said. "How it works is—"

Veben punched him in the faux nose. She screamed and pulled her hand back, shaking it all over again.

"Worth it," she gasped as Sno gave her a pitying look. "So worth it."

"Loch betrayed us, darling," Pol said.

"Stop calling me that," Veben snapped. "Not going to happen."

"You do know that this body can be modified any way you would like it to be," Pol said. "Enhanced and improved. Better than flesh and blood. If you catch my meaning."

Veben made an exaggerated gagging sound and feigned throwing up. Even though none of the guests were closer than a couple of meters from her, they all backed away quickly. Veben straightened up, brushed at the top of her dress, and gave Pol the finger. Sno couldn't help but notice the finger was immaculate and manicured to perfection. V was always V even in a life or death crisis.

"Never going to happen," Veben said. "You will have to spend your credits on your own. All alone out there in the big, bad, dark galaxy. Not a friend around you."

Pol was very quiet and very still.

"V, perhaps you two can discuss this later," Sno said, pointing at the ceiling. "At the moment, we have a Skrang problem to deal with."

"Yes, we can discuss this later," Pol said. "When you've had a chance to think this through."

"Oh, I've had plenty of—" Veben started, but Sno placed a hand on her shoulder and she snapped her mouth shut.

"How do you plan on getting us out of here, Pol?" Sno asked. "Black hole in front of us, Skrang behind us. This ship was not built for battle. It has incredible shielding so that it cannot be hijacked."

"Too late," Veben said.

"But other than the shielding, it has no other defenses. No anti-torpedo cannons. No plasma grid. No remote fighters."

"Ah, yes, about the fighters," Pol said. "I was anticipating the arrival of the Skrang. I had hoped that Ms. Tarcorf would be with us, but she is not. I have a feeling we can find some decent enough pilots to help with the effort while these lovely people finish their transactions."

Pol clapped his hands and the huge observation deck went almost totally silent.

"Two quick announcements, people," Pol boomed. His voice was amplified through the ship's PA again. "First announcement is that I need all money transfers to be finished within the hour. No exceptions. As you can tell by the screeching noises in your comm implants, attempting to call or alert anyone about your situation is pointless. Your only means of communication is between your banking interface and your banks. I would advise bringing up those holo protocols and get to swiping ASAP."

Terrified stares and gaping mouths were his answer. Pol sighed and it made shivers go up and down Sno's spine. Androids should not sigh.

"Second item of interest is that the Skrang have brought some serious firepower," Pol said. He swiped his hand up towards the ceiling and a holo projection filled the air. "As you can see, the Skrang are not messing around. Those are two heavy battleships. Destroyer class, if I know my Skrang classifications. Not as large as the Galactic Fleet destroyer class, but equally as deadly."

Pol tapped his left ear.

"They are currently hailing us and insisting they speak to Captain Loch," Pol continued. "Such foul language they are using. And those guttural Skrang voices. Ugh. I am not pleased that I am having to listen to them."

The holo projection zoomed in on the Skrang destroyers. They weren't racing towards the Mip, but holding steady close to the wormhole portal they came through. But a second later, Skrang fighters began pouring out of the destroyers. The battleships weren't carriers, so the number of Skrang fighters was only a small percentage of what they could have been, but still, Sno counted close to twenty-five fighters leaving each destroyer and heading straight for the Mip.

"Since I have been a gracious host, and allowed you all to have an hour for the money transfers, that means we will need to hold off these fighters during that hour," Pol said. "Agent Prime here has volunteered to lead a group of pilots to do just that: hold off the fighters for an hour. I will need more volunteers, so those of you with combat experience, please step forward."

"Volunteered, eh?" Sno said, but Pol ignored him.

No one stepped forward from the crowd. Pol shook his head.

"I have everyone's records up here," Pol said, tapping at his head again. "If I start calling names, then you forfeit your chance at survival. More importantly, your loved one or loved ones forfeit their chance at survival. Volunteer and I guarantee the safety of those that are onboard this ship with you." Pol grinned and several of the guests shrunk back involuntarily. "And the safety of those that are not on this ship. All of your records are in my mind. All of them. Including family records. Should I begin announcing their residences to make my point?"

Murmurs began to circulate then a dozen beings of various races began to separate themselves from the other guests.

"Wonderful," Pol said. "That is, let's see, twelve plus Agent Prime. Lucky thirteen. When this incident is written about, that should be the name assigned to you brave souls. The Lucky Thirteen."

Pol turned to face the stage where Loch was still standing, looking completely lost.

"Captain Loch?" Pol called.

"Yes, sir?" Loch replied instantly.

"I will leave you to oversee these fine folks," Pol said. "I expect the industrious movement of funds to continue unabated. They now have fifty-three minutes. Please make sure everything progresses smoothly. My bot friends will ensure that no one leaves or gets out of hand. All you have to do is confirm transfer of funds. Are we clear on your duties, Captain?"

"Crystal clear, sir," Loch said and saluted. There were a few quiet snickers in the crowd. Loch lowered his hand. "All will go as you desire, sir."

"I like the sound of that," Pol said. He returned his attention to Sno then the dozen volunteers. "We shall move this discussion to the bridge then."

Pol snapped his fingers.

Sno's world disappeared. He felt a pull just behind his navel then his head exploded, reassembled, exploded again, reassembled, and he was no longer on the First Class observation deck. Sno's stomach did a hundred backflips before calming down and he bent over, unsure of whether he was going to throw up or not. When he straightened, he was standing on the bridge with the rest of the Lucky Thirteen and Pol.

A single cleaning bot was mopping the floor, leaving streaks of technicolor blood here and there before circling back to take care of those. The rest of the bridge was spotless.

"Excellent work," Pol said and patted the bot which was only a meter tall. "You take pride in what you do, I can see that. You may finish later. Leave us."

The bot chirped and retreated through a hatch in the wall, leaving the Lucky Thirteen and Pol to stare out of the view shield at the two far-off Skrang destroyers and incoming Skrang fighters.

Pol sharpened the resolution and zoomed in on the fighters.

"Twenty-five fighters," Pol said. "Skrang fighters, so they are not light ships that can be destroyed with a couple taps from plasma cannons. Which is fine since I do not need you to destroy them, I only need you to hold them off until the hour is up and the ship can be moved."

Sno cocked his head, but didn't speak up. Pol had played part of his hand. The hour wasn't for the guests to be able to transfer their funds. The hour was for something else. Pol needed the hour in order for his plan to be complete. He had figured out that Loch had betrayed him, but he wasn't ready for the repercussions of that betrayal. Pol needed more time.

"We'll most likely die out there, Pol," Sno said. "I'm a good pilot, but I am not a combat pilot. I doubt any of these men and women are either."

"I flew sixteen combat missions for the GF Marines back during the War," a Shiv'erna woman said. Shiv'ernas were a lithe race, humanoid but with elephantine proboscises. The woman's proboscis raised slightly, aimed at Pol. "I can handle myself in a ship. But do you have ships that can take on Skrang fighters?"

"No, there are no ships aboard that can take on Skrang fighters," Pol said, sounding bored and irritated. "Like I said, all I need you to do is stall the Skrang for the remainder of the hour. You do not need ships equal to the Skrang fighters to do that."

"We only need ships with strong enough shielding that we can divert their attention away from the M'illi'ped," a Spilfleck man said. "Do we have access to ships like that?"

Pol grinned. Everyone stiffened, but no one recoiled. Sno began to reassess his assumptions of the guests on the Mip. They weren't all soft and scared oligarchs. Some had grit and guts.

"I do have ships like that," Pol said to the man. "I have removed the shielding from several ships in order to strengthen the shielding on fifteen ships. We only need thirteen, so we are in luck."

"But no weapons?" a Gwreq woman asked. The suit she wore clashed with her stone-grey skin, but the way she held herself made it clear she neither cared nor was it wise to point that fashion fact out to her. "Not even plasma blasters?"

"No weapons," Pol said. "Unfortunate, but there was no time to outfit the ships with weapons. The shielding will have to do."

"And if we hold off the Skrang for the remainder of the hour?" Sno asked. "What then? You let us land back on the Mip and we escape? How exactly can you do that, Pol? The ship is caught within the black hole's field of influence. The Skrang are blocking the wormhole portal. Can your tech truly get us free of the Mlo System?"

"My tech can get us free of the Mlo System," Pol said. "And all of you are welcome to return to the ship once the hour is up and I call you back."

"If we survive," Sno said.

"Well, yes, that would be a prerequisite," Pol said. He pointed a finger at the Shiv'erna woman. "To make this easier on all of you, I will give you numbers. Remember them. You are One."

He ticked off numbers as he pointed at each being. One was the Shiv'erna woman. Two was a human male. Three was a human female. Four a Slinghasp female. Five the Spilfleck male. Six a Tcherian male. Seven a Leforian female. Eight the Gwreq female. Nine a human male. Ten a Groshnel male. Eleven a Dornopheous male. Twelve a Slinghasp female. And Thirteen was Sno.

"I'll go by Agent Prime," Sno said. "I'd rather not be called Thirteen."

"There is no call for superstition here, Sno," Pol said.

"There is every call for superstition, Pol," Sno countered, pointing at the view shield and the Skrang fighters that were getting closer by the second. "If we are going to survive that, then I'll take every bit of hoodoo, mojo, lucky gump feet, bags of grave dirt, and whatever else is needed to get me through this."

Sno stepped closer to Pol and sneered.

"That way, when I do live, I can come back here and destroy you, Pol Hammon," Sno said. "Count on that."

"Denman Sno," Pol said, sounding pleased. "That fighting spirit right there is why you are Agent Prime."

"I don't need you to tell me that, asshole," Sno said. He turned from Pol and faced the rest of the Lucky Thirteen. "I believe we have ships to get to."

"Allow me," Pol said.

Again, Sno's world disappeared then he was standing in a docking hangar, staring at fifteen ships. Bots scurried this way and that, finalizing whatever work orders Pol had given them. The Lucky Thirteen all took deep breaths and steadied themselves. Then they each looked at Sno.

"What?" Sno asked. "I haven't flown combat missions. Do not look at me to be in charge."

"You're Agent Prime," the Shiv'erna woman said. "You work for the Galactic Fleet. We're all civilians now. It only makes sense for you to take command."

Sno growled low then nodded.

"Fine. Let's get to work then."

They each hurried to a separate ship and climbed in as side hatches and cockpits opened wide for them.

33.

Sno made sure to synchronize a countdown as soon as he sat down in the pilot's seat of the ship he chose. He had to scroll through a menu to find the right setting since he no longer had implants. He couldn't simply swipe his wrist over the control console.

The same was true for the pre-flight checklist and lift off from the hangar. He was doing it all manually, including the comm.

"This is Agent Prime checking comms," he called. "Reply if you can hear me."

"One can hear you."

"Two here."

"Three is loud and clear."

"Four here."

"Five is here."

"Six ready."

"Seven is loud and clear."

"Roger for Eight."

"Nine is a go."

"Ten here."

"Eleven ready."

"Twelve is loud and clear."

The hangar doors opened wide and the thirteen ships angled themselves then left the hangar in a close, orderly formation with Sno in the lead.

"Listen," Sno said as he aimed the ship for the incoming Skrang fighters. "Stay alive. Keep the fighters from going after the Mip, but try to stay alive. This doesn't have to be a suicide mission."

"It is not suicide if none of us want to die," One said. "This is a sacrifice mission."

"True, but we don't have to die," Sno said. "If we work together, we can corral the Skrang fighters and keep— Hey! Who is that?"

A large cruiser, one way too big to outmaneuver the Skrang fighters, broke formation and raced at the smaller enemy ships.

"Answer me!" Sno shouted.

"Five," came a tense voice. "One is right. This is a sacrifice mission. We should face that now before we fool ourselves with false hope. There are twenty-five of them and thirteen of us. If we use our ships wisely, we can take out the Skrang fighters quickly."

"Five, get your ass back in formation!" Eight shouted. "Don't do this!"

"Only thing I can do," Five replied. "Check your ships. Our shielding will hold off about eight or nine direct hits from the Skrang plasma cannons. We can duck and dodge all we want, but in the end, we are all dying in order to keep the Mip, and those we love onboard, safe."

There was a squelch of static and Five's comm cut off.

"Shit," Sno said as he pushed his ship faster to try to catch up with Five.

"Agent Prime," One called. "Don't. Five has made his decision. Let him."

"Dammit," Sno grumbled.

He slowed his ship and kept formation with the others.

Five's ship raced towards the Skrang fighters and six of them broke off from the rest to engage. It took about four minutes for them to close on each other. The Skrang fighters opened fire and Five's cruiser was lit up like a holo game. The cruiser dove sharply and the Skrang fighters pursued it closely.

Then the cruiser's fore thrusters engaged at full power and the ship braked hard. The Skrang fighters were about to collide with the ship and half began to break away. But before they could get clear, the cruiser exploded. A quick flash of brilliant white light then nothing but debris. None of the Skrang survived.

"He put his engine drives into critical," Three said. "Six Skrang fighters down."

"Nineteen for us," One said. "You see what has to be done, folks. Let's do it."

The Lucky Thirteen's formation broke into chaos and Sno watched in confusion and awe as the other ships shot out and away from him, all headed straight at the rest of the Skrang fighters.

"Stop!" Sno yelled into the comm as he watched the Skrang react. Their formations broke apart and the fighters flew in different directions. "They won't let that happen again!"

"No, they won't," One replied. "And we don't need them to."

The ships raced towards the Skrang. It took two minutes for them to reach the cluster of fighters. Sno glanced at the countdown and was surprised to see that there were only twenty minutes left in the hour.

"Listen up!" he shouted. "Twenty minutes! That's all we need to hold them off! Twenty minutes! Get back here! We can live through this!"

No one replied.

The eleven ships shot through the cluster of Skrang fighters, all of them taking a good amount of cannon fire as they passed. Sno blinked several times as he watched the eleven ships seem to completely ignore the Skrang fighters.

"Hey! What are you doing?" he called.

No one replied. There was zero chatter on the comm.

"You have got to be kidding," he muttered. "They shut me out."

Sno guessed that One took command, which was fine by him, really, and told the others to switch to a different comm channel. They left him behind and silent.

"Agent Prime," Pol said, his voice echoing from the bridge's loudspeakers. "Are you not going with them? Don't be a coward, Sno."

"Pol, stop all this insanity," Sno demanded. "Tell them to come back and then get us out of here. I am sure you have enough money transferred by now. Don't be a greedy asshole."

There was a long pause then, "Twelve minutes remain, Agent Prime. Best get in the fight. I have no intention of letting cowards back onboard the M'illi'ped. Go fight, go survive, then come back before we leave."

"You're mad," Sno said with disgust. "You are completely mad. And the GF brass are just as mad to deal with you. They should have known you'd double-cross them. Your reputation has shown that you are only capable of deceit."

"Deceit? Quite the accusation coming from an agent of the SSD," Pol said with a laugh. "And I do not intend to double-cross anyone, Sno. The Galactic Fleet will get what has been promised to them. And I will get to finally be free."

"They'll never rest, Pol," Sno said. "They will find you."

"Denman, Denman, Denman," Pol replied. "The GF will not only rest, they will pretend I never existed. Yes, there will be fallout from my extortion, as you call it, but that can be fixed with a special fund set up to compensate these spoiled beings for their losses. None of them will recoup all of what they transfer to me, simply because none of them will report the full amount. Doing so might contradict the legal accounting their estates have been reporting for centuries. Can you imagine the back taxes and fines that would accrue if the actual amounts were discovered? No. They will get back enough to be comfortable once again, but not one of these families will have the same influence as they did before going on their little luxury cruise."

Sno shook his head.

"Mad," was his reply.

"We agree to disagree," Pol responded. "Now, go help the others or remain in Mlo forever, Agent Prime. Or until your ship runs out of power and you are sucked into the black hole."

"I will find you, Pol," Sno said.

"No, Denman, you will not," Pol said and the comm went dead.

Sno stared at the eleven ships that were well past the Skrang fighters. He knew what they were doing and it was working. All eleven ships were headed straight for the Skrang destroyers. They were going to try to ram the huge ships.

The majority of the Skrang fighters turned and pursued the eleven ships. But five did not. They were racing right at Sno.

"Dammit," Sno said as he hit the throttle and headed straight at the fighters. "Eight Million Gods dammit!"

The five fighters broke into two teams of two, those two teams breaking off to flank Sno while the fifth fighter kept its course head on for Sno's ship.

"What can I do? What can I do?" Sno wondered to himself.

His fingers raced across the control console and he brought up every system and protocol the ship had. Nothing even close to an offensive weapon. The shields would take a beating but not for too long, and not from all five of those fighters. He'd be dead in minutes.

Minutes.

Sno glanced at the countdown and saw that there were only nine minutes left before the hour was up. If his calculations were close, then that left him with a minute to spare. He could keep the fighters occupied until the Mip did whatever Pol had planned. Then maybe he could get free and try to slip around the Skrang destroyers to get through the wormhole portal.

Sno laughed loud at his idiocy. He wasn't going to survive the Skrang fighters, let alone get past two destroyers in order to get through a wormhole portal. He was a dead man flying.

"Then don't fly," he said out loud.

Sno stood up and left the bridge. The ship had five levels and he took the lift down to the bottom level. After some hunting, he found what he needed. Lined up in racks, and probably never used, were two dozen environmental suits.

Racing to the closest rack, Sno pulled down a suit then stripped to his undergarments. He'd been trained for deep space isolation and knew that the suit would be more efficient if he didn't have clothes on. The systems could better track his temperature and life signs if his skin was bare.

Sno slid into the suit and grabbed a helmet. He secured the helmet, went through the suit's safety checklist, twice, then stepped to a panel on the wall and tapped at it until he got a schematic of the ship. Sno studied the schematic, saw where he needed to go, and took off running.

Klaxons blared as the ship began to shake and shudder as it took on fire from the Skrang fighters. Sparks flew around Sno as he reached the lift. He tapped at the control panel, but the doors didn't open. A thin line of smoke was coming from the seam between the doors.

"Shit," he said then spun about until he located a side hatch.

Sno ran to the hatch, popped it open, ducked his head inside, and growled at the ladder, and long climb, before him. He didn't hesitate. He didn't have time to. Sno grabbed onto the ladder and ascended up through the levels of the ship.

Smoke began to fill the shaft, and Sno was nearly knocked loose from the ladder several times as the Skrang kept up their attack. Sno checked a reading on the wrist panel on his suit and saw he had two minutes left. He doubled his effort and kept climbing.

One minute was left to spare when he reached the emergency airlock at the top of the shaft. Sno grabbed onto the manual controls and twisted the handle twice to the left, twice to the right, then slammed it back into its recessed port. The hatch above him opened and before Sno could do anything, he was sucked out into open space. He hadn't attached a safety tether because the last thing he wanted was to be connected to a doomed ship.

Sno was tumbling out of control, but at least he was headed in the right direction. Every half revolution he could see that the Mip was dead ahead. If he was lucky, he might reach it in time.

Then his ship exploded. He was close enough that before the concussive force could dissipate into the void of open space, he was buffeted and sent tumbling even faster towards the Mip.

"Come on, come on, come on," Sno said over and over.

Closer, closer, closer, almost there. Sno started to smile, but the smile fell from his face as he came out of a half rotation and there was no Mip. The luxury liner was gone. All that he could see was the black hole devouring that half of the Mlo System.

And Sno was still tumbling.

Training kicked in and Sno used the small thrusters on the environmental suit to steady himself. The tumbling stopped and he turned away from the black hole. No need to keep facing that nightmare.

Instead, Sno focused his attention on what was happening with the Skrang. No implants meant no ability to access the environmental suit's face shield. He couldn't zoom in on the action. All Sno could see was far off micro-explosions, that he was sure weren't so micro close up, and their aftermaths. Light from the system's star glinted off a sea of debris.

At least the fighters that had gone after Sno were gone. The afterburn from their engine drives were dots in the nearly dark void.

There were several more far off micro-explosions then Sno was shocked to see a massive detonation. One of the Lucky Thirteen had gotten through and took out a Skrang destroyer.

"Good for you," Sno said to himself as he slowly drifted towards the black hole.

He wondered if any of the Lucky Thirteen realized they didn't need to fight anymore. The Mip was gone. But he had his answer soon when the dots of the last Skrang fighters disappeared, followed quickly by the far-off shape of the last Skrang destroyer. The unmistakable swirl of the wormhole portal opening then closing was easy to see from where he was.

"Hello?" Sno called, activating the helmet's comm. "Anybody out there? Anyone left alive?"

There was no response. None of the Lucky Thirteen replied to his calls.

"Great," Sno said. "Well, here I am."

A polite chime sounded in his helmet.

"Air levels at critical," an electronic voice said. "Please return to the ship."

"Yeah, I'll get right on that," Sno said.

He tried to find the cutoff for the voice, but couldn't. The controls weren't on the wrist panel. If he'd had implants, he could have ordered the voice to shut all the Hells up.

So, Sno relaxed in the suit, thought about his life, and consigned himself to the fact he was going to die. He activated the thrusters and spun around so he could face the black hole. He'd asphyxiate before he reached the impressive phenomenon, but he'd die with a great view.

34.

Once again, Sno woke up in a med pod.

"Hey, buddy," B'urn said, smiling down at him through the med pod lid. "Welcome home."

Sno blinked then started laughing. The laughter turned slightly maniacal which caused B'urn's face to become concerned which caused Sno to laugh even harder.

"How about we get you out of there," B'urn said.

The med pod lid opened and Sno sat up. He got himself under control and wiped at his eyes.

"Toss me some clothes," Sno said.

"Don't you want to know how you got here?" B'urn asked.

"I think the story would be best heard while wearing underpants," Sno said.

"Fair enough," B'urn said and shrugged. He fetched a pile of clothes on a chair close by and handed them to Sno. "It's a great story, by the way."

Sno got dressed then shook B'urn's hand as he nodded at the med bay's doors.

"Hungry. Thirsty. Very," Sno said.

"I see your syntax has gone primitive," B'urn replied and laughed as the two walked out of the med bay. "Maybe that brain of yours was deprived of a little too much oxygen."

Sno looked about. "Division?"

"Where else would we be?" B'urn asked.

"I thought I was going to die in that environmental suit," Sno said. "Barring that, I expected to wake up at GF headquarters, not Division."

"Oh, the GF brass wanted to have you taken to headquarters, but Crush and Gerber argued that you should be brought here for medical treatment and debriefing first," B'urn said. "Gods knows how many favors Gerber had to cash in to make that happen."

People passed the two agents and nodded. Many seemed quite pleased at the sight of Sno, while others looked downright pissed off.

"There was a pool going to see when I'd wake up, wasn't there?" Sno asked when they reached the lift and stepped inside. "What was the winning guess?"

"Forty-seven days," B'urn said reluctantly.

"Forty-seven days?" Sno exclaimed. "I've been out for forty-seven days?"

"Oh, Hells no," B'urn said. "You've been here at Division for forty-seven days. You've been out for eighty-eight days. Approximately. The smugglers that dropped you off at the closest GF outpost weren't exactly detailed in their reporting."

"Smugglers?" Sno nodded. "Right. Smugglers. The Mlo System."

"Let's get that food and drink then I'll fill you in on the whole story," B'urn said.

Sno agreed and they stayed quiet until they were in Sno's quarters. Tana was waiting for them.

"You son of a bitch," she said as she wrapped Sno in her arms. She kissed him on the lips, on the cheeks then gave him a hard shove. "You son of a bitch!"

"Why exactly am I a son of a bitch?" Sno asked, heading straight for the wet bar.

"No!" Tana ordered. "Food first. You just got out of a coma, you moron."

"Comas make me thirsty," Sno said, but didn't pour a drink. He started to tap at his wrist then paused. "Uh, could someone order food for me? I'm a little naked in the implant department."

"Nah, they fixed that two weeks ago, buddy," B'urn said. "No way Agent Prime could be allowed to wander around without tech in him."

"Ledora?" Sno called.

"Hello, Agent Prime," Ledora responded in his ear. Sno smiled at the sound he'd taken for granted for so long. "How may I help you, Agent Prime?"

Sno began to speak then stopped.

"She's secure," Tana said. "She can't be hacked anymore."

"How do you know about that?" Sno asked.

"Veben Doab has been pretty honest with the GF interrogators," B'urn said with a chuckle. "I think she scared a few of them during her debriefing. She told everyone about Ledora, about Pol Hammon, about the planned auction, Pol's descent into madness, the murders, Captain Loch, everything."

Sno looked at Tana.

"Everything," Tana agreed with a nod.

"Pol let her live?" Sno asked, shocked.

"Pol Let everyone live," B'urn said. "Or he let those still alive after transport live. There were quite a few deaths before their arrival, but you know that, right?"

"Yeah, I know that," Sno said. "Ledora?"

"Yes, Agent Prime?"

"Steaks. Massive steaks. I need protein," he said. "And a side salad for balance."

"Oh, yes, gotta have balance," B'urn said. He laughed and placed his order. Same with Tana.

When the food was placed on the dining table by a bot, which Sno watched closely until it left the room, the three sat down and Sno began to devour his meat. He'd eaten an entire steak before he came up for air and even looked at the salad bowl.

"What happened to everyone on the Mip?" Sno asked.

"They've all been returned home," B'urn said.

"We probably shouldn't talk in too much detail about this until Sno is debriefed," Tana said.

"Give me the bullet points," Sno said. "I didn't expect anyone to live, myself included. Where did the M'illi'ped appear?"

"In orbit over GF headquarters," B'urn said. "One moment not there, next moment there."

"I don't think fighter squadrons have ever been scrambled faster than when that ship showed up," Tana said. "Not even during the War."

"Once the GF realized the ship wasn't a threat, they boarded and began processing the passengers," B'urn said.

"The ship's logs were wiped," Tana added. "So all the GF has are the personal accounts of the passengers. There isn't a single bit of surveillance data left."

"There wasn't any system left," B'urn said. "Other than life support and basic maneuvering controls, that ship's systems were reset and shutdown. Pol Hammon left the M'illi'ped as empty as it was when it first left dry dock after manufacture."

"I knew he would do that," Sno said. "He had no intention of sharing his tech with anyone."

B'urn and Tana glanced at each other then away quickly.

"What?" Sno asked. "You said he wiped the ship clean."

"We'll leave this part of the discussion between you and Gerber," Tana said. "We're stepping into tricky waters here."

"Bullet points only, buddy," B'urn said. "Finish that steak and let's get some drinks in ya. We have some great stories from the missions we were on while you were napping."

"Fine," Sno said. "I've waited eighty-odd days, I can wait a little longer before I find out what all happened while I was napping."

When they finished eating, a cleaning bot appeared to take the dishes and Sno nearly jumped out of his seat, his hand going for his sidearm which he was not wearing.

"That's new," Tana said as she took him by the arm and led him to the couch. "Have a seat while B'urn gets us drinks."

"Something happen between you and a bot?" B'urn asked as he poured two glasses of whiskey, handed them to Sno and Tana then returned for his own. He shook his head. "Never mind. Don't answer that."

"Let's say that I may hire living beings when I get home," Sno said as he sipped his whiskey. "I think I have had my fill of bots for a lifetime."

"Your fill of bots? Buddy, your life is gonna be a twitchy ride if you're gonna jump out of your skin each time you come across a bot," B'urn said. "They're kinda everywhere."

"Speaking of, let me tell you what I've been dealing with," Tana said. "You'll get a kick out of this."

Sno listened as first Tana then B'urn told him all about their missions while he was in the med pod. Sno nodded, laughed, smiled, feigned outrage, and commiserated in all the right places. It wasn't long before Tana and B'urn were sharing glances again.

B'urn set his empty glass down and stood up.

"Well, you may have just woken up, buddy," he said to Sno. "But some of us have been awake for close to twenty hours now. I'm gonna go get some sleep. Gotta head out in the morning on a new mission."

"Oh?" Sno replied. "Anything fun?"

"Watch and wait duty," B'urn said with a frown. "Group of diplomats meeting to discuss some trade thing that I can't care less about. I'm there to make sure no one has brought their own spies. If I catch a snoop, I neutralize the snoop and keep the talks going."

"Full neutralization?" Tana asked.

"I wish," B'urn said and laughed. "That would make the job interesting. Goodnight. I'll catch you when I get back."

They said goodnight to B'urn then Sno and Tana were left alone.

"How about we hit the bed too," Tana said. "Despite your med pod vacation, you look exhausted."

"I am," Sno said. "Gravity has that effect on a body that hasn't been used to it for eighty days."

Tana stood and offered her hand. Sno took it and stood up. They embraced, kissed then stood there with Tana's cheek resting against Sno's chest.

"I was able to see part of Veben's report," Tana said. "I'm sorry about the swift ship pilot. It sounded like you two bonded."

"We did," Sno said, kissing the top of Tana's head. "And thank you."

"Bed?" Tana asked.

"Yes, that would be great," Sno said, letting her lead him to his bedroom. "But, um…"

"Don't worry," Tana said. "We'll actually sleep. I've been up for twenty hours too, Sno. I'm beat. It'll be nice to just be next to you. You had me worried."

"Sorry," Sno said as he stripped out of his clothes and threw the bed sheets back. He climbed in and sighed. "Oh, that feels good."

"It does," Tana said as she joined him, draping her arm across his chest and nuzzling into him. "Sno?"

"Hmmm?"

"What are you going to do about Veben?"

"I'm not going to do anything," Sno replied. "Her fate is up to the GF."

Tana didn't respond. Sno lifted his head and looked at her.

"What?" he asked.

"Nothing," Tana said. "It can wait. Gerber will fill you in, I'm sure. If he doesn't, then Crush will tell you everything you need to know."

"Tana…"

"Get some sleep, Sno," Tana said. "You have a very big day tomorrow."

Sno let the matter drop. In minutes, Tana was snoring gently against him. Sno remained awake for a good hour as memories of his mission came back to him. He struggled to shove the memory of Velly's death from his mind, but unfortunately, that was the last image he saw before he drifted off into a difficult sleep.

35.

Sno awoke with a start as his mind registered the whirring noise of a cleaning bot entering his bedroom.

"Out!" he shouted as he slapped at his bedside table for a pistol. There was no pistol.

The cleaning bot was gone before Sno slid out from under a still sleeping Tana. He wasn't surprised she didn't wake up at his shout. When Tana was comfortable, she could sleep through a solar storm. Sno brought up his chrono and saw he had a message from Crush ordering him to be present for his debriefing at 0900 on the dot. It was currently 0600.

Sno watched Tana sleep then got up and headed for the lavatory. He turned the steam on to full, enjoyed a long overdue piss then hopped in the shower after cleaning his teeth. Bits of dream swirled in his head, but the steam soon relaxed him enough that he let the uncomfortable images dissolve away.

"Hey," Tana said as she stepped into the steam with him. "You hear from Crush or Gerber yet?"

"0900," Sno said before giving her a kiss.

The kiss turned into more, much more, and Sno and Tana spent the next hour in the steam, at times frantically making love and at others simply being with each other. A chime sounded as they held each other, both completely sated, and Sno laughed.

"Yes, Ledora?"

"Sorry to interrupt, Agent Prime," Ledora said, her voice coming over the speaker in the lavatory instead of Sno's comm. "But an urgent call for Agent Stand has come through."

"Duty calls," Tana said as she pulled away from Sno. "Literally."

She got out of the steam and wrapped herself in a large towel.

"Put the call through to my comm," Tana said as she left the lavatory.

Sno stayed in the steam for a few minutes more then got out, dried off, and got dressed. When he stepped into the bedroom, the bed was made and there was no sign of Tana. She wasn't in the living room or kitchen. A note was on his fridge.

"Lunch later?" it read.

Sno smiled at the note then got a large cup of caff and drank it down, hot and black.

He paced for a while until it was time for his meeting then left his quarters and made his way to Crush's office.

Sno greeted those that greeted him, dodged questions he didn't want to answer, ignored jabs at how it was his fault people lost the betting pool, returned a few jabs of his own then was at the doors to Crush's office. He took a deep breath and entered.

"Go right in," Crush's assistant said as the door behind the reception desk opened wide. "They are expecting you."

Sno walked into the office, stood at attention, and waited to be offered a seat.

"Sit down, Sno," Crush said from behind his desk. Gerber was seated in a corner to Sno's left. "Sit."

Sno took the chair in front of Crush's desk then looked back over his shoulder at General Gerber.

"I'm only hear to listen, Agent Prime," Gerber said. "Pretend like I'm not in the room."

"We both know that isn't going to happen," Crush said with some irritation. He swiped at a holo interface then leaned back in his seat and fixed all of his eyes on Sno. "This debriefing is being recorded, as you are aware. You are required to tell the whole truth and answer every question asked of you honestly and to the best of your knowledge. Are we understood, Agent Prime?"

"Understood," Sno replied.

"Then let's get this over with," Crush said. "Start from the beginning."

Sno started from the moment he walked into his estate house. He realized that was the true beginning of the mission for him when he found Veben cooking in his kitchen and then Pol Hammon waiting in his sitting room. By that time, a plan had been hatched, or was in the process of being hatched, between Veben and Pol, Sno was certain of that.

Then Sno proceeded to honestly and faithfully recall every moment from there on. He even admitted that he'd been manipulated into suggesting the luxury liner as a mode of transportation. He described his time on the Mip, even his time with Velly Tarcorf, and ended his report with the last thing he remembered.

"Have you ever seen the black hole in Mlo?" he asked Crush. "It is impressive."

"I am sure it is," Crush said. A couple of his eyes looked towards Gerber then back at Sno. "Is that all, Agent Prime?"

"It is," Sno said. "As far as I can recollect. If I remember any other details, I will be sure to report them."

"Appreciated," Crush said. "General Gerber? Any questions for Agent Prime?"

"Not at the moment," Gerber said.

"Then I will fill you in on what you have missed, Sno," Crush said. "Or as much as I am authorized to fill you in on."

Crush described the chaos of when the Mip appeared suddenly in the GF headquarters' orbit. He described the ordeal of processing all of the guests and the GF's surprise at finding the ship's systems wiped clean. Then he glanced at Gerber again.

"Go ahead," Gerber said.

"Despite everything, we are pleased to say that the mission was a success, Agent Prime," Crush announced. "It was a galactic mess that will take months to sort out fully, but the primary objective was achieved."

"I'm sorry, I don't understand," Sno said. He looked at Gerber then back at Crush. "The mission was to deliver Pol Hammon with his tech. I did neither of those."

"We do not need Pol Hammon," Gerber said. Sno turned to him. "The GS M'illi'ped was outfitted with his tech fully operational when it arrived. That is how it traveled from the Mlo System to GF headquarters. The tech is still being studied, but from all reports, we'll be able to duplicate it without much difficulty. So, as Commander Crush said, despite the galactic mess that has been dropped in our laps, your mission was completed. Congratulations, Agent Prime."

Sno sat there and let that sink in. His superiors were referring to all the death and misery that beings endured on the Mip as a "galactic mess." There was no way Sno could fit his experience on that ship into such a handy label.

"Agent Prime? Are you not happy about this?" Crush asked.

"No, I am happy, Commander," Sno replied. "But I am left with a question."

"Only one?" Crush said and nodded his body. "What's the question, Sno?"

"Veben Doab," Sno said.

"That's a name, not a question," Gerber said.

"What is her fate?" Sno asked.

"Her fate?" Crush responded. "How should we know? That's her responsibility."

"Veben Doab has been released," Gerber said. "She cooperated fully, which we verified by some rather invasive scans of her mind, so she has been released to live out her life any way she feels fit."

"As long as she doesn't pull any of this crap again," Crush said. "She is to stay off the GF's radar for the remainder of her days."

"She's free?" Sno asked, stunned. "She was complicit in a lot of what Pol Hammon accomplished."

"The reality is a little more muddled than that, Sno," Gerber said. "Technically, she was complicit in a plan to auction off Pol Hammon's tech to the highest bidder. There is nothing illegal about that. The GF had a deal with Pol Hammon, not Veben Doab. Legally, she was helping an acquaintance sell private property."

"She was complicit in more than that," Sno said.

"A case could be made to support that, yes," Gerber said. "But it was decided that she be set free due to her complete and unwavering honesty with us. Sometimes the GF knows when to back off, Sno."

Sno started to speak, but Gerber held up a hand.

"A lesson you need to take from all of this," Gerber continued. "Sometimes know when to back off, Agent Prime."

"If you come across Ms. Doab again, then what you two discuss is up to you," Crush said. "She is not allowed to tell her story to anyone without proper security clearance. You have such clearance, so I am sure if you two do converse, it will be more than open and honest."

"That's an understatement," Sno said. He waited, but neither Crush nor Gerber said more. "So, is that it?"

"That is it," Crush said. "I will most certainly have follow-up questions once I have a chance to go over your report, but for now, you are on indefinite leave."

"I'm sorry?" Sno said. "Indefinite?"

"Go home and rest, Sno," Gerber said. "Not just physically, but psychologically and emotionally. You are no good to the SSD while these past events are still fresh in your mind."

"I've been inactive for over eighty days, Commander," Sno said, addressing Crush. "I think that's enough leave."

"I don't," Crush replied. "So go home. And this time, there won't be a secret mission waiting for you." Crush gave Gerber a look then returned his eyes to Sno. "Go. Home."

"End of discussion," Gerber said. "You are dismissed, Agent Prime."

Sno didn't argue. He bit back the words he wanted to say, stood up, saluted his superiors then left the office.

"Hey," Sno said into his comm as he walked to the lift. "I'm going to have to skip lunch. Sorry."

"Skip lunch? You off on a mission already?" Tana asked over the comm. "I didn't expect Crush to put you right back in the field."

"No, I've been sent home. Again," Sno said. "This time for real. I'm on indefinite leave until Crush feels I'm fit to return to duty."

"Oh," Tana said. "So, you're going back to Nab then."

"Back to Nab," Sno said. "Where I will probably sit by the lake in a perpetual drunken stupor. It should be nice."

Sno paused.

"Care to join me?"

There was a sound of Tana taking in a sharp breath then she responded with, "Yes. But I have to handle some work first. It's a short mission and even more boring than B'urn's. Shouldn't take me more than a week at the most. Can I come to Nab then? I actually have a good amount of leave banked and I'm sure I can cash it in. Crush won't argue. Hells, I might tell him it is for Agent Prime's speedy recovery. Then it'll be work and I won't have to spend my leave time."

"Yes, I am sure Crush will go for that," Sno said dryly. "However it works out, arrive when you can. I'll be waiting."

"By the lake in a drunken stupor," Tana said.

"More than likely," Sno said.

"Hey, Denman?"

Sno stopped before he got to the lift. "Yes?"

"Take care of yourself, will ya? Don't let that drunken stupor take you to places you don't want to go. Make it a fun drunken stupor. If you need to feel something, wait until I get there. It's best you aren't alone with whatever you need to deal with."

"So, you're saying to schedule my inevitable breakdown for when you get there so you can prop me up?" he asked.

"Pretty much," Tana replied. "Will you do that for me?"

"Of course," Sno said. "No breakdowns until I am safely back in your embrace, Agent Stand."

"Good," Tana said, sounding relieved. "And don't think I won't be calling Ledora to check up on you."

"I expect you to," Sno said and laughed.

"Take care, Denman," Tana said. "See you soon."

The com went silent and Sno stepped onto the lift. He made pleasantries with the various SSD personnel he encountered until the lift stopped and he made his way to the docking hangar.

"Mix, what have you got for me?" Sno asked as he approached the Master Sergeant.

"I have your new ship ready," Mix said. "Another Raven, but this time it has full shielding and I've already been instructed to lock in a course for Nab. I hope that's where you want to go because that is where you are going. The boss said to make it happen so I made it happen."

"Nab is fine, Mix. Thank you," Sno said. "Be good while I'm gone."

"I'm going to try not to," Mix said as Sno boarded his ship.

Sno made it to the bridge and sat down in the pilot's seat.

"Shall I fly us home, Agent Prime?" Ledora asked.

"Yes, please, Ledora," Sno said. "Home sounds nice, actually."

The ship lifted off, navigated through the swarm of ships close to SSD headquarters then accelerated once given the go-ahead by traffic control. Sno leaned back in his seat and closed his eyes.

Then his eyes shot open at the whirring sound behind him. He spun about and pointed at the small bot that appeared.

"Nope. Out," he shouted. "No bots allowed."

"Is this a new directive, Agent Prime?" Ledora asked.,

"Yeah, it is," Sno said. "Same at home. I don't want to see bots, hear bots, or even know bots are anywhere near the house."

"I will relay that order to the house's system, Agent Prime," Ledora said. "It should not be a problem."

"Good," Sno said and relaxed back into his seat. "Good. What's our travel time, Ledora?"

She relayed the travel time, but Sno had already stopped listening. His mind was on home and whether or not Veben would have the guts to face him, if she was even on Nab. If she did, she did. If she didn't, she didn't. He'd deal with whatever happened when it happened.

Which was how he lived anyway.

It was the only way one could live when living as Agent Prime.

The End

Author Bio:

Jake Bible, Bram Stoker Award nominated-novelist, short story writer, independent screenwriter, podcaster, and inventor of the Drabble Novel, has entertained thousands with his horror, sci/fi, thriller, and adventure tales. He reaches audiences of all ages with his uncanny ability to write a wide range of characters and genres.

Jake is the author of the bestselling Z-Burbia series set in Asheville, NC, the bestselling Salvage Merc One, the Apex Trilogy (DEAD MECH, The Americans, Metal and Ash) and the Roak: Galactic Bounty Hunter series for Severed Press. He is also the author of the YA zombie novel, Little Dead Man, the Bram Stoker Award nominated Teen horror novel, Intentional Haunting, the ScareScapes series, and the Reign of Four series for Permuted Press, as well as Stone Cold Bastards and the Black Box, Inc. series for Bell Bridge Books.

Find Jake at jakebible.com. Join him on Twitter @jakebible and find him on Facebook.

Look for other novels in Jake's Galactic Fleet universe:
Salvage Merc One
Salvage Merc One: The Daedalus System

Drop Team Zero

Outpost Hell

Roak: Galactic Bounty Hunter
Nebula Risen- A Roak: Galactic Bounty Hunter Novel
Razer Edge- A Roak: Galactic Bounty Hunter novel

Galactic Vice

CHECK OUT OTHER GREAT SCIENCE FICTION BOOKS

DERELICT: MARINES
by Paul E. Cooley

Fifty years ago, Mira, humanity's last hope to find new resources, exited the solar system bound for Proxima Centauri b. Seven years into her mission, all transmissions ceased without warning. Mira and her crew were presumed lost. Humanity, unified during her construction, splintered into insurgency and rebellion.

Now, an outpost orbiting Pluto has detected a distress call from an unpowered object entering Sol space: Mira has returned. When all attempts at communications fail, S&R Black, a Sol Federation Marine Corps search and rescue vessel, is dispatched from Trident Station to intercept, investigate, and tow the beleaguered Mira to Neptune.

As the marines prepare for the journey, uncertainty and conspiracy fomented by Trident Station's governing AIs, begin to take their toll. Upon reaching Mira, they discover they've been sent on a mission that will almost certainly end in catastrophe.

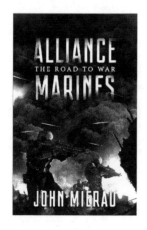

ALLIANCE MARINES
by John Mierau

One by one, all of Earth's colonies have gone dark and silent. Reach, the last colony, teeters on the verge of civil war against its Earth-loyal overlords...and Reach-born rebel Lee Zhang has sworn to push the planet over the edge.

As the colony descends into total war, a convoy from Earth races across the galaxy, carrying news of a threat unlike anything mankind has faced before. The colonies have all been destroyed by a vast alien horde, and now Earth has fallen, too. Time is running out for sworn enemies to learn to trust and unite, or the human race is extinct. The Takers are coming to destroy mankind. If we don't do the job for them first.

CHECK OUT OTHER GREAT SCIENCE FICTION BOOKS

SPACE MARINE AJAX
by Sean-Michael Argo

Ajax answers the call of duty and becomes an Einherjar space marine, charged with defending humanity against hideous alien monsters in furious combat across the galaxy.

The Garm, as they came to be called, emerged from the deepest parts of uncharted space, devouring all that lay before them, a great swarm that scoured entire star systems of all organic life. This space borne hive, this extinction fleet, made no attempts to communicate and offered no mercy.

Humanity has always been a deadly organism, and we would not so easily be made the prey. Unified against a common enemy, we fought back, meeting the swarm with soldiers upon every front.

PLANET LEVIATHAN
by D.J. Goodman

The cyborg commandos of the Galactic Marines are the greatest warriors in the galaxy, but sometimes one will go bad. Too unstable to be let back into the general population and too powerful for a normal prison to hold them, there is only one place they can be sent: Planet Leviathan.

CHECK OUT OTHER GREAT
SCIENCE FICTION BOOKS

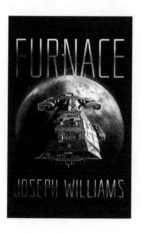

FURNACE
by Joseph Williams

On a routine escort mission to a human colony, Lieutenant Michael Chalmers is pulled out of hyper-sleep a month early. The RSA Rockne I lummel is well off course and—as the ship's navigator—it's up to him to figure out why. It's supposed to be a simple fix, but when he attempts to identify their position in the known universe, nothing registers on his scans. The vessel has catapulted beyond the reach of starlight by at least a hundred trillion light years. Then a planetary-mass object materializes behind them. It's burning brightly even without a star to heat it. Hundreds of damaged ships are locked in its orbit. The crew discovers there are no life-signs aboard any of them. As system failures sweep through the Hummel, neither Chalmers nor the pilot can prevent the vessel from crashing into the surface near a mysterious ancient city. And that's where the real nightmare begins.

LUNA
by Rick Chesler

On the threshold of opening the moon to tourist excursions, a private space firm owned by a visionary billionaire takes a team of non-astronauts to the lunar surface. To address concerns that the moon's barren rock may not hold long-term allure for an uber-wealthy clientele, the company's charismatic owner reveals to the group the ultimate discovery: life on the moon.

But what is initially a triumphant and world-changing moment soon gives way to unrelenting terror as the team experiences firsthand that despite their technological prowess, the moon still holds many secrets.

Made in the USA
Middletown, DE
21 July 2023

35545320R00123